GUARDIAN OF THE NIGHT . . .

While watching was a daytime job, listening was done after dark, requiring greater concentration. Madame Phloi listened for noises in the walls. She heard termites chewing, pipes sweating, and sometimes the ancient plaster cracking, but mostly she listened to the ghosts of generations of deceased mice.

One evening, shortly after the incident in the elevator, Madame Phloi was listening, Thapthim was asleep, and the other two were quietly turning pages of books, when a strange and horrendous sound came from the wall. The Madame's ears flicked to attention, then flattened against her head.

An interminable screech was coming out of that wall, like nothing the Madame had ever heard. . . .

—from "The Sin of Madame Phloi"
by Lilian Jackson Braun

MAGICATS II

EDITED BY
JACK DANN & GARDNER DOZOIS

ACE BOOKS, NEW YORK

MAGICATS II

An Ace Book / published by arrangement with
the editors

PRINTING HISTORY
Ace edition / December 1991

ISBN: 0-441-51533-9

Ace Books are published by The Berkley Publishing Group,
200 Madison Avenue, New York, New York 10016.
The name "ACE" and the "A" logo
are trademarks belonging to Charter Communications, Inc.

PRINTED IN THE UNITED STATES OF AMERICA

10 9 8 7 6 5 4 3 2 1

Acknowledgment is made for permission to reprint the following material:

"Kreativity for Kats" by Fritz Leiber, copyright © 1961 by Galaxy Publishing Corporation; first published in *Galaxy*, April 1961; reprinted by permission of the author and the author's agent, Richard Curtis.

"Life Regarded as a Jigsaw Puzzle of Highly Lustrous Cats" by Michael Bishop, copyright © 1991 by Omni Publications International, Ltd.; first published in *Omni*, September 1991; reprinted by permission of the author.

"Bright Burning Tiger" by Tanith Lee, copyright © 1983 by Davis Publications, Inc.; first published in *Isaac Asimov's Science Fiction Magazine*, 1983; reprinted by permission of the author.

"I Love Little Pussy" by Isaac Asimov, copyright © 1988 by Davis Publications, Inc.; first published in *Isaac Asimov's Science Fiction Magazine*, November 1988; reprinted by permission of the author.

"The Boy Who Spoke Cat" by Ward Moore, copyright © 1973 by Ward Moore; first published in *Venus*, December 1973; reprinted by permission of the author's agent, Virginia Kidd.

"The Jaguar Hunter" by Lucius Shepard, copyright © 1985 by Mercury Press, Inc.; first published in *The Magazine of Fantasy and Science Fiction*, May 1985; reprinted by permission of the author.

"The Sin of Madame Phloi" by Lilian Jackson Braun, copyright © 1962 by Davis Publications, Inc.; first published in *Ellery Queen's Mystery Magazine*, 1962; reprinted by permission of the author and the author's agent, Blanche C. Gregory, Inc., and The Berkley Publishing Group.

"The Mountain Cage" by Pamela Sargent, copyright © 1987 by Pamela Sargent; first published in *The Best of Pamela Sargent*, Edited by Martin Harry Greenberg (Academy Chicago, 1987); reprinted by permission of the author.

"May's Lion" by Ursula K. Le Guin, copyright © 1983 by Ursula K. Le Guin; first published in *The Little Magazine*, Volume 14, combined Numbers 1 & 2; reprinted by permission of the author and the author's agent, Virginia Kidd.

"The Color of Grass, the Color of Blood" by R.V. Branham, copyright © 1989 by Davis Publications, Inc.; first published in *Isaac Asimov's Science Fiction Magazine*, Mid-December 1989; reprinted by permission of the author.

"A Word to the Wise" by John Collier, copyright 1940 by *Esquire*.

"Duke Pasquale's Ring" by Avram Davidson, copyright © 1985 by TSR Hobbies, Inc.; first published in *Amazing Stories*, May 1985; reprinted by permission of the author and the author's agent, Richard D. Grant.

ACKNOWLEDGMENTS

The editors would like to thank the following people for their help and support:

Susan Casper, who helped with much of the word-crunching and lent us the use of her computer; Jeanne Van Buren Dann; Janet Kagan; Ricky Kagan; Sheila Williams; Ian Randall Strock; Scott L. Towner; Russell Atwood; Ellen Datlow; Michael Swanwick; Virginia Kidd; Pamela Sargent; the staff of Borders bookstore in Philadelphia; Greg Frost; and special thanks to our own editors, Susan Allison and Ginjer Buchanan.

CONTENTS

Kreativity for Kats
by
Fritz Leiber

With a forty-year career that stretches from the "Golden Age"
Astounding *of the 1940s to the present day, with no sign of
slackening of vigor or faltering of imagination, Fritz Leiber is
an indispensable figure in the development of modern science
fiction and fantasy. Leiber is considered to be one of the fathers
of modern "heroic fantasy," and his long sequence of stories
about Fafhrd and the Gray Mouser remains one of the most
complex and intelligent bodies of work in the entire subgenre
of "Sword & Sorcery" (which term Leiber himself is usually
credited with coining). He may also be one of the best—if not
the best—writers of the supernatural horror tale since Love-
craft and Poe, and practically invented the updated "modern"
or "urban" horror story with classic tales such as "Smoke
Ghost."*

Leiber is also a towering ancestral figure in science fiction
as well, having been one of the major writers of both
Campbell's "Golden Age" Astounding *of the '40s and H.L.
Gold's* Galaxy *of the '50s, then going on to contribute a steady
stream of superior fiction to the magazines and anthologies of
the '60s, the '70s, and the '80s as well. Leiber has won six
Hugos and four Nebulas, plus three World Fantasy awards—
one of them the prestigious Life Achievement Award—and a
Grandmaster of Fantasy Award. Leiber's books include* The
Green Millennium, A Specter Is Haunting Texas, The Big
Time, *and* The Silver Eggheads; *the collections* The Best of
Fritz Leiber, The Book of Fritz Leiber, The Change War,
Night's Black Agents, Heroes and Horrors, The Mind Spider,
and The Ghost Light; *and the eight volumes of Fafhrd–Gray
Mouser stories, the most essential of which are probably* The
Swords of Lankhmar, Swords in the Mist, *and* The Knight and
Knave of Swords.

Here he gives us a cat story—the little-known sequel, in fact,

*to his famous story "Space-Time for Springers"—but it's no
ordinary cat story, and it's about no ordinary cat, for Gummitch, its protagonist, is, as you will see, a cat with a profound
appreciation for the finer things in life.* . . . .

*   *   *

Gummitch peered thoughtfully at the molten silver image of
the sun in his little bowl of water on the floor inside the kitchen
window. He knew from experience that it would make dark
ghost suns swim in front of his eyes for a few moments, and
that was mildly interesting. Then he slowly thrust his head out
over the water, careful not to ruffle its surface by rough
breathing, and stared down at the mirror cat—the Gummitch
Double—staring up at him.

Gummitch had early discovered that water mirrors are very
different from most glass mirrors. The scentless spirit world
behind glass mirrors is an upright one sharing our gravity
system, its floor a continuation of the floor in the so-called real
world. But the world in a water mirror has reverse gravity. One
looks down into it, but the spirit-doubles in it look *up* at one.
In a way water mirrors are holes or pits in the world, leading
down to a spirit infinity or ghostly nadir.

Gummitch had pondered as to whether, if he plunged into
such a pit, he would be sustained by the spirit gravity or fall
forever. (It may well be that speculations of this sort account
for the caution about swimming characteristic of most cats.)

There was at least one exception to the general rule. The
looking glass on Kitty-Come-Here's dressing table also opened
into a spirit world of reverse gravity, as Gummitch had
discovered when he happened to look into it during one of the
regular visits he made to the dressing table top, to enjoy the
delightful flowery and musky odors emanating from the fragile
bottles assembled there.

But exceptions to general rules, as Gummitch knew well, are
only doorways to further knowledge and finer classifications.
The wind could not get into the spirit world below Kitty-Come-
Here's looking glass, while one of the definitive characteristics
of water mirrors is that movement can very easily enter the
spirit world below them, rhythmically disturbing it throughout,
producing the most surreal effects, and even reducing it to

chaos. Such disturbances exist only in the spirit world and are in no way a mirroring of anything in the real world: Gummitch knew that his paw did not change when it flicked the surface of the water, although the image of his paw burst into a hundred flickering fragments. (Both cats and primitive men first deduced that the world in a water mirror is a spirit world because they saw that its inhabitants were easily blown apart by the wind and must therefore be highly tenuous, though capable of regeneration.)

Gummitch mildly enjoyed creating rhythmic disturbances in the spirit worlds below water mirrors. He wished there were some way to bring their excitement and weird beauty into the real world.

On this sunny day when our story begins, the spirit world below the water mirror in his drinking bowl was particularly vivid and bright. Gummitch stared for a while longer at the Gummitch Double and then thrust down his tongue to quench his thirst. Curling swiftly upward, it conveyed a splash of water into his mouth and also flicked a single drop of water into the air before his nose. The sun struck the drop and it flashed like a diamond. In fact, it seemed to Gummitch that for a moment he had juggled the sun on his tongue. He shook his head amazedly and touched the side of the bowl with his paw. The bowl was brimful and a few drops fell out; they also flashed like tiny suns as they fell. Gummitch had a fleeting vision, a momentary creative impulse, that was gone from his mind before he could seize it. He shook his head once more, backed away from the bowl, and then lay down with his head pillowed on his paws to contemplate the matter. The room darkened as the sun went under a cloud and the young golden dark-barred cat looked like a pool of sunlight left behind.

Kitty-Come-Here had watched the whole performance from the door to the dining room and that evening she commented on it to Old Horsemeat.

"He backed away from the water as if it were poison," she said. "They have been putting more chlorine in it lately, you know, and maybe he can taste the fluorides they put in for dental decay."

Old Horsemeat doubted that, but his wife went on, "I can't figure out where Gummitch does his drinking these days. There never seems to be any water gone from his bowl. And we haven't had any cut flowers. And none of the faucets drip."

"He probably does his drinking somewhere outside," Old Horsemeat guessed.

"But he doesn't go outside very often these days," Kitty-Come-Here countered. "Scarface and the Mad Eunuch, you know. Besides, it hasn't rained for weeks. It's certainly a mystery to me where he gets his liquids. Boiling gets the chlorine out of water, doesn't it? I think I'll try him on some tomorrow."

"Maybe he's depressed," Old Horsemeat suggested. "That often leads to secret drinking."

This baroque witticism hit fairly close to the truth. Gummitch *was* depressed—had been depressed ever since he had lost his kittenish dreams of turning into a man, achieving spaceflight, learning and publishing all the secrets of the fourth dimension, and similar marvels. The black cloud of disillusionment at realizing he could only be a cat had lightened somewhat, but he was still feeling dull and unfulfilled.

Gummitch was at that difficult age for he-cats, between First Puberty, when the cat achieves essential maleness, and Second Puberty, when he gets broad-chested, jowly and thick-ruffed, becoming a fully armed sexual competitor. In the ordinary course of things he would have been spending much of his time exploring the outer world, detail-mapping the immediate vicinity, spying on other cats, making cautious approaches to unescorted females and in all ways comporting himself like a fledgling male. But this was prevented by the two burly toms who lived in the houses next door and who, far more interested in murder than the pursuit of mates, had entered into partnership with the sole object of bushwacking Gummitch. Gummitch's household had nicknamed them Scarface and the Mad Eunuch, the latter being one of those males whom "fixing" turns, not placid, but homicidally maniacal. Compared to these seasoned heavyweights, Gummitch was a welterweight at most. Scarface and the Mad Eunuch lay in wait for him by turns just beyond the kitchen door, so that his forays into the outside world were largely reduced to dashes for some hiding hole, followed by long, boring but perilous sieges.

He often wished that old Horsemeat's two older cats, Ashurbanipal and Cleopatra, had not gone to the country to live with Old Horsemeat's mother. They would have shown the evil bushwackers a thing or two!

Because of Scarface and the Mad Eunuch, Gummitch spent most of his time indoors. Since a cat is made for a half-and-half existence—half in the wild forest, half in the secure cave—he took to brooding quite morbidly. He thought over-much of ghost cats in the mirror world and of the Skeleton Cat who starved to death in a locked closet and similar grisly legends. He immersed himself in racial memories, not so much of Ancient Egypt where cats were prized as minions of the lovely cat-goddess Bast and ceremoniously mummified at the end of tranquil lives, as of the Middle Ages, when European mankind waged a genocidal war against felines as being the familiars of witches. (He thought briefly of turning Kitty-Come-Here into a witch, but his hypnotic staring and tentative ritualistic mewing only made her fidgety.) And he devoted more and more time to devising dark versions of the theory of transmigration, picturing cats as Silent Souls, Gagged People of Great Talent, and the like.

He had become too self-conscious to re-enter often the make-believe world of the kitten, yet his imagination remained as active as ever. It was a truly frustrating predicament.

More and more often and for longer periods he retired to meditate in a corrugated cardboard shoebox, open only at one end. The cramped quarters made it easier for him to think. Old Horsemeat called it the Cat Orgone Box after the famed Orgone Energy Accumulators of the late wildcat psychoanalyst Dr. Wilhelm Reich.

If only, Gummitch thought, he could devise some way of objectifying the intimations of beauty that flitted through his darkly clouded mind! Now, on the evening of the sunny day when he had backed away from his water bowl, he attacked the problem anew. He knew he had been fleetingly on the verge of a great idea, an idea involving water, light and movement. An idea he had unfortunately forgotten. He closed his eyes and twitched his nose. I must concentrate, he thought to himself, concentrate. . . .

Next day Kitty-Come-Here remembered her idea about Gummitch's water. She boiled two cupfuls in a spotless enamelware saucepan, letting it cool for half an hour before using it to replace the seemingly offensive water in the young cat's bowl. It was only then she noticed that the bowl had been upset.

She casually assumed that big-footed Old Horsemeat must have been responsible for the accident, or possibly one of the two children—darting Sissy or blundering Baby. She wiped the bowl and filled it with the water she had dechlorinated.

"Come here, Kitty, come here," she called to Gummitch, who had been watching her actions attentively from the dining room door. The young cat stayed where he was. "Oh, well, if you want to be coy," she said, shrugging her shoulders.

There was a mystery about the spilled water. It had apparently disappeared entirely, though the day seemed hardly dry enough for total evaporation. Then she saw it standing in a puddle by the wall fully ten feet away from the bowl. She made a quick deduction and frowned a bit worriedly.

"I never realized the kitchen floor sloped *that* much," she told Old Horsemeat after dinner. "Maybe some beams need to be jacked up in the basement. I'd hate to think of collapsing into it while I cooked dinner."

"I'm sure this house finished all its settling thirty years ago," her husband assured her hurriedly. "That slope's always been there."

"Well, if you say so," Kitty-Come-Here allowed doubtfully.

Next day she found Gummitch's bowl upset again and the remains of the boiled water in a puddle across the room. As she mopped it up, she began to do some thinking without benefit of Concentration Box.

That evening, after Old Horsemeat and Sissy had vehemently denied kicking into the water bowl or stepping on its edge, she voiced her conclusions. "I think *Gummitch* upsets it," she said.

"He's rejecting it. It still doesn't taste right to him and he wants to show us."

"Maybe he only likes it after it's run across the floor and got seasoned with household dust and the corpses of germs," suggested Old Horsemeat, who believed most cats were bohemian types.

"I'll have you know I *scrub* that linoleum," Kitty-Come-Here asserted.

"Well, with detergent and scouring powder, then," Old Horsemeat amended resourcefully.

Kitty-Come-Here made a scornful noise. "I still want to know where he gets his liquids," she said. "He's been off milk for weeks, you know, and he only drinks a little broth when I give him that. Yet he doesn't seem dehydrated. It's a real mystery and—"

"Maybe he's built a still in the attic," Old Horsemeat interjected.

"—and I'm going to find the answers," Kitty-Come-Here concluded, ignoring the facetious interruption. "I'm going to find out *where* he gets the water he does drink and *why* he rejects the water I give him. This time I'm going to boil it and put in a pinch of salt. Just a pinch."

"You make animals sound more delicate about food and drink than humans," Old Horsemeat observed.

"They probably are," his wife countered. "For one thing they don't smoke, or drink Martinis. It's my firm belief that animals—cats, anyway—like good food just as much as we do. And the same sort of good food. They don't enjoy canned catfood any more than we would, though they *can* eat it. Just as we could if we had to. I really don't think Gummitch would have such a passion for raw horsemeat except you started him on it so early."

"He probably thinks of it as steak tartare," Old Horsemeat said.

Next day Kitty-Come-Here found her salted offering upset just as the two previous bowls had been.

Such were the beginnings of the Great Spilled Water Mystery that preoccupied the human members of the Gummitch household for weeks. Not every day, but frequently, and sometimes two and three times a day, Gummitch's little bowl was upset. No one ever saw the young cat do it. But it was generally accepted that he was responsible, though for a time Old Horsemeat had theories that he did not voice involving Sissy and Baby.

Kitty-Come-Here bought Gummitch a firm-footed rubber bowl for his water, though she hesitated over the purchase for some time, certain he would be able to taste the rubber. This bowl was found upset just like his regular china one and like the tin one she briefly revived from his kitten days.

All sorts of clues and possibly related circumstances were seized upon and dissected. For instance, after about a month of the mysterious spillings, Kitty-Come-Here announced, "I've been thinking back and as far as I can remember it never happens on sunny days."

"Oh, Good Lord!" Old Horsemeat reacted.

Meanwhile Kitty-Come-Here continued to try to concoct a kind of water that would be palatable to Gummitch. As she continued without success, her formulas became more fantastic. She quit boiling it for the most part but added a pinch of sugar, a spoonful of beer, a few flakes of oregano, a green leaf, a violet, a drop of vanilla extract, a drop of iodine. . . .

"No wonder he rejects the stuff," Old Horsemeat was tempted to say, but didn't.

Finally Kitty-Come-Here, inspired by the sight of a greenly glittering rack of it at the supermarket, purchased a half gallon of bottled water from a famous spring. She wondered why she hadn't thought of this step earlier—it certainly ought to take care of her haunting convictions about the unpalatableness of chlorine or fluorides. (She herself could distinctly taste the fluorides in the tap water, though she never mentioned this to Old Horsemeat.)

One other development during the Great Spilled Water Mystery was that Gummitch gradually emerged from depression and became quite gay. He took to dancing cat schottisches and gigues impromptu in the living room of an evening and so forgot his dignity as to battle joyously with the vacuum-cleaner dragon when Old Horsemeat used one of the smaller attachments to curry him; the young cat clutched the hairy round brush to his stomach and madly clawed it as it *whuffled* menacingly. Even the afternoon he came home with a shoulder gashed by the Mad Eunuch he seemed strangely light-hearted and debonair.

The Mystery was abruptly solved one sunny Sunday afternoon. Going into the bathroom in her stocking feet, Kitty-Come-Here saw Gummitch apparently trying to drown himself in the toilet. His hindquarters were on the seat but the rest of his body went down into the bowl. Coming closer, she saw that his forelegs were braced against the opposite side of the bowl, just above the water surface, while his head thrust down sharply between his shoulders. She could distinctly hear rhythmic lapping.

To tell the truth, Kitty-Come-Here was rather shocked. She had certain rather fixed ideas about the delicacy of cats. It speaks well for her progressive grounding that she did not shout at Gummitch but softly summoned her husband.

By the time Old Horsemeat arrived the young cat had refreshed himself and was coming out of his "well" with a sudden backward undulation. He passed them in the doorway with a single mew and upward look and then made off for the kitchen.

The blue and white room was bright with sunlight. Outside the sky was blue and the leaves were rustling in a stiff breeze. Gummitch looked back once, as if to make sure his human congeners had followed, mewed again, and then advanced briskly toward his little bowl with the air of one who proposes to reveal all mysteries at once.

Kitty-Come-Here had almost outdone herself. She had for the first time poured him the bottled water, and she had floated a few rose petals on the surface.

Gummitch regarded them carefully, sniffed at them, and then proceeded to fish them out one by one and shake them off his paw. Old Horsemeat repressed the urge to say, "I told you so."

When the water surface was completely free and winking in the sunlight, Gummitch curved one paw under the side of the bowl and jerked.

Half the water spilled out, gathered itself, and then began to flow across the floor in little rushes, a silver ribbon sparkling with sunlight that divided and subdivided and reunited as it followed the slope. Gummitch crouched to one side, watching it intensely, following its progress inch by inch and foot by foot, almost pouncing on the little temporary pools that formed, but not quite touching them. Twice he mewed faintly in excitement.

"He's *playing* with it," Old Horsemeat said incredulously.

"No," Kitty-Come-Here countered wide-eyed, "he's *creating* something. Silver mice. Watersnakes. Twinkling vines."

"Good Lord, you're right," Old Horsemeat agreed. "It's a new art form. Would you call it water painting? Or water sculpture? Somehow I think that's best. As if a sculptor made mobiles out of molten tin."

"It's gone so quickly, though," Kitty-Come-Here objected, a little sadly. "Art ought to last. Look, it's almost all flowed over to the wall now."

"Some of the best art forms are completely fugitive," Old Horsemeat argued. "What about improvisation in music and dancing? What about jam sessions and shadow figures on the wall? Gummitch can always do it again—in fact, he must have been doing it again and again this last month. It's never exactly the same, like waves or fires. But it's beautiful."

"I suppose so," Kitty-Come-Here said. Then coming to herself, she continued, "But I don't think it can be healthy for him to go on drinking water out of the toilet. Really."

Old Horsemeat shrugged. He had an insight about the artistic temperament and the need to dig for inspiration into the smelly fundamentals of life, but it was difficult to express delicately.

Kitty-Come-Here sighed, as if bidding farewell to all her efforts with rose petals and crystalline bottled purity and vanilla extract and the soda water which had amazed Gummitch by faintly spitting and purring at him.

"Oh, well," she said, "I can scrub it out more often, I suppose."

Meanwhile, Gummitch had gone back to his bowl and, using both paws, overset it completely. Now, nose a-twitch, he once more pursued the silver streams alive with suns, refreshing his spirit with the sight of them. He was fretted by no problems about what he was doing. He had solved them all with one of his characteristically sharp distinctions: there was the *sacred* water, the sparklingly clear water to create with, and there was the water with character, the water to *drink*.

Life Regarded as a Jigsaw Puzzle of Highly Lustrous Cats

by
Michael Bishop

Michael Bishop is one of the most acclaimed and respected members of that highly talented generation of writers who entered SF in the 1970s. His short fiction has appeared in almost all the major magazines and anthologies, and has been gathered in three collections: Blooded on Arachne, One Winter in Eden, *and* Close Encounters With the Deity. *In 1981 he won the Nebula Award for his novelette "The Quickening," and in 1983 he won another Nebula for his novel* No Enemy but Time. *His other novels include* Transfigurations, Stolen Faces, Ancient of Days, Catacomb Years, Eyes of Fire, *and* The Secret Ascension. *His most recent book is the novel* Unicorn Mountain. *Bishop and his family live in Pine Mountain, Georgia.*

In the wry and subtle story that follows, he demonstrates that everyone's life is made up of many intricately interlocking pieces, and that some of the most interesting of those pieces may well turn out to be some highly lustrous cats . . .

*   *   *

Your father-in-law, who insists that you call him Howie, even though you prefer Mr. Bragg, likes jigsaw puzzles. If they prove harder than he has the skill or the patience for, he knows a sneaky way around the problem.

During the third Christmas season after your marriage to Marti, you find Howie at a card table wearing a parka, a blue watch cap with a crown of burgundy leather, and fur-lined shoes. (December through February, it is freezing in the Braggs' Tudor-style house outside Spartanburg.) He is assembling a huge jigsaw puzzle, for the Braggs give him one every

Christmas. His challenge is to put it together, unaided by
drop-in company or any other family member, before the Sugar
Bowl kick-off on New Year's Day.

This year, the puzzle is of cats.

The ESB procedure being administered to you by the Zoo Cop
and his associates is keyed to cats. When they zap your
implanted electrodes, cat-related memories parachute into your
mind's eye, opening out like fireworks.

The lid from the puzzle's box is Mr. Bragg's—Howie's—
blueprint, and it depicts a population explosion of stylized cats.
They are both mysterious beasts and whimsical cartoons. The
puzzle lacks any background, it's so full of cats. They run,
stalk, lap milk, tussel, tongue-file their fur, snooze, etc., etc.
There are no puzzle areas where a single color dominates, a
serious obstacle to quick assembly.

Howie has a solution. When only a handful of pieces remain
in the box, he uses a razor blade to shave any piece that refuses
to fit where he wants it to. This is cheating, as even Howie
readily acknowledges, but on New Year's Eve, with Dick
Clark standing in Times Square and the Sugar Bowl game only
hours away, a man can't afford to screw around.

"Looking good," you say as the crowd on TV starts its
rowdy countdown to midnight. "You're almost there."

Howie confesses—complains?—that this puzzle has been a
"real mindbender." He appreciates the challenge of a
thousand-plus pieces and a crazy-making dearth of internal
clues, but why this particular puzzle? He usually receives a
photographic landscape or a Western painting by Remington.

"I'm not a cat fancier," he tells you. "Most of 'em're sneaky
little bastards, don't you think?"

Marti likes cats, but when you get canned at Piedmont Freight
in Atlanta, she moves back to Spartanburg with your son,
Jacob, who may be allergic to cats. Marti leaves in your
keeping two calico mongrels that duck out of sight whenever
you try to feed or catch them. You catch them eventually, of
course, and drive them to the pound in a plastic animal carrier

that Marti bought from Delta, or Eastern, or some other airline out at Hartsfield.

Penfield, a.k.a. the Zoo Cop, wants to know how you lost your job. He gives you a multiple-choice quiz:

    A. Companywide lay-off
    B. Neglect of duty and/or unacceptable job performance
    C. Personality conflict with a supervisor
    D. Suspicion of disloyalty
    E. All, or none, of the above

You tell him that there was an incident of (alleged) sexual harassment involving a female secretary whose name, even under the impetus of electrical stimulation of the brain (ESB), you cannot now recall. All you can recall is every cat, real or imaginary, ever to etch its image into your consciousness.

After your firing, you take the cats, Springer and Ossie (short for Ocelot), to the pound. When you look back from the shelter's doorway, a teen-age attendant is giving you, no doubt about it, the evil eye. Springer and Ossie are doomed. No one in the big, busy city wants a mixed-breed female. The fate awaiting nine-year-old Jacob's cats—never mind their complicity in his frightening asthma—is the gas chamber, but, today, you are as indifferent to the cats' fate as a latter-day Eichmann. You are numb from the molecular level upward.

"We did have them spayed," you defend yourself. "Couldn't you use that to pitch them to some nice family?"

You begin to laugh.

Is this another instance of Inappropriate Affect? Except for the laughing gas given to you to sink the electrodes, you've now been off all medication for . . . you don't know how long.

On the street only three years after your dismissal, you wept at hoboes' bawdy jokes, got up and danced if the obituaries you'd been sleeping under reported an old friend's death.

Once, you giggled when a black girl bummed a cigarette in

the parking lot of Trinity United Methodist: "I got AIDS, man.
Hain't no smoke gonna kill me. Hain't time enough for the old
lung cee to kick in, too."

Now that Penfield's taken you off antipsychotics, is Ye Olde
Inappropriate Affect kicking in again? Or is this fallout from
the ESB? After all, one gets entirely different responses (rage
and affection; fear and bravado) from zapping hypothalamic
points less than 0.02 inch from each other.

Spill it, Adolf, Penfield says. What's so funny?

Cat juggling, you tell him. (Your name has never been
Adolf.)

What?

Steve Martin in *The Jerk*. An illegal Mexican sport. A joke,
you know. Cat juggling.

You surrender to jerky laughter. It hurts, but your glee isn't
inappropriate. The movie was a comedy. People were *supposed* to laugh. Forget that when you close your eyes, you
see yourself as the outlaw juggler. Forget that the cats in
their caterwauling orbits include Springer, Ossie, Thai Thai,
Romeo, and an anonymous albino kitten from your dead
grandparents' grain crib on their farm outside Mont-
gomery. . . .

As a boy in Hapeville, the cat you like best is Thai Thai, a male
Siamese that your mama and you inherit from the family
moving out. His name isn't Thai Thai before your mama starts
calling him that, though. It's something fake Chinese, like
Lung Cee or Mouser Tung. The folks moving out don't want to
take him with them, their daddy's got a job with Otero Steel in
Pueblo, Colorado. Besides, Mouser Tung's not likely to
appreciate the ice and snow out there. He's a Deep South cat,
Dixie-born and -bred.

"You are who you are," Mama tells the Siamese while he
rubs her laddered nylons, "but from here on out your *name* is
Thai Thai."

"Why're you calling him that?" you ask her.

"Because it *fits* a cracker Siamese," she says.

It's several years later before you realize that Thailand is

Siam's current name and that there's a gnat-plagued town southeast of Albany called, yeah, Ty Ty.

Your mama's a smart gal, with an agile mind and a quirky sense of humor. How Daddy ever got it into his head that she wasn't good enough for him is a mystery.

It's her agile mind and her quirky sense of humor that did her in, the Zoo Cop says, pinching back your eyelid.

Anyway, Daddy ran off to a Florida dog-track town with a chunky bottle-blonde ex-hairdresser who dropped a few pounds and started a mail-order weight-loss-tonic business. He's been gone nine weeks and four days.

Thai Thai, when you notice him, is pretty decent company. He sheathes his claws when he's in your lap. He purrs at a bearable register. He eats leftover vegetables—peas, lima beans, spinach—as readily as he does bacon rinds or chicken scraps. A doll, Mama calls him. A gentleman.

This ESB business distorts stuff. It flips events, attitudes, preferences upside-down. The last shall be first, the first shall be last. This focus on cats, for example, is a *major* distortion, a misleading reenvisioning of the life that you lived before getting trapped by Rockdale Biological Supply Company.

Can't Penfield see this? Uh-uh, no way. He's too hot to screw Rockdale Biological's bigwigs. The guy may have right on his side, but to him—for the moment, anyway—you're just another human oven-cake. If you crumble when the heat's turned up, great, zip-a-dee-zoo-cop, pop me a cold one, justice is served.

Thing is, you prefer dogs. Even as a kid, you like them more. You bring home flea-bitten strays and beg to keep them. When you live in Alabama, you covet the liony chow, Simba, that waits every afternoon in the Notasulga schoolyard for Wesley Duplantier. Dogs, not cats. Until Mouser Tung—Thai Thai—all the cats you know prowl on the edges of your attention. Even Thai Thai comes to you and Mama, over here in Georgia, as a kind of offhand house-warming gift. Dogs, Mister Zoo Cop, not cats.

Actually, Penfield says, I'm getting the idea that what was in the *forefront* of your attention, Adolf, was women. . . .

After puberty, your attention never *has* a forefront. You are divebombed by stimuli. Girls' faces are billboards. Their bodies are bigger billboards. Jigsawed ad signs. A piece here. A piece there. It isn't just girls. It's everything. Cars, buildings, TV talking heads, mosquito swarms, jet contrails, interchangeable male callers at suppertime, battle scenes on the six o'clock news, rock idols infinitely glitterized, the whole schmear fragmenting as it feeds into you, Mr. Teen-age Black Hole of the Spirit. Except when romancing a sweet young gal, your head's a magnet for all the flak generated by the media-crazed twentieth century.

"You're tomcatting, aren't you?" Mama says. "You're tomcatting just like Webb did. God."

It's a way to stay focused. With their faces and bodies under you, they cease to be billboards. You're a human being again, not a radio receiver or a gravity funnel. The act imposes a fleeting order on the ricocheting chaos working every instant to turn you, the mind cementing it all together, into a flimsy cardboard box of mismatched pieces.

Is that tomcatting? Resisting, by a tender union of bodies, the consequences of dumping a jigsaw puzzle of cats into a box of pieces that, assembled, would depict, say, a unit of embattled flak gunners on Corregidor?

Christ, the Zoo Cop says, a more highfalutin excuse for chasing tail I've never heard.

Your high school is crawling with cats. Cool cats, punk cats, stray cats, dead cats. Some are human, some aren't.

You dissect a cat in biology lab. On a plaster-of-Paris base, guyed upright by wires, stands the bleached skeleton of a quadruped that Mr. Osteen—he's also the track and girls' softball coach—swears was a member of *Felis catus*, the common house cat.

With its underlying gauntness exposed and its skull gleaming brittle and grotesque, this skeleton resembles that of something prehistoric. Pamela van Rhyn and two or three other girls want to know where the cats in the lab came from.

"A scientific supply house," Coach Osteen says. "Same place we get our bullfrogs, our microscope slides, the insects in that there display case." He nods at it.

"Where does the supply house get them?" Pamela says.

"I don't know, Pammie. Maybe they raise 'em. Maybe they round up strays. You missing a kitty?"

In fact, rumor holds that Mr. Osteen found the living source of his skeleton behind the track field's south bleachers, chloroformed it, carried it home, and boiled the fur off it in a pot on an old stove in his basement. Because of the smell, his wife spent a week in Augusta with her mother. Rumor holds that cat lovers hereabouts would be wise to keep their pets indoors.

Slicing into the chest cavity of the specimen provided by the supply house, you find yourself losing it. You are the only boy in Coach Osteen's lab to contract nausea and an overwhelming uprush of self-disgust; the only boy, clammy-palmed and light-headed, to have to leave the room. The ostensible shame of your departure is lost on Pamela, who agrees, in Nurse Mayhew's office, to rendezvous with you later that afternoon at the Huddle House.

"This is the heart," you can still hear Osteen saying. "Looks like a wet rubber strawberry, don't it?"

As a seven-year-old, you wander into the grain crib of the barn on the Powell farm. A one-eyed mongrel queen named Sky has dropped a litter on the deer hides, today stiff and rat-eaten, that Gramby Powell stowed there twenty or more years ago. Sky one-eyes you with real suspicion, all set to bolt or hiss, as you lean over a rail to study the blind quintet of her kittening.

They're not much, mere lumps. "Turds with fur," Gramby called them last night, to Meemaw Anita's scandalized dismay and the keen amusement of your daddy. They hardly move.

One kitten gleams white on the stiff hide, in the nervous curl of Sky's furry belly. You spit at Sky, as another cat would spit, but louder—*ssssphh! ssssphh!*—so that eventually, intimidated, she gets up, kittens falling from her like bombs from the open bay of a B-52, and slinks to the far wall of the crib.

You climb over the rail and pick up the white kitten, the Maybe Albino as Meemaw Anita dubbed it. "Won't know for sure," she said, "till its eyes're open."

You turn the kitten in your hands. Which end is which? It's sort of hard to say. Okay, here's the starchy white potato print of its smashed-in pug of a face: eyes shut, ears a pair of napkin folds, mouth a miniature crimson gap.

You rub the helpless critter on your cheek. Cat smells. Hay smells. Hide smells. It's hard not to sneeze.

It occurs to you that you could throw this Maybe Albino like a baseball. You could wind up like Denny McLain and fling it at the far wall of the grain crib. If you aim just right, you may be able to hit the wall so that the kitten rebounds and lands on Sky. You could sing a funny song, "Sky's being fallen on, / Oh, Sky's being fallen on, / Whatcha think 'bout that?" And nobody'll ever know if poor little Maybe Albino has pink eyes or not. . . .

This sudden impulse horrifies you, even as a kid, *especially* as a kid. You can see the white kitten dead. Trembling, you set the kitten back down on the cardboardy deer hide, climb back over the crib rail, and stand away from the naked litter while Sky tries to decide what to do next.

Unmanfully, you start to cry. "S-s-orry, k-kitty. S-s-sorry, Sk-sky. I'm r-r-really s-sorry." You almost want Gramby or Meemaw Anita to stumble in on you, in the churchly gloom and itch of their grain crib, to see you doing this heartfelt penance for a foul deed imagined but never carried out. It's okay to cry a bit in front of your mama's folks.

I'm touched, Penfield says. But speak up. Stop mumbling.

For several months after your senior year, you reside in the Adolescent Wing of the Quiet Harbor Psychiatric Center in a suburb of Atlanta. You're there to neutralize the disorienting stimuli—flak, you call it—burning out your emotional wiring, flying at you from everywhere. You're there to relearn how to live with no despairing recourse to disguises, sex, drugs.

Bad drugs, the doctors mean.

At QHPC, they give you good drugs. This is actually the case, not sarcastic bullshit. Kim Yaughan, one of the psycho-therapists in the so-called Wild Child Wing, assures you that this is so; that antipsychotics aren't addictive. You get twenty milligrams a day of haloperidol. You take it in liquid form in paper cups shaped like doll-house-sized coffee filters.

"You're not an addict," Kim says. (Everyone at QHPC calls her Kim.) "Think of yourself as a diabetic, of Haldol as insulin. You don't hold a diabetic off insulin, that'd be criminal."

Not only do you get Haldol, you get talk therapy, recre-ational therapy, family therapy, crafts therapy. Some of the residents of the Wild Child Wing are druggies and sexual-abuse victims as young as twelve. They get these same therapies, along with pet therapy. The pets brought in on Wednesdays often include cats.

At last, Penfield tells an associate. That last jolt wasn't a mis-hit, after all.

The idea is that hostile, fearful, or withdrawn kids who don't interact well with other people will do better with animals. Usually, they do. Kittens under a year, tumbling with one another, batting at yarn balls, exploring the pet room with their tails up like the radio antennas on cars, seem to be effective four-legged therapists.

One teen-age girl, a manic-depressive who calls herself Eagle Rose, goes ga-ga over them. "Oh," she says, holding up a squirmy smoke-colored male and nodding at two kittens wrestling in an empty carton of Extra Large Tide, "they're so soft, so neat, so . . . so *highly lustrous*."

Despite Kim Yaughan's many attempts to involve you, you stand aloof from everyone. It's Eagle Rose who focuses your attention, not the kittens, and E.R.'s an untouchable. Every patient here is an untouchable, that way. It would be a terrible betrayal to think anything else. So, mostly, you don't.

The year before you marry, Marti is renting a house on North Highland Avenue. A whole house. It's not a big house, but she has plenty of room. She uses one bedroom as a studio. In this room, on the floor, lies a large canvas on which she has been painting, exclusively in shades of blue, the magnified heart of a magnolia. She calls the painting—too explicitly, you think—*Magnolia Heart in Blue*. She's worked on it all quarter, often appraising it from a stepladder to determine how best to continue.

Every weekend, you sleep with Marti in the bedroom next to the studio. Her mattress rests on the floor, without box springs or bedstead. You sometimes feel that you're lying in the middle of a painting in progress, a strange but gratifying sensation that you may or may not carry into your next week of classes at GSU.

One balmy Sunday, you awake to find Marti's body stenciled with primitive blue flowers, a blossom on her neck, more on her breasts, an indigo bouquet on the milky plane of her abdomen. You gaze at her in groggy wonderment. The woman you plan to marry has become, overnight, an arabesque of disturbing floral bruises.

Then you see the cat, Romeo, a neighbor's gray Persian, propped in the corner, belly exposed, so much like a hairy little man in a recliner that you laugh. Marti stirs. Romeo preens. Clearly, he entered through a studio window, walked all over *Magnolia Heart in Blue*, then came in here and violated Marti.

My wife-to-be as a strip of *fin de siècle* wallpaper, you muse, kissing her chastely on one of the paw-print flowers.

You sleep on the streets. You wear the same stinking clothes for days on end. You haven't been on haloperidol for months. The city could be Lima, or Istanbul, or Bombay, as easily as Atlanta. Hell, it could be a boulder-littered crater on the moon. You drag from one place to another like a zombie, and the people you hit up for hamburgers, change, MARTA tokens, old newspapers, have no more substance to you than you do to them, they could all be holograms or ghosts. They could be androids programmed to keep you dirty and hungry by dictating your behavior with remote-control devices that look like wristwatches and key rings.

Cats mean more to you than people do. (The people may not

be people.) Cats are fellow survivors, able to sniff out nitrogenous substances from blocks away. Food.

You follow a trio of scrawny felines down Ponce de Leon to the rear door of a catfish restaurant where the Dumpster overflows with greasy paper and other high refuse. The cats strut around on the mounded topography of this debris while you balance on an upturned trash barrel, mindlessly picking and choosing.

Seven rooms away from Coach Osteen's lab, Mr. Petty is teaching advanced junior English. Poetry. He stalks around the room like an actor doing Hamlet, even when the poem's something dumb by Ogden Nash, or something beat and surface-sacrilegious by Ferlinghetti, or something short and puzzling by Carlos Williams.

The Williams piece is about a cat that climbs over a cabinet—a "jamcloset"—and steps into a flowerpot. Actually, Mr. Petty says, it's about the *image* created by Williams's purposely simple diction. Everyone argues that it isn't a poem at all. It's even less a poem, lacking metaphors, than that Carl Sandberg thing about the fog coming on little, for Christ's sake, cat's feet.

You like it, though. You can see the cat stepping cautiously into the flowerpot. The next time you're in Coach Osteen's class, trying to redeem yourself at the dissection table, you recite the poem for Pamela van Rhyn, Jessie Faye Culver, Kathy Margenau, and Cynthia Spivy.

Coach Osteen, shaking his head, makes you repeat the lines so that he can say them, too. Amazing.

"Cats are digitigrade critters," he tells the lab. "That means they walk on their toes. Digitigrade."

Cynthia Spivy catches your eye. *Well, I'll be a pussywillow,* she silently mouths. *Who'd've thunk it?*

"Unlike the dog or the horse," Coach Osteen goes on, "the cat walks by moving the front and back legs on one side of its body and then the front and back legs on the other. The only other animals to move that way are the camel and the giraffe."

And naked crazy folks rutting on all fours, you think,

studying Cynthia's lips and wondering if there was ever a feral child raised by snow leopards or jaguars. . . .

Thai Thai develops a urinary tract infection. Whenever he has to pee, he looks for Mama pulling weeds or hanging out clothes in the backyard, and squats to show her that he's not getting the job done. It takes Mama two or three days to realize what's going on. Then you and she carry Thai to the vet.

Mama waits tables at a Denny's near the expressway. She hasn't really got the money for the operation that Thai needs to clear up the blockage, a common problem in male Siamese. She tells you that you can either forfeit movie money for the next few months or help her pay to make Thai well. You hug Mama, wordlessly agreeing that the only thing to do is to help your cat. The operation goes okay, but the vet telephones a day later to report that Thai took a bad turn overnight and died near morning.

Thai's chocolate and silver body has a bandage cinched around his middle, like a wraparound saddle.

You're the one who buries Thai because Mama can't bring herself to. You put him in a Siamese-sized cardboard box, dig a hole under the holly in the backyard, and lay him to rest with a spank of the shovel blade and a prayer consisting of grief-stricken repetitions of the word please.

Two or three months later, you come home from school to find a pack of dogs in the backyard. They've dug Thai Thai up. You chase the dogs away, screeching from an irate crouch. Thai's corpse is nothing but matted fur and protruding bones. Its most conspicuous feature is the bandage holding the maggoty skeleton together at its cinched-in waist.

This isn't Thai, you tell yourself. I buried Thai a long, long time ago, and this isn't him.

You carry the remains, jacketed in the editorial section of the *Atlanta Constitution*, to a trash can and dump them with an abrupt, indifferent thunk. Pick-up is tomorrow.

One Sunday afternoon in March, you're standing with two hundred other homeless people at the entrance to Trinity United Methodist's soup kitchen, near the state capitol. It's drizzling. A thin but gritty-looking young woman in jeans and sweatshirt, her hair lying in dark strands against her forehead, is passing out hand-numbered tickets to every person who wants to get into the basement. At the head of the outside basement steps is a man in pleated slacks and a plaid shirt. He won't let anyone down the steps until they have a number in the group of ten currently being admitted. He has to get an okay from the soup-kitchen staff downstairs before he'll allow a new group of ten to pass.

Your number, on a green slip of paper already drizzle-dampened, is 126. The last group down held numbers 96 to 105. You think. Hard to tell with all the shoving, cursing, and bantering on the line. One angry black man up front doesn't belong there. He waves his ticket every time a new group of ten is called, hoping, even though his number is 182, to squeeze past the man set there to keep order.

"How many carahs yo ring?" he asks. "I sick. Mon n lemme eah fo I fall ouw. Damn disere rain."

When the dude holding number 109 doesn't show, the stair guard lets number 182 pass, a good-riddance sort of charity.

You shuffle up with the next two groups. How many of these people are robots, human machines drawn to the soup kitchen, as you may have been, on invisible tractor beams? The stair guard isn't wearing a watch or shaking a key ring. It's probably his wedding band that's the remote-control device. . . .

"My God," he cries when he sees you. "Is that really you? It is, isn't it?"

The stair guy's name is Dirk Healy. He says he went to school with you in Hapeville. Remember Pamela van Rhyn? Remember Cynthia What's-her-name? When you go down into the basement, and get your two white-bread sandwiches and a Styrofoam cup of vegetable soup, Dirk convinces another volunteer to take over his job and sits down next to you at one of the rickety folding tables where your fellow street folk are single-mindedly eating. Dirk—who, as far as you're concerned, could be the Man in the Moon—doesn't ask you how you got in this fix, doesn't accuse, doesn't exhort.

"You're off your medication, aren't you?" Your hackles lift.

"Hey," he soothes, "I visited you at Quiet Harbor. The thing to do is, to get you back on it."

You eat, taking violent snatches of the sandwiches, quick sips of the soup. You one-eye Dirk over the steam the way that, years ago, Sky one-eyed you from her grain-crib nest.

"I may have a job for you," Dirk says confidentially. "Ever hear of Rockdale Biological?"

One summer, for reasons you don't understand, Mama sends you to visit your father and his ex-hairdresser floozie—whose name is Carol Grace—in the Florida town where they live off the proceeds of her mail-order business and sometimes bet the dogs at the local greyhound track.

Carol Grace may bet the greyhounds at the track, but, at home, she's a cat person. She owns seven: a marmalade-colored tom, a piebald tom, three tricolor females, an orange Angora of ambiguous gender, and a Manx mix with a tail four or five inches long, as if someone shortened it with a cleaver.

"If Stub was pure Manx," Carol Grace says, "he wouldn't have no tail. Musta been an alley tom in his mama's Kitty Litter."

Stroking Stub, she chortles happily. She and your mother look a little alike. They have a similar feistiness, too, although it seems coarser in Carol Grace, whom your balding father—she calls him Webby, for Pete's sake—unabashedly dotes on.

A few days into your visit, Carol Grace and you find one of her females, Hedy Lamarr, lying crumpled under a pecan tree shading the two-story house's south side. The cat is dead. You kneel to touch her. Carol Grace kneels beside you.

"Musta fell," she says. "Lotsa people think cats are too jack-be-nimble to fall, but they can slip up, too. Guess my Hedy didn't remember that, pretty thing. Now look."

You are grateful that, today, Carol Grace does the burying and the prayer-saying. Her prayer includes the melancholy observation that anyone can fall. Anyone.

Enough of this crap, Penfield says. Tell me what you did, and for whom, and why, at Rockdale Biological.

Givin whah I can, you mumble, working to turn your head into the uncompromising rigidity of the clamps.

Adolf, Penfield says, what you're giving me is cat juggling.

Alone in the crafts room with Kim Yaughan while the other kids in Blue Group (QHPC's Wild Child Wing has two sections, Blue and Gold) go on a field trip, you daub acrylics at a crude portrayal of a cat walking upside down on a ceiling. Under the cat, a woman and a teen-age boy point and make hateful faces.

"Are they angry at the cat or at each other?" Kim asks.

You give her a look: What a stupid question.

Kim comes over, stands at your shoulder. If she were honest, she'd tell you that you're no artist at all. The painting may be psychologically revealing, but it refutes the notion that you have any talent as a draftsman or a colorist.

"Ever hear of British artist Louis Wain?" Kim says. "He lived with three unmarried sisters and a pack of cats. His schizophrenia didn't show up until he was almost sixty. That's late."

"Lucky," you say. "He didn't have so long to be crazy."

"Listen, now. Wain painted only cats. He must've really liked them. At first, he did smarmy, realistic kitties for calandars and postcards. Popular crap. Later, thinking jealous competitors were zapping him with X-rays or something, the cats in his paintings got weird, really hostile and menacing."

"Weirder than mine?" You jab your brush at it.

"Ah, that's a mere puddy-tat." Then: "In the fifteen years he was institutionalized, Wain painted scads of big-eyed, spiky-haired cats. He put bright neon auras and electrical fields around them. His backgrounds got geometrically rad. Today, you might think they were computer-generated. Anyhow, Wain's crazy stuff was better—fiercer, stronger—than the crap he'd done sane."

"Meaning I'm a total loss unless I get crazier?" you say.

"No. What I'm trying to tell you is that the triangles, stars, rainbows, and repeating arabesques that Wain put into his paintings grew from a desperate effort to . . . well, to impose order on the chaos *inside* him. It's touching, really touching. Wain was trying to confront and reverse, the only way he could, the disintegration of his adult personality. See?"

But you don't. Not exactly.

Kim taps your acrylic cat with a burgundy fingernail. "You're not going to be the new Picasso, but you aren't doomed to suffer as terrifying a schizophrenia as Wain suffered, either. The bizarre thing in your painting is the cat on the ceiling. The colors, and the composition itself, are reassuringly conventional. A good sign for your mental health. Another thing is, Wain's doctors couldn't give him antipsychotic drugs. We can."

"Cheers." You pantomime knocking back a little cup of Haldol.

Kim smiles. "So why'd you paint the cat upside-down?"

"Because *I'm* upside-down," you say.

Kim gives you a peck on the cheek. "You're not responsible for a gone-awry brain chemistry or an unbalanced metabolism, hon. Go easy on yourself, okay?" Dropping your brush, you pull Kim to you and try to nuzzle her under the jaw. Effortlessly, she bends back your hand and pushes you away. "But that," she says, "you're going to have to control. Friends, not lovers. Sorry if I gave you the wrong idea. Really. Really."

"If the pieces toward the end don't fit," Howie tells you, "you can always use a razor blade." He holds one up.

You try to take it. Double-edged, it slices your thumb. Some of your blood spatters on the cat puzzle.

A guy in a truck drives up to the specimen-prep platform and loading dock behind Rockdale Biological Medical Supply. It's an unmarked panel truck with no windows behind the cab. The guys who drive the truck change, it seems, almost every week, but you're a two-month fixture on the concrete platform with the slide cages and the euthanasia cabinet. Back here, you're Dirk Healy's main man, especially now that he's off on a business trip somewhere.

Your job is both mindless and strength-sapping. The brick wall around the rear of the RBMS complex, and the maple trees shielding the loading dock, help you keep your head together. Healy has you on a lower dosage of haloperidol than you took while you and Marti were still married. Says you were overmedicated before. Says you were, ha ha, "an apathetic drug slave." He should know. He's been a hotshot in national medical supply for years.

"We'll have you up in the front office in no time," he assured you a couple weeks ago. "The platform job's a kind of trial."

The guy in the truck backs up and starts unloading. Dozens of cats in slide cages. You wear elbow-length leather gloves, and a heavy apron, and feel a bit like an old-timey Western blacksmith. The cats are pieces of scrap iron to be worked in the forge. You slide the door end of each cage into the connector between the open platform and the euthanasia cabinet, then poke the cats in the butt or the flank with a long metal rod until they duck into the cabinet to escape your prodding. When the cabinet's full, you drop the safety door, check the gauges, turn on the gas. It hisses louder than the cats climbing over one another, louder than their yowling and tumbling, which noises gradually subside and finally stop.

By hand, you unload the dead cats from the chamber, slinging them out by their tails or their legs. You cease feeling like a blacksmith. You imagine yourself as a nineteenth-century trapper, stacking fox, beaver, rabbit, wolf, and musk-rat pelts on a travois for a trip to the trading post. The pelts are pretty, though many are blemished by vivid skin diseases and a thick black dandruff of gassed fleas. How much could they be worth?

"Nine fifty a cat," Dirk Healy has said. That seems unlikely. They're no longer moving. They're no longer—if they ever were—highly lustrous. They're floppy, anonymous, and dead, their fur contaminated by a lethal gas.

A heavy-duty wheelbarrow rests beside the pile of cats on the platform. You unwind a hose and fill the barrow with water. Dirk has ordered you to submerge the gassed cats to make certain they're dead. Smart. Some of the cats are plucky boogers. They'll mew at you or swim feebly in the cat pile even before you pick them up and sling them into the wheelbarrow. The water in the wheelbarrow ends it. Indisputably. It also washes away fleas and the worst aspects of feline scabies. You pull a folding chair over and sort through the cats for the ones with flea collars, ID collars, rabies tags. You take these things off. You do it with your gloves on, a sodden cat corpse hammocked in your apron. It's not easy, given your wet glove fingers.

If it's sunny, you take the dead cats to the bright part of the platform and lay them out in neat rows to dry.

Can't you get him to stop mumbling? Penfield asks someone in the room. His testimony's almost unintelligible.

He's replaying the experience inwardly, an indistinct figure says. But he's starting to go autistic on us.

Look, Penfield says. We've got to get him to verbalize clearly—or we've wasted our time.

Two months after the divorce, you drive to Spartanburg, to the Braggs' house, to see Jacob. Mr. Bragg—Howie—intercepts you at the front gate, as if appraised of your arrival by surveillance equipment.

"I'm sorry," he says, "but Marti doesn't want to see you, and she doesn't want *you* to see Jake. If you don't leave, I'll have to call the police to, ah, you know, remove you."

You don't contest this. You walk across the road to your car. From there, you can see that atop the brick post on either side of Mr. Bragg's ornate gate reposes a roaring granite lion. You can't remember seeing these lions before, but the crazed and reticulated state of the granite suggests they've been there a while. It's a puzzle. . . .

As you lay out the dead cats, you assign them names. The names you assign are always Mehitabel, Felix, Sylvester, Tom, Heathcliff, Garfield, and Bill. These seven names must serve for all the cats on the platform. Consequently, you add Roman numerals to the names when you run out of names before you do cats:

Mehitabel II, Felix II, Sylvester II, Tom II, and so on. It's a neat, workable system. Once, you cycled all the way to Sylvester VII before running out of specimens.

As a fifth grader in Notasulga, you sit and watch a film about the American space program.

An old film clip shows a cat—really more a kitten than a cat—suspended from a low ceiling by its feet. It's a metal ceiling, and the scientist who devised the experiment (which has something to do with studying the kitten's reactions to upside-downness, then applying these findings to astronauts aboard a space station) has fastened magnets to the cat's feet so that they will adhere to the metal surface.

The scientist has also rigged up a pair of mice in the same odd way, to see if they will distract, entice, or frighten the hanging kitten. They don't. The kitten is terrified not of the mice (who seem to be torpid and unimaginative representatives of their kind), but of the alien condition in which it finds itself. Insofar as it is able, the kitten lurches against the magnets, its ears back, its mouth wide open in a silent cry. On the sound track, a male voice explains the import and usefulness of this experiment.

No one can hear him, though, because most of the other kids in Miss Beischer's class are laughing uproariously at the kitten. You look around in a kind of sick stupefaction.

Milly Heckler, Agnes Lee Terrance, and a few other girls appear to be as appalled as you, but the scene doesn't last long—it's probably shorter than your slow-motion memory of it—and it seems for a moment that you *are* that kitten, that everything in the world has been wrenchingly upended.

"I know it *seemed* to you that evil people were trying to invade and control your thoughts," Dr. Hall, the director of Quiet Harbor, tells you. He pets a neutered male just back from a visit to the Gerontological Wing. "But that was just a symptom of the scrambled condition of your brain chemistry. The truth is . . ."

Fatigued, you slouch out the rear gate of Rockdale Biological. Your apartment—the three-roomer that Healy provided—is only a short distance away. A late-model Lincoln Town Car pulls alongside you as you walk the weed-grown sidewalk. The tinted window on the front-seat passenger's side powers down, and you catch your first glimpse of the raw-complexioned man who introduces himself as David Penfield. An alias? Why do you think so?

"If you like," he says, "think of me as the Zoo Cop."

It's a permission you don't really want. Why would you choose to think of a well-dressed, ordinary-featured man with visible acne scarring as something as *déclassé* as, Jesus, the Zoo Cop. Is he a detective of some sort? What does he want?

The next thing you know you're in the car with Penfield and two other tight-lipped men.

The next thing you know you're on the expressway and one of the Zoo Cop's associates—goons?—has locked the suction-cup feet of one of those corny Garfield toys on his tinted window as a kind of—what?—mockery? rebuke? warning?

The next thing you know you're in a basement that clearly isn't the soup kitchen of Trinity United Methodist. The next thing you know you're flat on your back on a table. The next thing you know you don't know anything. . . .

. . . Marti's body is stenciled with primitive blue flowers, a blossom on her neck, more on her breasts, an indigo bouquet on the milky plane of her abdomen. You gaze at her in groggy wonderment. The woman you one day marry has become, overnight, an arabesque of disturbing floral bruises.

"Marti," you whisper. "Marti, don't leave me. Marti, don't take my son away."

Penfield, a.k.a. the Zoo Cop (you realize during your descent into the puzzle box), isn't a real cop. He hates you because what you've been doing for Healy is vile, contemptible, *evil*. So it is, so it is. He wants to get Healy, who hasn't been around this last week at all, who's maybe skipped off to Barbados or the Yucatan or Saint-Tropez.

Penfield is an animal-rights eco-terrorist, well-financed and determined, and the ESB zappings to which he and his associates are subjecting you are designed to incriminate, pinpoint, and doom old Dirk and *his* associates, who obviously deserve it. You, too. You deserve it, too. No argument there. None.

Christ, Penfield says, unhook the son of a bitch and carry him upstairs. Dump him somewhere remote, somewhere rural.

You visit the pound for a replacement for Springer and Ossie, gassed three or four years ago. The attendant tells you there are plenty of potential adoptees at the shelter. You go down the rows of cages to select one. The kittens in the fouled sawdust tumble, paw, and miaow, putting on a dispirited show.

"This one," you finally say.

"Cute." The attendant approves. Well, they'd fire her if she didn't. The idea is to adopt these creatures out, not to let them lapse into expendability.

"It's for Jake, my son," you tell her. "His asthma isn't that bad. I think he may be growing out of it."

"Look at my puzzle," Howie says, yanking the razor blade away from you. "You've bled all over it. . . ."

—For Jeanne Schinto

Bright Burning Tiger
by
Tanith Lee

*Tanith Lee is one of the best known and most prolific of modern
fantasists, with well over a dozen books to her credit, including
(among many others)* The Birth Grave, Drinking Sapphire
Wine, Don't Bite the Sun, Night's Master, The Storm Lord,
Sung in Shadow, Volkhavaar, Anackire, Night Sorceries, *and
the collections* Tamastara *and* The Gorgon. *Her short story
"Elle Est Trois (La Mort)" won a World Fantasy Award in
1984, and her brilliant collection of retold folk tales,* Red as
Blood, *was also a finalist that year, in the Best Collection
category. Her most recent books are the massive collection*
Dreams of Dark and Light, *and a new novel,* The Blood of
Roses.*

*Here she takes us deep into the haunted jungles of India and
even deeper into the primordial jungles of the mind, to a place
where terror can reach the intensity of ecstasy, beauty can cut
like a knife, and truth can be as fiery and searing as a bright
burning tiger. . . .*

*   *   *

Long, long ago in London a girl of my acquaintance, finding
her ginger feline asleep by the gas fire, struck a pose, one foot
lightly on the cat's back, announcing: "Shot it in Injuh,
y'know," and she had so perfectly caught, in voice and stance,
the pompous waking dream of the British raj, that it became a
game often repeated; only ended at last by the intolerance of
the cat to playing tiger's skin. As for me, the joke summed up
a basic personal attitude. I had then an allergic indifference to
a type of man and his pursuits, as unlike myself and mine as
those of an alien species. Later, when I learned more of the
facts, some of the glibness of the joke had to be rethought.
There are occasionally among tigers maneaters, which can prey
on the remoter villages of the jungle-forest, cruel, maddened

35

things that seem to hate, killing from lust rather than hunger, leaving the half-devoured bodies of women among the stalks of the fields at sunrise; by night a nightmare shadow, so a man will be afraid to go out of his hut to make water in case death has him. There is sometimes a need for a bullet, which the sneer and the attitude had formerly cloaked. Much later again, when I met Pettersun, I came to understand, unwillingly at first, maybe always unwillingly, something of what drives one hunter, something actually of the uncanny bond which can come to obtain between one who hunts, one who is hunted. Certainly to perceive the slender division that exists, always interchangeable. For the man may misfire, the weapon stall, the beaters run away, and the dark come down which is the tiger's country, the land of night. And in the forests of the night, the golden beast with his nocturnal sight, the unalloyed weapons of his mouth, the blades of his feet, his great strength—the creature capable of eating men—that is no mean adversary. It isn't in me to enter, to want to enter, the magic circle of any of this. Not merely that I lack the courage, though I do lack it, but because I could never kill anything either ritually or callously that I absolutely did not have to. And luckily, I never have had to kill anything, beast or man. For this reason, perhaps, I can tell my story, safe by a sort of mitigating accident. I wonder.

It was just outside the Victoria Memorial in Calcutta that I met the fat man. Part of my living comes from carrying out paid research for others, and my mind was still idling somewhere between here and the Jadu Ghar, my feet already turning toward the hotel. Softening the slums and palaces, an orange sun bled low over the Maidan. The fat man blocked the view, halting before me on the steps and introducing himself. I can't recall who he said he was, but he knew me from an article that had carried my photograph. I was thinking with annoyance he would now engage me in argument over something I had written and forgotten, when he told me Pettersun was dead.

"How?" I was shocked by aptness, not surprise, and the query was half rhetorical. It was fairly obvious what must have occurred, nor was I mistaken.

"A tiger killed him. Funny business. Damn funny. I've given myself the responsibility, you might say, to let people know, people who knew him."

"I never knew him well."

"Didn't you? That's all right then. But still, a funny business." I looked at the blankness of his dark silhouette with the amber sunset crackling around the fat edges of it. He wanted to say some more. "Funny," he said.

"You mean amusing, or peculiar?"

"Oh, not amusing. Not at all. Peculiar. Yes, that's it."

"Why?" I said.

"Well, he wasn't off hunting it, you know. He was in bed."

"In—*bed*—"

"Exactly. And the thing came in, right into the bungalow, and tore him in pieces. Pretty horrible, I gather. Yes, pretty damn horrible."

It certainly sounded odd. Monkeys, rats, snakes, these come into houses, not tigers that I ever heard of. The fat man stood, gloating over his own dismay, mine. I was compelled to go on, ask questions.

"Where did this happen?"

"North," he said, and named a small town. "About ten miles from there. A couple of villages. One of the old rangers' bungalows. He was living there, out in the jungle. Just drinking a lot, not doing anything. Then there was a scare apparently, a maneater. They'd heard about Pettersun and came and asked him if he'd take it on, and Pettersun said, No, he was through with all that. But he started cleaning his gun—you remember that gun of his with ivory—"

"Yes, I remember."

"Then there's a panic, you know how they are. The tiger's everywhere. In the village. In the other village. Up a tree, in the fields, down the well— He was going out the next night, or that's how I heard it, torches and beaters, the whole bloody show. A little before dawn he was lying there with the gin bottle for company and—whap! One of his beaters found him and ran out screaming. It was mucky."

"How do you know all this?"

"Doctor at Chadhur was called in to look at the body. I know Hari pretty well. Second-hand news, but reliable."

"It sounds unbelievable."

The fat man didn't take offense. He shrugged.

"It does, doesn't it. But the Bombay papers had it, you know, a paragraph or two."

"How long ago was all this?"

"A couple of months. Well, that's life. I could do with something cool."

The dim wild cry of sunset worship was beginning to rise from distant mosques. I excused myself to the fat man and went away to get a drink alone.

I digested Pettersun's death slowly in the shadow of the turning fans, like huge insects in the ceiling. How else must a hunter die, but logically under the hoof or claw or fang of the entity he has so long himself stood over, his foot on its neck, the rifle smoking. Shot it in India. Though he had not been one for tigerskin rugs.

I hadn't, as I said, known him well. I hadn't liked him, God forbid, or admired him, except possibly for his bravery, for there had been stories of that I had heard from other sources. I suppose to some extent he fascinated me, the forbidden fruit of what our own ethic tells us is wrong, which to another is only an ordinary facet of existence. I'd met him at a sprawling English party in Bombay, full of men in penguin costume and women in gold lamé dresses, all of them brown as tanned leather, which made the coffee flesh of the waiters look almost blue. We spoke generally for a while, part of a group, which gradually drifted away, leaving Pettersun alone with me. He then said, smiling, as if he'd been waiting the chance, "You don't like me much do you." No question, no aggression; a statement. I said nothing. He swirled the last of his drink, drank it and said, "Or rather, you don't like what I do. Orion the Hunter. The wicked man who kills the nice animals."

I shrugged, considering the neatest way of escaping, which hadn't yet suggested itself. One of the waiters came by with more drinks, and Pettersun took off four, the fourth of which he handed to me.

"Thanks," I said.

"Yes," he said. He drank the first of his new drinks straight down, and said, "Call me names, if you like. I don't shoot men."

"Just tigers," I said, before I could stop myself.

"Just tigers? A tiger is never *just* tiger."

"For sport," I said.

"No," he said. Still the smile, throwing me, enjoying it? "I'd never call it that."

This was becoming boring and uncomfortable.

"Well," I said, helpfully, "a maneater obviously—"

"So you won't stand up for your principles," he said, and drank that second drink. "You think I'm an offense on God's green earth, but you're not about to tell me so."

"Mr. Pettersun," I said, "what you do is your problem."

"Afraid I'll hit you if you speak up, break the chiseled nose, is that it? I won't. I'm a peaceable man. I like booze, preferably free. I kill tigers. Note, I didn't say I *liked* killing them. That's it. The sum of my parts."

"Excuse me," I said. As I turned, he put the third glass into my other hand, which duly stayed me, because he had obviously wanted it himself. "Have a drink?" he said.

I stood there with a glass in either hand, looking at him, wondering.

"What do you want?" I said.

"I think," he said, "I want to talk to you, tell you—about the very thing you don't want to hear about."

"In other words, you want to be a nuisance."

"No."

"Convert me? Not a chance."

"Well of course not," Pettersun said. "There's no pleasure in conversion. And debate is normally pointless, isn't it?" I stayed where I was, caught despite myself because he had said something I myself believed. "So, what can it be?"

I started to drink the drink he had given me. I said: "Drunken egomania needing to find a voice?"

He laughed. "This affair stinks," he said. "I know a place on the waterfront where a girl dances with cobras on all the tables. You like that kind of thing?"

"Yes, I sometimes like that kind of thing."

In the "place" where the barefoot girl did her dance every two hours, swishing her black hair like a horse's tail, the milked snakes knotted on her arms, at her waist, we drank something alcoholic curdled in *lassi*. I wasn't even then sure what had made me go there with him. It would be easy enough, with hindsight, to say I sensed he needed to confess, last rites before execution. As someone I once knew said, there is something of the priest about me, somehow, somewhere, apparent both to myself and, under particular circumstances, to others.

The preliminary conversation rambled, I don't recollect much of it, but when he began to *talk* to me, as he had said he wished to, there came a kind of clarity which I do remember and maybe always shall. No sentences are left, but I retain their kernel. For this was when the free-masonry of the hunt was made known to me, and I was just drunk enough that it came in over or under the barriers of my mind and ethics, and I understood, and I still understand, though I won't condone. Condone it less, probably, since I saw the attraction, the religious element, the extraordinary bonding that might occur (at least in the human's mind), which must then be sought after like a drug. While it was some bloody old duffer with his rifle and his notions of sport it stayed safely and obscenely remote. But the sorcerous quality of the ritual of the hunt, arcane and special, and there, I suspect, in many of us, had a seductive frisson that had to be resisted—which in fact made it all the more repulsive—the venus flytrap.

I recall too, well into the night, staggering back along by the seashore, the black water and the towering ghosts of apartment buildings, and the moon like ivory, like the ivory inlay on the rifle, of which he carried a snapshot, just as other men carry photos of their women or their children, or lacking those, their dogs.

In the morning, waking with a hangover, I thought it had been a waste of time, ridiculous. But very soon the teachings— for he had taught me his philosophy, under the wild fig tree of the dancing girl's shade—came back. Hunter and hunted, the stalker and the prey, woven by reeds, by leaves, by shadows, by bloodthirst and fear, and by desire. And which was which?

Then getting up to put my head in the basin full of lukewarm water, I thought angrily: Rubbish. A man with a gun. What chance had the wretched tiger? Who did Pettersun think he was fooling? But he hadn't been trying to fool me. He had only been saying, This is how it is, for some, for me. Right or wrong. This. I had never had much patience with Hemingway, but I reread *The Old Man and the Sea* a week later, in the blazing Indian veranda. The relationship between the fisherman and the great beautiful hooked fish—aside from necessity, thick-headed, wanton, unaware—anything its detractors will prove it—but powerfully illustrative, in its way, of the mystique Pettersun had revealed to me. But if it is possible to murder with honor and love and pity, then all the more reason to stop.

I never met Pettersun again. A few months later, the fat man met me instead on the Memorial steps in Calcutta and said, "A tiger killed him. Funny business."

So, then. Just over twelve months later, doing this time some research on my own behalf, I ended up more or less randomly in Chadhur.

Once I had my own professional affairs in hand, I went over to the hospital building. Here I loitered, pondering if I really wanted or intended to chase the matter. But someone asked me, as they do Europeans, who I was looking for. I replied with the name of the doctor the fat man had called familiarly, "Hari."

Graceful and gregarious, Doctor Hari invited me into his office for very good coffee, and I broached my subject tentatively. The response was not tentative at all. Doctor Hari had had for Pettersun all the rage of the good physician for the intransigent patient. "If the tiger had not done for him, his alcoholism would have seen to it. His system was in revolt. On the path he had chosen he had a year or less."

"But it's true, then. I heard the animal got into—"

"—the bungalow and attacked him in bed? Quite true. Do you have a strong stomach?"

Pettersun had been disemboweled, the heart and throat torn out—the rest of the corpse had been bitten, rent, virtually slit like a sack. "It was quite a mess. The villagers are used to death and mishap, but they were terribly afraid and superstitious. I too have seen a number of men killed by tigers or panthers. Never a body exactly in this condition, and all uneaten."

"Then it wasn't the tiger he was out to get?"

"Well, perhaps. The second village trapped a tiger about ten days after—an old tiger turned to man-flesh, as they sometimes do, because men are easier game. I should say this tiger was not strong enough to have done to the body what had been done. Naturally, sometimes they will kill and not eat, but then not maul so savagely, splitting open, almost a dissection. While the room was untouched."

"How did it get in?"

"The door was open. He had left it open—wide, like an invitation, one might almost say. Very strange. Very unpleasant. And sad. There are other villages in the area with cause to be grateful to Pettersun."

I had a dead feeling, the letdown of anticlimax. I didn't know what I had expected to hear. Then, as I was leaving, Doctor Hari said, "Of course, the drinking had made him do curious things. On the wall of the bungalow, for example, he had written something in big letters. A poem of some sort, some modern English or American verse, unrhyming. About a tiger, naturally. The villagers still refuse to go near the house at night."

To go out to the bungalow was the next thing to do, so I put off doing it. Pettersun's death was stale a year now, and nothing to me or to do with me. My interest did not seem purely ghoulish, but probably was. Against that, I knew I couldn't leave without following events to their proper conclusion. Finally I got a car and took to the new highway, which bore me all the way to the town of the fat man's tale. From there the wisest course was horseback, colonial style, along the dusty road and into the blistered, streaked, striped heart of the jungle. Here I almost gave myself entirely to the spirit of the place, the intense enclosure of the massive trees skirted with broad leaves and thickets of bamboo. A few times women passed me on the track, walking what I call the sari-walk, wound in their jewel-bright garments, basket or pot on head. They were lean and proud and sometimes beautiful beyond measure. Presently I saw a village, downhill in a valley, where the jungle broke and scattered. Grain stood straight up at the sky, children ran about, a herd of buffalo wallowed in summer mud.

The sky had turned briefly to a wall of glowing maroon beyond the trees, when I reached the bungalow—and nearly missed it. The jungle, as in Kipling, had been let in, vines and high grass all over everything, barely the glint of dirty-white veranda posts to show me. There was a cookhouse round at the back and a couple of huts, but these also were overgrown; the roofs had fallen in.

I stirred about for a while, the horse cropping the grass, unconcerned. The doors to the house had been boarded up by authority, and I had no intention of forcing them in the dark. There seemed nothing dangerous abroad, but as the night smoked through the forest, I remounted and made my way back to the village. Here I was greeted with curiosity amounting to joy. I didn't mention my errand or that I had been to the bungalow, merely did a little trading over the rice and spiced vegetables. Later a child of five appeared, who spoke to the men in Hindi of his wife and family, the family cow and goat, the ailment of his youngest daughter. It was the memory of the recent past life. Such things are not uncommon in India. The child's mother presently came in and comforted him, telling him all would be well. He would soon forget prior responsibilities, as this life and its obligations claimed him. When the child had been taken off, I mentioned tigers, and at once a deep silence fell. The men looked at one another. Eventually someone told me, "There are no tigers here. They have gone away."

"But surely," I said, "someone was attacked by a tiger in these parts, about a year ago . . . quite a well-known hunter—Porter, Potter—some name like that."

"Yes," said another gravely. "That tiger was killed. There are no more."

I looked at their gaunt, passionless faces, so handsome some of them, enduring all. Outside, across the space of nighttime earth, the forlorn child, burdened by obligations he could no longer uphold, slept on his mother's breast. They had shared food with me and would shelter me, and I could force no more of my own wants on them. I didn't sleep that night behind their safe stockade, lying listening to the rustle of leaves and stars. At first light I left, walking the horse through endless-seeming ranks of goats being arranged for milking, and girls walking to the well.

Up in the jungle-heart the bungalow had not altered, still locked up in its boards and creepers. Leaving the tethered horse I forced one of the windows, and climbed through into what had been Pettersun's sleeping room. The low Indian bed, its lacquer peeling and webbing broken, still stood dutifully at one wall, the rotted netting hanging down about it like cobwebs. Some shelves, a desk, a chair, these things remained, but no niceties, if there had ever been any. There was no idiosyncratic odor in the room. Becoming one with the invading jungle, it had the jungle smell, tinders and juices. Lianas had come through the foundations even, and covered the floor, so that any stains there were hidden.

The verse Doctor Hari had told me of was on the wall facing the bed, written in paint with long letters that leaned in all directions. It was dark enough, I had trouble making any of it out. When I did, an unnerving pang of recognition went through me, still displaced. Pettersun had written this:

> Symmetry fearful thy frame could
> Eye? Or Hand Immortal—What?
> Night—the; of forests. The in—
> Bright burning Tiger! Tiger!

I stood there, breathing audibly, startled, hearing the birds and the monkeys calling through the jungle, silently reading the words over, until suddenly, of course, that *Tiger! Tiger!* gave me the key. It was nothing else but Blake's poem, but all bizarrely reversed, the last line first, the second to last second, second line third, first line last. And each word in each line also reversed, first word last, last first, and so on. Gibberish. No astonishment Hari had thought it some avant-garde piece

coined in Greenwich Village. The punctuation, too, was
scarcely Blake's.

"Madman," I said aloud, jolted to an abrupt disgust and
compassion neither of which had I thought to feel so forcibly,
if at all. "Poor bloody drunken murdering madman." And,
having spoken, I read the nonsense on the wall also aloud, to
the quiet box of bungalow held in noisy jungle.

Something clicked in my brain as I did so. I stumbled
mentally after it. Elusive, it was gone. In some preposterous
manner, the lunatic reversal of the fragment of poem—made
sense. As if, blindfolded, one touched a cat's fur in darkness,
not knowing, yet instinct to say: Ah, but *this* is—before the
acceptable name came or light to disclose.

Then, letting in the jungle, something else was let in.
Standing there with a shaft of olive green sunlight on the vine
carpet, I visualized the tawny shadow of death-by-night
shouldering through the opened doorway. Every hair stood up
on my body and my loins were cold and empty with horror. It
was imperative to escape. I fled through the window, tearing
skin and clothing, pursued by demons of the mind. Pettersun's
mind.

When I had calmed down, I got on the horse and rode in the
direction of the other village the fat man, and Doctor Hari, had
informed me of.

The simple explanation of what happened next is that I
misjudged my road, got off the track, blundered about and
made things worse for myself, ending up the proverbial
panic-stricken lost traveler of song and story. I suppose that is
what happened, though generally I rarely lose my way, or if I
do I regain it fairly quickly. Not so in this instance. The track
all at once dissolved, and carefully retracing my way for some
distance, or trying to, I failed to rediscover it. Various
formations of trees, angles of illumination, which I had noted
and which might have provided guidance, seemed mysteri-
ously changed, though the greenish jungle sun streamed
through and the shadows massed and the monkeys screamed to
each other, all as they had been doing minutes before. If
anything, something was at fault in my own perception.

I fell into the pit of compounding my error by then defiantly pressing on. I was sure I would soon pick up the path again, discover a fresh one, or merely ride through a break in the foliage and so into the village, by a sort of serendipity. None of these things happened. In the end sheer heat and exhaustion forced me to halt, dismount in the shade and drink water. Here I very foolishly went to sleep for almost an hour, an idiotic thing to do. As a rule, the beasts of the forest do not attack sleeping creatures, but Pettersun had probably been asleep when so attacked—what price faith? Besides, snakes haunt the wilderness, and sometimes itinerant human beings, the worst predators of all.

When I woke, irritated by everything, mostly myself, I had given up on my quest. The second village was plainly enchanted, and had vanished. Using the compass, and occasionally aided by glimpses of afternoon sun marking the west, I turned back toward the first village which was real. Although I had been floundering for some while and my bearings were hopelessly out, that group of huts and persons, and the reincarnated child, lay directly over to the east, and the tracks which led to and from the place were good. I had no doubts I should get there well before sunset.

Hours later, bathed in sweat, the horse shambling, the hollows bowing into shadow and the glimpsed sky throwing hot bars against the trees, I began to be dully afraid. It seemed I had now lost my clue to anywhere. The jungle had me, bound me in its veils and towering stems. There was no way back, no way out. I stopped then, and tried not to lose my nerve too. It was difficult.

The red flame died and the grayness came in a rush, and in another rush the black of night. I sat the horse, as the sounds of day receded and the choruses of the frogs grew loud, mocking me, for this black fearful interior was home to them. And to others.

The *Ramayana*, which speaks of the roaring of wild animals, the tangled walks, the fatigue and privation of this landscape of trees, says the forest is the realm of the wind, darkness, hunger and great terrors.

There was nothing now to be done till morning. I had water and some crumbs to make my magnificent evening *khana*. I possessed no weapon, save the means of starting fire, which I would arrange at once. My sleep I had had. I would watch tonight.

I kept my vigil well. Maybe tiredness came to assist me, for I passed swiftly into that Benzedrine state where sleep seems superficial anyway, an invention of time-wasters. Slight fear was here, too, a constant. Slight fear like a condiment sprinkled on the enormous lulling beauty of the night. Not that I could see very much, beyond the sharp gold splashings of my fire. The beauty was in the blackness, and only the blackness lay out there, fold on fold of it, vision coming solely through the ears. Everywhere was the steady burring of frogs and nocturnal insects, which frequently fell death-still, as it does, not for any sinister reason, at least no reason that might be sinister for me. A couple of times, too, came the pandemonic uproar of monkeys disturbed, bursting adrenaline through my bloodstream, after each of which alarums I relapsed, smiling a little. The forests, "realm of terrors," are essentially and potentially dangerous, but there will seldom be actual violence. The venomous serpent, dropping on the neck like coiled rope from the ceiling of boughs, the big cat, famished and rearing from the bushes, these are the stuff of the book and film industry.

Periodically I looked at my watch, pleased at the timelessness I had achieved, where minutes passed like hours, and where two hours could go in what seemed only minutes. That sacerdotalism I've mentioned perhaps lay behind the sense I had of the peace of contemplation the *sadhu* pursues to such spots. For yes, here you might feel the depth and shallowness of created things, their oneness, the bottomless, endless, blissful nothing that is everything, and which contains the vibrating root of the soul. I was delighted also that I had avoided the cliché of supposing I had been brought there by fate. The idea of silly accident sustained me. At length, I could say it would be dawn in scarcely more than an hour, and with the new day I should find my way wherever I wished.

I had no thought of Pettersun, who inadvertently had caused

me to be where, now I was. He seemed far off from my contemplations. As if I were forgetting him.

The light came when the dawn remained most of an hour away. This was not sunrise.

It was separated light, like that of my own fire. I formed the opinion at once, with mingled hope and distrust, that mankind had arrived with torches, and whether friend or foe I had no means of telling. I sat on with my spine to the tree, my hearth before me, trying to make out figures round the alien glare.

Presently my uneasiness increased. I had realized whoever carried the torches was playing some sort of puzzling game. First of all, they did not approach, but seemed to be circling me to the left, the flame flashing on and off as stands of fern or trunks interposed. Secondly, unless small children or midgets were concerned, whoever flourished the brands must be crawling on their knees.

My blood was undiluted adrenaline by now, and rising I moved away from my fire as quietly as I could, taking up a position against a neighboring tree. My anticipation was of robbers, even some revival of the stranglers of Kali Ma. My horse, tethered nearby, was snorting and prancing in the undergrowth. Perhaps the answer would be to slash the tether with the knife I had picked up and now defensively cradled, leap on the horse's back and make a wild dash through the pitch-black jungle. But such a headlong course was precarious and I was not sure I preferred it. Bluff, lies, and a gift of rupees might be handier.

I had reached this partial decision when something else struck me about the circling, low-down blaze of torchlight. And now I was rather stunned, completely disinclined to attempt or plan escape because everything seemed inappropriate, faced by the fact that, though the light stayed all together—some thirteen or fourteen feet of it—it reflected on nothing, lit up nothing, could not therefore be *light* at all.

Just then the vegetable strands of the darkness parted, and the lightless light flamed through.

I remember I said, "Oh God," quietly, as if I were expected to. That was all. It was pointless to say or do anything.

There is a kind of terror that is no longer truly terror, but some type of refined and developed emotion that terror has bred—a sort of ecstasy in which fear, actually, has no part, nor the will to resist that fear usually supplies. I had heard it once or twice described. Now I felt it.

I could make excuses at this juncture, or alternately could pile the expletives up to mountain height and let off fireworks from the top—both methods resorted to out of nervousness. Because what I must put down now will, of course, not be believed. I didn't imagine it, or dream it, I do believe in it myself, but only because I saw it.

What had appeared in front of me was a tiger; it was Pettersun's tiger, and I choose that possessive with care. It had a tiger's shape, and a tiger's aura, from the canine swagger of the hindquarters found always in the greater felines, to the sculpted almost toylike modeling of the head. The blazon of the tiger it had too, it was the color of apricots laced with zebra stripes, as if the scars of a beating had been inlaid with jet. It stood longer and higher than any tiger I had seen or heard of; if it came closer, as undoubtedly it would, its head might nearly level with my own. But freaks occur in nature, men or beasts mightier, larger, than their fellows. The light was inexplicable. For the tiger, Pettersun's tiger, burned bright, bright as the fire I had mistaken it for, and on this conflagration which shed no gleam to either side, or anywhere, the black stripes seemed like the bars of a furnace, holding the power of it barely contained.

The eyes were also fire, or apertures into the fire which composed it, not green as the lenses of cats become by night, but golden like the rest. The eyes saw me, perhaps not my flesh, but piercing like an X ray through to my bones. In my ecstasy of terror I understood this much: I was no prey to it. To kill me would be incidental—how it had killed Pettersun— death a by-product of the thing it was. And yet, this was not so, not the truth—even in that extremity I knew I had made a mistake and if I died, would die without the extreme unction of an answer. And then the tiger moved. It moved like a forest fire, plunging in a straight igniting line, right at me. My heart stopped. Started again as the gush of gold veered and crossed my path. At the last, its eyes avoided mine, uninterested. Its dog's ears were pricked, listening, but not to me, the trembling of my body and my mind. The unstrung bow of its tail brushed through the grasses that should have exploded into arson, that only dipped aside, falling over to lave my hands with coolest dew not sparks.

Having seen everything, I then covered my eyes with my hands.

When I looked again, the forests were stirring; a subtle penciling in of forms hinted at the dawn; all other fires were out.

I put down the beginning of Blake's poem, though so well known, to facilitate this final act, as one sets out each stage meticulously, when solving a mathematical problem. It runs:

> Tyger! Tyger! Burning bright,
> In the forests of the night,
> What immortal hand or eye
> Dare frame thy fearful symmetry?

When the scald of morning lifted the black rind off the jungle, I started to walk, leading the horse, due east. If I had needed proof, which I did not, that something out of the ordinary had touched the vicinity, the horse would have furnished it. Sweating, shivering, and skittish, trying to kick at me, frothing, rolling its eyes—this was what my docile mount of yesterday had become. I led it with the utmost difficulty. It was clearly not afraid of anything that lay ahead, only unhinged; my own state, relegated to the primal.

After about fifteen minutes, I came into the clearing where a hint of dirty whiteness—a veranda rail and posts—announced the bungalow. This was how near I had been to it all night. I don't think the knowledge would have enhanced my pleasure. To find it now merely added a suitable footnote to what had gone before.

I skirted the building with pedantic caution. I wanted no part of it, and once it was behind me, the urge to bolt was almost irresistible. Somehow I controlled it, just as, somehow, I controlled the horse. When we reached the village, we were welcomed with courtesy and without comment. No doubt, the wound of the supernatural was raw for all to see, but I was not theirs, and they did not try to pry or comfort me.

A week later, when I had got back to Chadhur, I hung about in the hotel, waiting for myself to go off the boil like a kettle removed from the scene of the heat. My nerves were jarred in such a way that I could not put my finger on what the disorder was, or how it should be cured. I had accepted that I had brushed with things occult, but they had done me no physical harm. Reasonably elastic and rational as it generally was, my intellect would surely learn to cope with this; already I had perspective. Time would resolve the rest. Yet so far time had only made me worse. It was nothing so mundane as loss of appetite or sleep. I slept perhaps rather more readily than was my wont. And if my dreams were hectic, they were not about tigers, rather about a multitude of unimportant stupid items, that awake one would dismiss—a fly in the room, a dull, unidentified noise, trying to recall the name of someone never met. Awake, I ate and took healthy exercise, was no longer jittery; sudden sounds did not bring me to my feet with a wail. No, it was nothing I could lay my hand on, pick up and examine and so be done with. And yet it was as if my balance on the tightrope of life were gone. I could do all I should, could even be relaxed about it. Yet I knew I had fallen and somehow was suspended in midair.

After two days, I walked across to the hospital and located Doctor Hari's office and good coffee. He knew, without being informed, where I had been, and said nothing of it, only remarking as he poured the second cup, "You look a little not yourself. Can I do anything for you?"

"Only if you have a prescription for psychic whiplash."

"Ah ha! The phantom tiger of the forests."

I was not amazed he'd heard of it. I had come to believe that gaudy beast of golden fire was often sighted, and word passed on to credible and skeptic alike.

"Yes," I said. "And there really is one."

"Well," he said. "And why not?"

"You haven't said: Did you see it? Does that mean you've seen it yourself?" He only smiled. I thought perhaps he had not. I said, "What you can do for me, if you would, is ask your resident scholar if he'd consider letting me have a translation of this."

Hari accepted the sheet of paper mildly. The "resident scholar," his pet patient, was convalescing in an unusual condition of hermitage.

"I realize I'm being a damn nuisance," I said. "But I would be very grateful, and naturally I'd compensate him for his time in whatever way he felt was suitable."

"I am not hesitating for that. Your Hindi is fine, and I know from what you have written that you can read the language perfectly well."

"In this case, though, shall I say I need a second opinion?"

Hari glanced at the brief array of words. He may have recognized my own script, or some essence of text. He raised one long curved eyebrow, a dramatic gesture I respected, grinned and told me he would do what he could. Next evening, as the flying-foxes stormed the moon, he found me on the hotel roof and gave me the translation, its price an iced coconut juice. The scholar, it seemed, refused all payment.

I didn't read the translation then. I waited until I was alone, and then I waited until the hotel was noiseless, and the streets noiseless, and then until the streets and the hotel began to sound again with dawn. Then I chided myself, and opened the paper and read it through and put it away, and took it out again and read it again, and sat a long while as the window flooded with light, hearing goats and coughing cars, and bicycles and bullock carts, and the relentless drumming of my own heart, as my balance came back to me.

When I had said it aloud, that writing on the wall of Pettersun's bungalow, the phonetics had stolen in on me, and after gestation, offered themselves. They were basic enough; to replace "eye" with that which resembles it: "I." And in the vernacular that employs the word "thy" to guess that maybe the word "the" might become the word "thee." And primed by that, I had written out the back-to-front verse again, with its alterations, thus: *Symmetry fearful thy frame could I? Or Hand Immortal—What? Night—thee; of forests. Thee in—Bright burning Tiger! Tiger!* And again, a fraction closer, that *click* of intuitive knowledge—cat's fur touched blindfolded—yet not enough. And then I hit upon the obvious. I translated the bizarre sentences, as they stood, flatly into Hindi, and gave them to a bi-lingual scholar for free and profound translation back into our native tongue, Blake's, mine, and Pettersun's. And so I received my answer. It wasn't, I think, an invocation. Although Pettersun knew, he did *not* know. Although he wanted, he had no notion of wanting. Or at least of what the wanting was and how it might be satisfied. It had to tear him in pieces to get out, that monstrous and fantastical birth—the beast within, the glittering core of what he had tried to possess through pursuing, to become through destroying, the alter image, the bond, the magic circle, hunter and hunted—the place where the margin wears so thin that one may become the other. To the villages perhaps, it is the transmigration principle. He died and returned to pay *Karma* as a tiger. But no, he is the tiger's child, as surely as he gave birth to it—to *himself*. The Id foresaw, if Pettersun did not. The Id always foresees. And that was why, stumbling through the medium of Blake, knowing no other, he wrote on his wall what the kindly Brahman translated for me, this prayer to the infinite Possibility:

Flawless and fearful One, could I assume thy form?
Or, Immortal moving Fate, what is my portion?
Thou art Night, thou art the forests' night. Thou art within—
Bright burning Tiger! Tiger!

I Love Little Pussy
by
Isaac Asimov

A gentle children's poem was the inspiration for this tale of an aging spinster's love for her kitten, and the bizarre and funny consequences that follow upon a misguided attempt to strengthen the ties that bind. . . .

*A good case could be made for the proposition that Isaac Asimov is the most famous SF writer alive. He is the author of more than four hundred books, including some of the best-known novels in the genre (*The Caves of Steel, I, Robot, *and the* Foundation *trilogy, for example); his last several novels kept him solidly on the nationwide bestseller lists throughout the '80s; he has won two Nebulas and two Hugos, plus the prestigious Grandmaster Nebula; he has written an enormous number of nonfiction books on a bewilderingly large range of topics, everything from the Bible to Shakespeare, and his many books on scientific matters have made him perhaps the best-known scientific popularizer of our time; his nonfiction articles have appeared everywhere from* Omni *to* TV Guide; *he is one of the most sought-after speakers in the country, has appeared on most of the late-night and daytime talk shows, and has even done television commercials—and he is also the only SF writer famous enough to ever have had an SF magazine named after him,* Isaac Asimov's Science Fiction Magazine. *A mere sampling of Asimov's other books, even restricting ourselves to fiction alone (we should probably say, to SF alone, since he is almost as well known in the mystery field), would include* The Naked Sun, The Stars Like Dust, The Currents of Space, The Gods Themselves, Foundation's Edge, The Robots of Dawn, Robots and Empire, *and* Foundation's Earth. *His most recent fiction titles include the collection* Azazel, *and two expansions of famous Asimov short stories* *into novel form,* The Ugly Little Boy *and* Nightfall, *written in collaboration with Robert Silverberg.*

* * *

George and I were sitting on a park bench on a perfect late spring day when a rather ordinary tabby cat wandered into our vicinity. I knew there were feral cats in the park that would be dangerous to approach, but this specimen had the inquisitive look of a tame pussy. Since I am proud of the fact that cats are attracted to me, I held out my hand and sure enough she sniffed at it and allowed me to stroke her head.

I was rather surprised to hear George mutter, "Wretched little beast."

"Don't you like cats, George?" I asked.

"Would you expect me to, in the light of my sad history?" he said, sighing heavily.

"I know your history is sad," I said. "Inevitably so, considering your character, but I didn't know that cats had a role in it."

"That," said George, "is because I never told you of my second cousin, Andromache."

"Andromache?"

Her father [said George] was a classical scholar, hence the name. He also had a little money, which he left to Cousin Andromache on the occasion of his early death and she, by shrewd investment, considerably increased it.

He did not include me in his bounty. I was a child of five at the time of his death and he could scarcely have left me anything outright, but a more generous soul would have set up a trust fund.

As I grew older, however, I realized that Cousin Andromache, who was twenty-two years older than I, might well predecease me. It did occur to me—for I was a precocious lad, thoughtful and far-sighted—that, in that case, I might receive a sizable share of the loot.

—Yes, provided, as you say, that I sucked up to her. Please do not try to anticipate my words, however, for that is not the phraseology I intended to use. What I was going to say was that

I realized I might inherit a portion of her estate if I gave her the warmth and affection she so richly deserved.

As it happened, Cousin Andromache needed warmth and affection not only richly, but also desperately. When I was still in my teens and she was approaching forty, I realized that she was a dedicated spinster, untouched by human hands. Even at my tender age, I found the situation understandable. She was tall and rawboned, with a long plain face, large teeth, small eyes, limp hair, and no figure worth mentioning.

I said to her once, out of a natural curiosity to determine how unlikely an event might be and yet come to pass, "Cousin Andromache, has any fellow ever asked you to marry him?"

She turned a threatening face on me and said, "Asked me to marry *him?* Hah! I'd like to see some fellow ask me to marry *him!*"

(I rather thought she would indeed like to see it happen, but I had early reached the years of discretion and did not put the thought into words.)

She went on. "If any man ever has the *gall* to ask me to marry *him*, I'll give *him* what for. I'll show *him* a thing or two. I'll teach *him* to approach a respectable woman with any of his lollygagging notions."

I didn't quite see what was lollygagging about a marriage proposal, or what might be in it to offend a respectable woman, but I didn't think it would be wise—or even safe—to ask.

For a few years, I kept hoping that some person perverse enough to be interested in Cousin Andromache might indeed make a suggestion or two because I wanted to see what she would do—while I remained at a safe distance, to be sure. There seemed, however, no chance of that. Not even her gathering wealth seemed to suffice to make her an object of marriageability to the male half of the population. One and all, it seemed, weighed the price that would have to be paid, and one and all turned away.

An abstract consideration of the situation showed me that it was exactly what I wanted. A Cousin Andromache without husband and without children would be less apt to dismiss a second cousin as a testamentary possibility. Furthermore, since she was an only child, the vicissitudes of life had left her with no relative closer than I was. That seemed an appropriate situation for me, since it meant I didn't have to work *too* hard at supplying affection. A little bit, now and then, to reinforce my position as the natural heir, would be quite enough.

When she passed that fortieth milestone, however, it must have seemed to her that if no human male wished to dare her wrath with a proposal of marriage, she would make use of a non-human companion, instead.

She disliked dogs, because she had the notion that, one and all, they lusted to bite her. I would have liked to reassure her that no dog, however gaunt, would find her a toothsome morsel, but I had the feeling this would not reassure her, and would cripple me, so I kept silent on the matter.

She also thought that horses were too large for comfort, and hamsters too small, so she finally persuaded herself that what she wanted was a cat.

Thereupon, she obtained a little grey female kitten of non-descript appearance and bestowed every bit of her ungainly affection upon it.

With an appalling lack of even a modicum of wit, she named the kitten "Pussy" and that name was retained by the cat forever after, despite changes in sizes and temperament.

What's more, she took to cuddling the kitten and saying, in a revoltingly hoarse sing-song:

> "I love little pussy, her coat is so warm
> And if I don't tease her, she'll do me no harm.
> I'll pet her and stroke her, and give her some food,
> And pussy will love me because I'm so good."

It was simply nauseating.

I won't conceal from you, old man, that I was quite perturbed at first. Thoughts danced through my mind of besotted old maids who left all their money to their pampered, uncaring pets.

It did occur to me, as to whom would it not, that the kitten could easily be kidnapped and drowned, or taken to the zoo and fed to the lions, but the Cousin Andromache would merely get another.

Besides, she might suspect me of a hand in the felicide. Considering the paranoia peculiar to spinsters, I knew that it was perfectly possible for her to get into her head that I was primarily after her money and that she could interpret many things in that light and come fearsomely near the truth. In fact, I strongly suspected that she had already gotten it into her head.

It occurred to me, therefore, to invert matters. Why not display a passionate love of the kitten? I took to playing moronic games with it, dangling a piece of string for it to fight with, stroking it (sometimes, a little longingly, in the region of its neck), and feeding it tidbits—sometimes even (when Cousin Andromache was watching) from my own plate.

I must say it worked. Cousin Andromache softened distinctly. I presume she reasoned that I couldn't possibly be after Pussy's money, for she had none, so she chalked it up to the pure and unalloyed love I had for all of God's creatures. I helped strengthen that notion by telling her, in fervent tones, of how pure my love for them was. It made her accept my love for her with fewer fears concerning any ulterior motives I happened to have.

However, the trouble with a kitten's that eventually it becomes a cat—oh, did Ogden Nash say that also? Well, my best bits are constantly being stolen. I'm quite resigned to it.

I don't know, old man, if you have ever owned a cat, but with age, they grow larger, more self-centered, more self-assured, more contemptuous of their owners, more inert, more utterly uninterested in anything but food and sleep. The last thing on their contemptible little minds is the comfort and peace of mind of the person who feeds them.

In addition, Pussy grew rather ill-tempered. It had always seemed to me that tabby cats are comparatively placid and that it is the tomcats who are aggressive. It was clear, however, that Pussy had the disposition of a tomcat, despite her sex, and an unaltered tomcat at that. What's more, she seemed quite intolerant of me and would deliberately go out of her path in order to pass near me and scratch me surreptitiously. I tell you, old man, I could almost believe the beast could read my mind.

Considering Pussy's disposition, it is not at all surprising that Cousin Andromache went into a small decline. I found her in tears one day, or as close to tears as her tough and scraggy temperament would allow her to be.

"Oh, Cousin George," she said to me, "Pussy doesn't love me."

Pussy was, at the time, sprawled in comfort five feet away and was looking at Cousin Andromache with haughty distaste—its usual expression except when it looked at me, at which time the expression became one of settled hate.

I called the creature to my side, whereupon it favored me with a sneer and a bit of a snarl and stayed where it was. I strode to her and picked her up. She weighed fourteen pounds of solid inertia and the task was not an easy one, particularly since she kept adjusting her right forepaw (the most dangerous one) into a position where a rapid swipe could be made.

I clutched both her forepaws to prevent that, whereupon she hung in such a way as to double the pull of gravity upon her. I believe that only cats and truly obnoxious human infants know the secret and I am constantly surprised that scientists do not investigate the phenomenon.

I placed her in Cousin Andromache's lap, pointed at the tableau and said, "See, Cousin Andromache, Pussy loves you."

But I had taken my mind off the malignant devil, so that she had the chance of biting my pointing finger, and promptly did so to the bone. She then got off Cousin Andromache's lap and walked away.

Cousin Andromache wailed, "You see, she doesn't love me!" Characteristically, she said nothing about my massacred finger.

I sucked bitterly at the damage and said, "That's the way cats are. Why not give Pussy to someone you hate and get a new kitten?"

"Oh no," said Cousin Andromache, turning on me one of her censorious looks. "I love little Pussy. Isn't there some way of training a cat to display affection?"

I longed to make some cleaver comment to the effect that it would be easier to train Cousin Andromache to be pretty, and was able to suppress the longing only because a brilliant idea had illuminated the interior of my skull.

I had recently formed my friendship with Azazel, whom I may have mentioned to you—oh, I did? Well, all right. You needn't add "ad nauseam" merely to display your knowledge of Latin.

In any case, why shouldn't I use Azazel's abilities in this respect? What was the use of having a two-centimeter extra-terrestrial being of advanced technological abilities on call, so to speak, if one didn't make use of it?

I said, "Cousin Andromache, I believe I could train Pussy to show you affection."

"You?" she said, nastily. It was a word, and an intonation, she had used on me before, and I often thought how effectively I would resent it if I were only in a position to do so safely.

But the idea was looking better and better to me as I pictured Cousin Andromache's gratitude to me if I could pull it off.

"Cousin Andromache," I said earnestly, "let me have Pussy for one day—*one day*. I will then bring back a loving Pussy who will ask for nothing better than to sit in your lap and purr in your ear."

Cousin Andromache hesitated. "Are you sure you will be kind to her while you have her? You know, Pussy is a very sensitive creature, shy and gentle."

Yes, indeed, about as shy and gentle as a particularly irritated grizzly bear.

"I would take very good care of her, Cousin Andromache," I murmured insinuatingly.

And, in the end, Cousin Andromache's longing for an affectionate pussy overcame her uncertainties and she gave her permission with many an injunction to keep the little thing from being harmed by the cruel outside world.

Of course, I had to buy a cage first, one with bars as thick as my thumb. This I felt might retain Pussy, if she didn't get too angry, and off we went together.

Azazel didn't get as angry in those days as he does now when I call him up. He was curious about Earth in those days.

On this occasion, though, what he was was terrified. He screamed all but ultrasonically. It pierced my eardrums like an icepick.

"What's the matter?" I said, my hands over the affected organs.

"That creature." Azazel's tail pointed to Pussy. "What is it?"

I turned to look at Pussy. It had flattened itself at the bottom of the cage. Its wicked green eyes stared at Azazel with fixed longing. Its tail twitched slowly and then it launched itself at the bars of the cage, which shook and rattled. Azazel screamed again.

"It's just a cat," I said, soothingly. "A little kitten."

"Put me in your pocket," shrieked Azazel. "Put me in your pocket."

On the whole, that seemed a good idea. I plunked him into my shirt-pocket where he trembled like a tuning fork and Pussy, angered and puzzled at his disappearance, spat her displeasure.

Finally, I could make out coherent words from within my pocket.

"Oh, my supple tail," moaned Azazel. "It is just like a drakopathan—just like. They're ferocious beasts that bite and claw and tear, but this cat thing is much bigger and more ferocious by the look of it. Why have you exposed me to this, O Excrescence of a Rubbishy Planet?"

"O Fearless Master of the Universe," I said, "it is precisely in connection with this animal, whose name is Pussy, that I need a demonstration of your matchless might."

"No, no," came his muffled cry.

"It is to make a better cat. I want Pussy to love my Cousin Andromache who owns the animal. I want Pussy to give my cousin affection and tenderness and sweetness—"

Azazel poked a frightened eye over the top of the pocket and stared at Pussy for a moment. He said, "That creature has no love in it for anything but itself. That is quite obvious from its C-aura."

"Exactly! You must add love for Cousin Andromache."

"What do you mean, add love? Have you never heard of the Law of Conservation of Emotion, you sub-technological dolt? You can't add love. You can only transfer it from one object within a creature's emotional nexus to another."

"Do so," I said. "Take from the superfluity of love Pussy devotes to herself and fashion a strong attachment to Cousin Andromache."

"Taking from the self-love of that super-drakopathan is a task too formidable. I have seen my people strain their intensifiers permanently at lesser tasks."

"Then take the love from elsewhere in Pussy, O Superlative One. Do you wish word to get out that you failed a challenge so small?"

Vanity was, of course, Azazel's besetting fault, and I could see the possibility I had mentioned was gnawing at him.

He said, "Well, I will try. Do you have a likeness of your cousin? A good likeness?"

I certainly had, though I doubt that any photograph of Cousin Andromache could be both a likeness and good at the same time. Putting that philosophical matter to one side, I had a large cabinet photograph of her that I always placed in a prominent position when she came on a visit. I did have to take the fig tree out of the living room on those occasions, though, for the photo had a tendency to wither its leaves.

Azazel looked at the picture dubiously, and sighed. "Very well," he said, "but remember that this is not magic, but science. I can only work within the limits of the Law of Conservation of Emotion."

But what did I care for Azazel's limits of action as long as he did his job?

The next day I brought Pussy back to Cousin Andromache. Pussy had always been a strong and malevolent cat, but her indifference to others had induced a customary apathy that had kept her evil nature within bounds. Now, apparently, with her sudden wild love for Cousin Andromache frustrated by the absence of her object of affection, she had turned into a demon. She made it quite plain that, were it not for the bars of her cage, which gave dangerously under her pressure, she would tear me into shreds, and I was sure she could do it.

Pussy's mood changed completely, however, when she spied her mistress. The spitting, snarling, slashing devil became at once a panting, purring, picture of delight. She turned on her back, exposing a massively sinewy belly that she clearly wanted scratched.

Cousin Andromache, with a cry of delight, placed a finger through the bars to oblige. I then opened the cage and Pussy went sailing out into Cousin Andromache's waiting arms, purring as loudly as a truck going over a cobbled road, and striving to strop its rasping tongue on my cousin's leathery cheek. I will draw the curtain over what followed, because it will not bear description. Suffice it to say that, among other things, Cousin Andromache said to the vile cat, "And did you miss your loving Andromache-Womickey?"

It was enough to make me vomicky, let me tell you.

Stolidly, however, I remained, for I was waiting to hear what I wanted to hear and, finally, Cousin Andromache looked up with a pallid glitter in her opaque little eyes and said, "Thank you, Cousin George. I apologize for doubting you, and I promise you I won't forget this to my dying day and will then make you a suitable return."

"It was my pleasure, Cousin Andromache," I said, "and I hope your dying day is far, far in the future."

What was more, if she had at that moment consented to settle a goodly sum to me effective immediately, I believe I would actually have meant what I said—within limits.

I stayed away from Cousin Andromache for a while, not wishing to push my luck, since my presence in her vicinity had, in the past, always seemed to sour her—I don't know why.

I did phone her every now and then, though, just to make sure all was well, and, to my continuing delight, all *was* well. At least, she would each time trill coyly into my ear, "I love little Pussy," and then cite nauseating details of the cat's affectionate behavior.

Then, about three months after I had brought back Pussy, Cousin Andromache called and asked me to drop in for lunch. Naturally, under the circumstances, Cousin Andromache's wish was my law, so I hurried over at the set time. Since she had sounded cheerful on the phone, I had no apprehensions.

Nor did I have any when I entered her apartment, even

though I nearly slipped to destruction on the throw-rug she kept on her polished floor near the entrance for what I could only assume were homicidal reasons. She greeted me with what was intended, I imagine, as a jolly grin.

"Come in, Cousin George," she said. "Say hello to little Pussy."

I looked down at little Pussy and shied in horror. Little Pussy, perhaps because it was so full of love, had grown still farther, and at a rapid pace. She seemed nearly three feet long exclusive of lashing tail and I judged her to weigh, conservatively, twenty-five pounds of whipcord and gristle. Her eyes were flat, her mouth was open in a silent snarl, her eye-teeth gleamed like burnished needles, and her eyes, as they glared at me, were filled with indescribable loathing. She stood between Cousin Andromache and me quite as though guarding the silly woman against any false move on my part.

I dared make no move at all, for who knew what that monstrous creature might consider false.

I tried to be strong, but there was a distinct quaver in my voice as I said, "Is Pussy safe, Cousin Andromache?"

"Perfectly safe," said Cousin Andromache, giggling rather in the same fashion a rusty hinge would, "for she knows you are a relative and mean me well."

"Good," I said hollowly, wondering if it were possible for Pussy to read my mind. I decided she couldn't or I would not at that moment have been alive, I'm sure.

Cousin Andromache seated herself on the couch and motioned me to take the armchair. However, I waited till Pussy had also jumped on the couch and had placed her head in Cousin Andromache's lap in luxurious abandon, before daring to move sufficiently to sit down myself.

"Of course," said Cousin Andromache, "my sweet little Pussy is just a little unreasonable when she thinks someone is trying to harm me. A couple of weeks ago, the newsboy threw the paper just as I was coming out the door. It hit me on the shoulder. It didn't really hurt, but Pussy was after him like a flash. If he hadn't pedaled his bicycle at top speed, I really don't know what would have happened to him. Now the boy won't return and I have to go out every morning and buy the paper at a newsstand. It is comfortable to know, though, that I'm protected from any mugger or burglar."

At the words, "mugger or burglar," Little Pussy seemed to be reminded of me, for she turned to look at me and her eyes blazed with the fires of Hell.

It seemed to me I saw what had happened. After all, hate is negative love.

Pussy had had a mild hatred for everything and everyone but herself and, just possibly, Cousin Andromache. To increase Pussy's love for Andromache, Azazel, following the dictates of the Law of Conservation of Emotion, had to withdraw love from all other objects. Since that love was already negative, it grew more negative than ever. And since Azazel had added love with no sparing hand, the other loves grew *much* more negative. In short, Pussy now hated everyone and everything with an extravagant hatred that had strengthened and enlarged her muscles, sharpened her teeth and claws, and turned her into a killing machine.

Cousin Andromache chattered on. "Last week," she said, "Pussy and I were out for a morning stroll and we met Mr. Walsingham with his Doberman pinscher. I had every intention of avoiding him and crossing the street, but the dog had seen Pussy and snarled at the little innocent creature. Pussy didn't seem to mind, but it frightened me—I don't like dogs at *all*—and I'm afraid I let out a small shriek. That activated dear little Pussy's protective instinct, and she fell on the dog at once. There was no hope of separating them, and the dog, I understand, is still at the vet's. Mr. Walsingham is trying to have Pussy declared a dangerous animal, but of course it was the dog that took the initiative and Pussy was merely acting in my defense."

She hugged Pussy as she said that, placing her face in actual contact with the cat's canines, and with no perceptible nervousness. And then she got to the real reason for the invitation to lunch.

She simpered horribly and said, "But I called you here to give you some news I felt I should tell you personally and not on the telephone—I have a gentleman caller."

"A what!" I jumped slightly, and Pussy at once rose and arched its back. I quickly froze.

I have since thought it out. It seems clear that the sensation of being loved—even if only by a cat out of Golgotha—had softened Cousin Andromache's sinewy heart and made her ready to gaze with eyes of affection on some poor victim. And who knows? Perhaps the consciousness of being loved had changed her inner being to the point of making her seem marginally toothsome to someone particularly dim of vision and particularly lacking in taste.

But that was a later analysis. At the time Cousin Andromache broke the news, my keen mind quickly grasped the vital point—my prosperous relative might possibly have someone else to whom to leave her cash and possessions.

My first impulse was to rise from the seat, seize Cousin Andromache, and shake some sense of family responsibility into her. My second impulse, following a millisecond later, was not to move a muscle. Pussy's hate-filled eye was on me.

"But, Cousin Andromache," I said, "you always told me that if any fellow came lollygagging around you, you'd show *him!* Why not let Pussy show him? That will fix him."

"Oh, no, Hendrik is *such* a nice man and he loves cats, too. He stroked Pussy, and Pussy *let* him. That's when I knew he was all right. Pussy is a good judge of character."

I suppose even Pussy would have trouble matching the look of hatred I let *her* have.

"In any case," said Cousin Andromache, "Hendrik is coming over tonight and I believe he will propose that we formalize conditions by getting married. I wanted you to know."

I tried to say something, but couldn't. I tell you I felt as though I had been thoroughly emptied of my internal organs and I was nothing but hollow skin.

She went on, "I want you also to know, Cousin George, that Hendrik is a retired gentleman, who is quite well off. It is understood between us that, if I predecease him, none of my small savings will go to him. They will go to you, dear Cousin George, as the person who turned Pussy into a loving and efficient companion and protector for me."

Someone had turned the sun and the daylight back on again and all my internal organs were in place once more. It occurred to me, in the merest trice, that if Hendrik predeceased Cousin Andromache, his estate would be very likely added to hers, and would also eventually come to me.

I said ringingly, "Cousin Andromache. Your money does not concern me. Only your love and your future happiness do. Marry Hendrik, be happy, and live forever. That's all I ask."

I said it with such sincerity, old fellow, that I came within this much of convincing myself I meant it.

And then, that evening—

I wasn't there, of course, but I found out about it later. Hendrik—seventy, if he was a day, a little over five feet tall and pushing a hundred and eighty pounds in weight—came to call.

She opened the door for him, and skipped skittishly away. He threw his arms wide, called out, "My love!" advanced heavily, slipped on the throw-rug, went hurtling forward into Cousin Andromache feet-first, and bowled her over.

That was all Pussy needed. She knew an attack on her mistress when she saw one. By the time the screaming Andromache pulled the screaming Pussy off screaming Hendrik, it was too late for any hope of a romantic marriage proposal that night. It was indeed very nearly too late for anything at all that would involve Hendrik.

Two days later, I visited him at the hospital at Cousin Andromache's hysterical request. He was still bandaged to the eyebrows and a team of doctors were discussing the various possible strategies of skin-grafting.

I introduced myself to Hendrik, who wept copiously, drenching his bandages, and begged me to tell my fair relative that this was a visitation upon him for being unfaithful to his first wife, Emmeline, dead these seventeen years, and for even dreaming of marrying anyone at all.

"Tell your cousin," he said, "we will always be the dearest of friends, but I dare not ever see her again, for I am but flesh and blood and the sight of her might arouse loving thoughts and I would then once more be attacked by a grizzly bear."

I carried the sad news to Cousin Andromache, who took to her bed at once, crying out that through her doing, the best of men had been permanently maimed—which was undoubtedly true.

The rest, old man, is unalloyed tragedy. I would have sworn that Cousin Andromache was incapable of dying of a broken heart, but a team of specialists maintained that that was exactly what she proceeded to do. That was sad, I suppose, but the unalloyed tragedy I refer to was that she had had time to alter her will.

In the new will, she expressed her great affection for me and her certainty that I was far too noble to concern myself over a few pennies so that she left her entire estate of $300,000, not to me, but to her lost love, Hendrik, hoping it would make up to him for the suffering and the medical bills he had incurred because of her.

All this was expressed in terms so affecting that the lawyer who read the will to me wept uncontrollably and so, as you can well imagine, did I.

However, I was not entirely forgotten. Cousin Andromache stated in her will that she left me something she knew I would value far more than the paltry dross of cash. In short, she had left me Pussy.

George just sat there, staring numbly at nothingness, and I couldn't help saying, "Do you still have Pussy?"

He started, focused on me with an effort, and said, "No, not exactly. The very day I received her, she was trampled by a horse."

"By a horse!"

"Yes. The horse died of its wounds the next day. A shame, for it was an innocent horse. It's fortunate, on the whole, that no one had seen me open Pussy's cage and shake her into the horse's stall."

His eyes glazed over again, and his lips mouthed, silently: Three—hundred—thousand—dollars!

Then he turned to me and said, "So can you lend me a tenner?"

What could I do?

The Boy Who Spoke Cat
by
Ward Moore

Parents are sometimes vain enough, or naive enough, or whimsical enough to believe that they can actually understand children and cats . . . . they are usually wrong, as the following sprightly, delightful, and almost unknown story—which comes down squarely on the side of nurture in the old "nature or nurture" argument—amply demonstrates.

The late Ward Moore had his most profound impact on the science fiction field with his famous novel Bring the Jubilee, *which is certainly a strong contender—along with other classics such as L. Sprague de Camp's* Lest Darkness Fall, *Keith Roberts's* Pavane, *and Philip K. Dick's* The Man in the High Castle—*for the title of the best Alternate Worlds novel ever written. Moore was not a prolific writer, and produced only a few other novels and a handful of short stories, but they included* Greener Than You Think, *an early ecological-catastrophe novel,* Joyleg, *written in collaboration with Avram Davidson, a comic novel about an immortal Civil War veteran, and "Lot" and "Lot's Daughter," two of the strongest atomic war stories of the '50s. Moore's other books include* Caduceus Wild, *written with Robert Bradford, and the mainstream novel* Breathe the Air Again.

*   *   *

Like everybody else, I suppose, I've always thought the things I did were ordinary and normal—like having my first baby at nineteen and my second at forty-three—but I hope I've never been rigid about it or set myself up as a standard from which all deviation is unnatural. If other women prefer to have children at different intervals, it's perfectly all right with me.

On the other hand, Stephanie was upset—perhaps horrified would not be too strong a word—when she heard about Ben. (Not that we knew he was to be Ben then; he might as well have been Suzy. Or both, though twins don't run in either Jack's family or mine.) In spite of my protest she was washing the dishes—I'm strictly a just-before-meals dishwasher myself—in her scientific, no-lost-motion way, while I kept coaxing or shooing the cats out of the kitchen. Ever since she was little, Stephanie has disliked cats, which is odd; for Jack and I have always enjoyed their company, and several usually let us share our home with them. Stephanie has a nicely groomed cocker spaniel for her children.

"But Mother! You're too old!"

Obviously I wasn't, but there was no use pointing out that gravidity and senility are mutually exclusive. In Stephanie's twenty-three-year-old eyes I was ready for a wheelchair, or ought to be. She is a dear girl, a good wife (so far as I can tell), a wonderful mother, and an efficient housekeeper. She loves orderliness and punctuality and recipes without surprises. I remember the time I put soy sauce in a batch of cookies (they came out with a really haunting taste): Stephanie could no more have done that than appear in public without lipstick or have the sort of baby Ben turned out to be. Make no mistake: I dote in the approved way on my grandchildren. Stephanie, even when she was tiny, was never so clean, well-behaved, or fed such a properly high-protein diet as Peter and Ann. Anyway, "Grandmother" connotes, if not infirmity, at least a certain dignity and retirement incompatible with what the ads call "anticipating."

I picked up the gray tomcat—not the one with white feet, that's his father, but the pure gray all over—and put him outdoors. He had been looking as if he were about to bound up onto the drainboard for a friendly visit. He was offended by such unexpected discourtesy, and made an elaborate show of being engrossed in some wild mustard brought up by the last rain and growing rubbery and lush just beyond the kitchen door.

The canyon was at its best this time of year, I thought, looking up at the hills washed green, with patches of pale blue where the greasewood blossomed. Already yucca were shooting up the spears which would open into belled pagodas. I smelled the air scented with still damp earth, germinating seeds and bursting buds. People who say there's no sharp difference in the southern California seasons must live in air conditioned vaults and not know a liveoak from an elderberry bush.

"Besides, it's so complicated," she went on, whisking the knives and forks through the rinse water. "The children will have an aunt or uncle younger than themselves. Oh, Mother, I'm sorry to be behaving this horrible way. What does Father say?"

I know Stephanie has always believed Jack would have been a good solid citizen in a doublebreasted blue suit if I hadn't encouraged him to follow his impulses. She couldn't have been more than nine when we went to live on the houseboat so he could grow culture pearls. "Why doesn't Father ever do something where he goes to work at the same time every day inside a building, like other fathers?" she had asked earnestly. "I'm sure he doesn't really want to do these *different* things; you oughtn't to let him." The funny thing was that Jack was reasonably successful with the pearls before he decided to move on to Culver City and work as a movie extra—for which he grew a black beard I've always been sorry he shaved off. Unwilling to shake her faith, I thought up something sedate and innocuous and suppressed his actual bawdy comment. One shock a day was enough for Stephanie.

"Anyway, now you'll give up this wild adventure and move back to civilization, of course."

"I don't think so, dear. Your father's always wanted a place like this, and I have a feeling he'll enjoy goat farming another four or five years before he starts sending for pamphlets and manuals on something else. Now that he's cleaned out the old well and re-roofed the house and fixed the barn, it would be silly to give it up just because we're going to increase and multiply along with the goats and chickens and rabbits."

"Oh, Mother!"

Stephanie goes to church, I don't—that is, not regularly—but it is she who always finds Biblical language too outspoken.

"I'll probably come in town to have the baby; I don't want to be annoyingly rugged or too smugly pioneering."

"But you can't raise a baby on a ranch."

"Why not? I raised one in an abandoned cannery, with quite

satisfactory results. And goat's milk is just the thing for babies. If we're fifty miles from a clinic or pediatrician"—I knew this would come up next—"why, we have a phone, and a car your father keeps going, and . . . Goodness, Stephanie, don't start worrying so soon."

People like my daughter are disconcertingly right just often enough to keep one respectful of convention and conservatism. I began having difficulties with Ben shortly after this visit; my blood pressure wasn't whatever it was supposed to be, and all sorts of poisons chased themselves through my veins. I had to give up salt and smoking and, which was much harder, more than one cup of coffee; and the doctor suppressed the anxiety in his voice just enough to make me careful without scaring me too badly. I had to move in with Stephanie three months before the baby was born, leaving Jack all alone to take care of the livestock and be company for the cats. For the first time in my life I had leisure to read *Finnegans Wake*, but at that I didn't get beyond page 44. I would have done better with Gene Stratton Porter.

Little Ben certainly justified the headshakings and cluckings that went on behind a curtain of cooing and joyful exclamation. In the scriptural phrase, my bowels yearned over him; he was so sad and puny. Sad in appearance, I mean, for there was vitality in the scrawny body, apparently composed of too much skin and too many bones. This vitality flashed in his smile even at an age when smiles are supposed to be only signs of air in the stomach.

It didn't seem possible he could grow into the disproportionately large hands and feet, or that his fragile neck would ever support his heavy head. He was so clearly the child of parents too old for plump and healthy babies that I had a wretched sense of guilt for having borne him, which made me all the more fiercely determined that he must survive.

There was no question the odds were greatly against him. He couldn't keep food down, no matter what formula we tried. There was a moment—an anxiously hopeful week—when he assimilated the milk from a particular goat and gained priceless ounces, but then his stomach rejected this also. Something was wrong with his insides, something which could only be remedied by probing and cutting and rearranging.

The terrified hour of surgery and the doubting, tremulous days that followed passed; Ben's vitality triumphed over the shock, the starvation, the debilitated body. He drank eagerly, earnestly, as though he could never be quite sure of making up for the long deprivation and must get every drop while the miracle of eating and retaining lasted. As our fears slowly retreated and we dared to delight in his progress, he began to change before our eyes. The frail arms rounded; the legs, no longer drawn up protectively, kicked out with vigor. Fuzzy baldness gave way to lank blond hair, not particularly handsome perhaps, but welcomed as an indication—at least I took it as an indication—that there was nourishment now for luxury growths like eyebrows and fingernails without robbing heart or lungs.

His face filled out, his brown eyes—so light as to be almost hazel—no longer bulged like a choleric old man's. Sometimes shielded by the long baby lashes dropped demurely, more often they looked with intense curiosity on everything around him. Only the smile was least changed; recognizably the same as in the days of his struggle to stay alive. It was a grave smile, happy yet reserved, the smile of one willing but not quite ready to trust entirely.

He ate, he learned to roll over, to sit up, to pull himself erect, to creep. He ate, became chubby, raged when he was wet or hungry, slept angelically. Jack and I spent hours simply looking at him with admiration, like very young parents. Even Stephanie said he was a good baby, a healthy baby, a lovely baby—though, of course, he did seem to be a little backward learning to walk.

"I don't know that there's any backward or forward to it," I said. "Some children walk early, some late. You were walking at eleven months, and Ben is barely a year old. I've heard of perfectly normal babies who never took a step 'til much, much later."

"Why, of course, Mother. I didn't mean to imply . . . Peter and Ann both walked at nine months."

"I know."

"It may simply be that Ben's just making up time."

"Making up time?"

"Between when he was born and was able to eat properly. No development. Normal development, I mean—because all his energies went into just staying alive. So there's always a lag. Maybe not always; perhaps his progress will become faster later on until he catches up and everything will turn out perfectly all right. Incidentally, Mother, I think one of the cats has been crawling into the crib with him."

"I wouldn't be surprised. They like babies because they're warm and clean."

"But Mother . . ."

"I hope you're not thinking of the old superstition about cats' snuffing out babies' breaths. There was usually a cat sleeping with you when you were Ben's age."

"Perhaps that's why I don't particularly care for them," said Stephanie, adding vaguely, "trauma . . ."

Not quite soon enough to discredit Stephanie's theory, and not quite late enough to confirm it for sure, Ben began to walk. He walked with a rolling, sidling, straddling gait which was deceptively fast; and he rarely resorted to the up-and-down, half walk, half crawl that children who are inclined to be timid or uncertain indulge in. In fact he seemed to have little conception of either timidity or uncertainty; persistence and curiosity were his most noticeable traits. He explored fearlessly, tirelessly, bumps or knocks being no more than momentary distractions.

From the first, he took to the cats. Naturally we kept kittens and nursing mothers out of his way, but the toms, as toms will, indulged him tolerantly. I had seen him pound his tiny fists on the gray tom's skull until the dazed animal must have seen stars, squeeze its sides relentlessly, and wind up by pulling on its tail, all of which the cat endured with patient dignity—it would have abandoned forever the house of an adult taking a fraction of such liberties—until, bored at last, or possibly feeling its temper beginning to fray, Tom yawned, stretched, flirted the abused tail, and leapt out of reach.

Stephanie was afraid Ben would be scratched or bitten or

infected by his habit of grasping a loose roll of skin and fur and chewing on it. "And Mother—what *is* that funny noise he's learned to make? It sounds something like a bird trill."

"*Rrrrr, rrrr,*" murmured Ben obligingly.

"Oh that," I said, proud of Ben but slightly embarrassed for Stephanie's predictable reaction. "He's just speaking cat."

"What on earth are you talking about?"

"Mary Borden or somebody wrote a story about it. Years ago. Speaking cat, I mean. Cats have a very limited vocabulary, you know, and Ben seems to have picked up a little of it."

"That's perfectly absurd," said Stephanie.

"*Rr, rr,*" said Ben.

"*Rrrrrr-owr,*" said the gray tom.

"Mother, listen. I understand, or I think I understand, now I'm older, why you and Father are eccen . . . unconventional, that is. I realize the value of some people having unusual outlooks and different values. But Mother, children don't *like* their parents to be whimsical. It makes them uncomfortable."

"I know, dear. I'm sorry. But Ben really does speak cat."

There was no doubt in my mind that he was increasing his proficiency all the time. As all know who have been allowed to house and feed cats, there are only a few basic—well, one hesitates, and not just in deference to the opinion of those who think communication is limited to humanity, to call them words—a few basic idea-sounds in cat. These are all shorter or longer variants of the root, *rrr*, with a couple of prefixes—*prrr* and *mrrr*—and a few suffixes, notably *owr, rrm,* and *rrmh?*, but the language is highly inflected, capable of fine distinctions conveyed by rising or falling tones in different places. I don't understand cat myself, except for the obvious phrases one just can't help picking up, such as *prrruh prrruh*, which seems to mean, "Come quickly; I've something you'll like," and *MrrrrROWrrr!*, apparently a frightful curse uttered preparatory to a fight to the death—not to be confused with *Mrrrow, Mrrrow, Mrrrowh?:* "Stay me with apples, comfort me with flagons, for I am sick of love."

There are undoubtedly subtleties which escape, not merely the alien human ear, but the average tabby, surfeited with milk and mice. Whenever I hear some particularly dramatic outburst from a feline throat straining to articulate an anguish of desire which shakes the poor thing, I can't help but wonder if the party addressed really appreciates the felicities of phrasing or the niceties of expression. We come to take so for granted the downright, straightforward, purr-and-rub-against-your-legs-for-a-saucer-of-milk side of the cat—because generally that's the only one we're permitted to see—that we have to adjust ourselves to the idea of a feline Cyrano, Villon, or Byron.

I don't want to give the impression that Ben spent all his time trilling cat or exploring its nuances. Often he played silently—those esoteric, amorphous games of infancy which require intense concentration, and which completely baffle adult logic—or gurgled, grunted, and made experimental noises with his lips which didn't seem necessarily intended to convey meaning. He played car or airplane, adding the proper background sounds, and at night before falling asleep, or in the morning on waking, he hummed softly and cheerfully to himself. Still, several times a day he greeted a cat with a happy, "*Rrrrh?*", or, after its retreat upon much mauling, called in farewell, "*Rrrrrrrmh?*"

At the same time there were indications he was rapidly picking up the meaning of human speech, even though he didn't seem interested in using it himself. It was as if English were an impediment we suffered, or a crude method of communication he was forced to understand because we lacked a more sophisticated one. He did not appear to recognize any biological or cultural imperative in it for him, personally.

Much as I tried to discount maternal pride I was sure he was unusually bright. I had every evidence he was quick and sensitive, easily bored—never the sign of a dull baby—but as his second birthday approached I had to admit that an ability to pile blocks or open successive nests of boxes or turn the pages of a book in solemn imitation or a growing fluency in cat were not adequate substitutes for intelligible speech. I had no defense against Stephanie's tactful: "We must remember Einstein was an abnormally late talker. Two-and-a-half, or even three, I think."

However, I was not moved to brood over Ben's idiosyncrasy. There had been no rain that year after the middle of January; the spring grass withered early, and the fire hazard here in the mountains was great. Deer and cottontails from higher in the hills came down hopefully seeking something green, the gray soil petrified and cracked, the water table kept falling; unless we got an unusually early rain we'd be in trouble. The sky was a blazing blue from dawn to sunset; we were too high and too far from the ocean for fogs ever to drift in and relieve the terrible heat. To cap everything, some predator, evidently following the deer, began attacking the goats, mauling and tearing newborn kids.

Stephanie drove for her bimonthly visit the day Jack found what was left of another carcass and decided it was not coyotes as he had first thought, but a mountain lion. "Coyotes would've picked the bones clean; mountain lions gorge themselves while the meat is warm and fresh, and leave what's left for the buzzards. Never come back to it."

"If you kept dogs, Father, they would have driven it off."

Jack is firm in his conviction that if Stephanie hadn't married Peter Gordon she would have been an individualist. This ingenuous doctrine completely ignores a long line of markers stretching back to the moment when Stephanie, aged thirty seconds, yelled a yell which was precisely and exactly the norm of all yells given by newborn babies. He gave her a quick hug that lifted her off the floor, and set her down gently. "Maybe you're right, Chick. Only I don't enjoy that senseless yapping at every shadow."

"But Father, there's something comforting in the bark of a watchdog. I'm sure Mother would feel safer . . ."

"Not me," I interrupted. "Neither safer or more important. Just mad at having the baby wakened."

"Oh Mother, every farm has a dog."

"Except this one, Chick," said Jack. "Anyway I'm going to stay up and lay for the lion with the rifle. There's a full moon tonight."

Ben, clad only in a diaper, shoes and socks, toddled into the kitchen and handed me an empty spool which showed signs of hard usage. "Thank you," I said. He looked doubtfully at the spool, then lay down flat and began drumming his heels in complex syncopation. Stephanie, glancing at him, said, "Mother, you and Ben better come home with me until Father disposes of the creature."

It was a temptation, the thought of getting away from the heat and into the land of venetian blinds, ferns on the mantelpiece, unlimited water in recessed tubs, street noises, TV, and smog. It wasn't entirely loyalty to Jack and the goats that stopped me: I'd have to iron and change and make all sorts of preparation for an absence and get Ben ready. And when we got to Stephanie's, he would be fretful and unhappy confined to crib or playpen, uneasy on spotless rugs, probably frightened of the spaniel, and unsolaced by the companionship of the cats.

"No, dear. I can't leave your father to do all the chores."

Ben finally stopped his drumming and crawled under the sink, emerging triumphantly with a sauce pan I hadn't seen for a week.

"I can manage all right; why don't you go?" Jack encouraged.

"No," I repeated. "I'm not afraid of mountain lions. At least, not more than lots of other things."

"Nothing to be afraid of," Jack reassured me over his shoulder as he went out. "They never bother humans."

Ben banged the saucepan experimentally against the nearest chair, discovered the water heater gave off a more satisfying noise. He looked up at Stephanie for some sign of approval, then he caught my eye and broke into a charming smile.

"Very well," she said firmly. "If you're going to be obstinate, I'll stay, too. Overnight, anyway."

She was at her admirable best now, phoning to arrange care for Peter and Ann, explaining to Peter senior, ridiculing the thought of any danger ("They're terrible cowards, really, and run away from people"; I wondered how she got this bit of information, and whether it actually was information, an elaboration of Jack's casual remark, or just a soothing fiction), going through the house in spite of the afternoon heat, setting things to rights so I knew it would be weeks before they lapsed into their accustomed state and I could find whatever I was looking for.

"I'll sleep in the bedroom with you and the baby 'til Father kills the thing, then I'll move to the couch."

I hadn't her confidence in Jack's marksmanship, but I was glad at the prospect of her nearness. *Mountain lion* is an alarming term; possibly that's why our greatgrandparents spoke jocosely of varmints, painters and catamounts, trimming the object of apprehension down by derision. Exactly what Stephanie could do if the beast decided to visit the house instead of the goat pens I had no idea, but I was sure it would be cooler and more reasonable than any reflex of mine.

As soon as the sun set, the promise of bearable temperatures made it possible for us to get supper while Jack fed the chickens and rabbits and milked the goats. Catching Ben at the moment his energies began to flag and before he got too tired to go right to sleep, I whisked him to bed, paying no more than polite attention to Stephanie's "Really, Mother, do you think it's good for Ben to be having a bottle still? It may give him an oral fixation."

Jack brought in the milk. I filtered it into quart bottles, setting out the foam and residue in a large pan for the cats.

Stephanie voiced the thought that had been in my mind. "Father . . . suppose it decides to come in the house instead of bothering the goats?"

"He won't; why should he? He's after food, not company. He'd kill the cats if he stumbled across them, out of meanness, or jealousy, or something, but he'd never go looking for them because he wouldn't eat them. Goats are another story—they taste like his favorite meat, deer."

"I hope he knows this as thoroughly as you do," I said.

"If you're nervous, I'll put a couple of shells in the shotgun," he offered. "Only don't fire it—your shoulder will be lame for a week."

About nine o'clock Jack took up his post, wearing his leather jacket; for the night was already cool and would be positively cold before dawn. Stephanie and I sat up for a couple of hours talking about Peter and Ann and Ben. Very delicately, she hinted at the desirability of some sort of psychiatric examina-

tion. Not, I understood, that she thought anything was really
wrong with Ben, but these queer little symptoms . . .

"You mean, like talking cat?"

"I mean like making animal noises instead of learning to
speak. I do think you owe it to him, Mother, to get a competent
opinion right away. Before he gets any older."

"You sound as if he were some sort of defective who would
have to be institutionalized, and that I ought to know it before
I get too attached to him."

"Mother! How can you say such horrible things? If I must be
utterly frank, what I meant was that babies of older parents are
more likely to have weaknesses, or failings, or susceptibilities
than those of young people. Like the pyloric stenosis he had.
Whatever else there is we don't know, except that it shows up
in retarded speech. It's quite possible something can be done
about it; there's no use blinding yourself . . ."

"I don't think I'm blinding myself. In the first place I was
forty-two and your father fifty when Ben was conceived.
Believe me, that's not outrageously old. Sarah was ninety and
Abraham a hundred when Isaac . . ."

"Oh, the Bible!"

"Don't forget you're a Christian, Stephanie·dear. And in the
second place, I see no 'little symptoms', as you call them. Ben
is very bright and understands what you say to him. He can
make all his wants known—and he does—by gestures, pointing, holding out his arms, bringing things to me, tugging at my
dress. He doesn't *have* to speak yet in order to be understood."

"But that's exactly what I mean, Mother. Don't you
see . . ."

"No, I don't. I only see that when the time comes when he
has to speak, or wants to badly enough, he will. In the
meantime he chooses to talk cat. Why shouldn't he? No doubt
it's a very limited language; it doesn't contain phrases like, 'for
your own good', 'disagreeable necessity', 'stern measures',
'economic adjustment', 'gravest consequences', 'weeding out' or
any of the thousand expressions humans use when they're about
to do something mean and nasty while taking a lofty tone about
cats torturing birds or mice. Why, if everyone talked cat, most of
the diplomats would be out of jobs, likewise lawyers; the

Congressional Record would be pocket-size; demagogues would be cured of laryngitis; soap opera would burst like a bubble. Perhaps Ben, instead of being retarded, is really *homo superior*, the man of the future, who will talk cat instead of gobbledegook."

"How fanciful, Mother," said Stephanie. "Let's go to bed."

I didn't sleep; I don't think she did either. After moving and turning restlessly for a long time, Ben gave a whimper; I knew he wouldn't sleep properly again until he was dry.

"You can turn on the light, Mother. I'm awake."

"I'll change him in the dark," I whispered back. "I'm used to it, and a light would only disturb him."

Dark was only a formal word; as Jack had said, the moon was full. Ben's crib was under an open window giving out on the nakedly polished yard that ought to have been a garden if we'd had water to spare for growing things. I could see the goats in huddled heaps within the pens and, beyond, Jack sitting on a box, his back turned to the house, the stock and barrel-tip of the rifle visible as it lay across his knees.

Usually, if I changed Ben at night, he babbled a little and went back to sleep. Now, perhaps because of Stephanie's presence, or the tension in the air since Jack went out, he stayed wide awake, quietly but firmly resisting my efforts to lay him down, standing in his crib and peering with me out of the window.

I had just about decided to warm a bottle for him regardless of Stephanie's disapproval, when a cat slunk across the yard. A tom on the prowl, I thought, waiting for the raucous call and marveling how the tricky light magnified and distorted familiar figures.

And then I realized, deceptive moonlight or not, that this thing was the size of three toms—three good, hefty toms. And we had no cat whose color was that of dirty sulphur or whose tail was disproportionately long and of perfectly even thickness all the way to the curl just sweeping clear of the ground.

I could not frighten Ben or Stephanie. Moving as casually as I could with my knees trembling so, I went back to the bed and groped for the shotgun. It was much heavier than I remembered.

"What is it, Mother?"

"Shush," I said, carrying the gun to the window.

I heard her get out of bed softly and follow me, and I hoped she wouldn't scream when she caught sight of the mountain lion. Ben, holding on to the sides of the crib, was dancing silently up and down in nervous excitement.

The animal outside had crept closer while my back was turned; the two eyes reflected like thick, flawed glass in the moonlight. It was maddening to regard the impassive back of Jack's head; he should have known instinctively that we were in danger and discovered the intruder. I dared not call out to him for fear of what might happen before the rifle could be brought up to an angle which wouldn't make us targets as well as the mountain lion. It was all very well to talk of what cowards the beasts were, but suppose this particular one happened to be an exception—and with a taste for two-year-old baby? I leveled the shotgun out of the window.

Behind me Stephanie caught her breath sharply, and I waited for the cry she suppressed. Ben must have seen the cougar, also; for he stopped dancing and stared as intently as we did, still making no sound at all.

I tried to keep the gun trained on the eyes and pull both triggers together, but the weight made it waver and my hands shook. I don't know if this was the buck fever hunters talk about or simply the paralysis of mounting terror. I felt my nervousness would pass, but for the moment I was incapable of action.

"Here, Mother—let me," Stephanie whispered.

She took the firearm out of my hands, which remained rigid as though still holding it. The mountain lion had stopped, one paw upraised, the tip of that ropy tail quivering faintly. He was a perfect target; I waited for the explosion as I felt, rather than saw, Stephanie's finger strain at the trigger.

"*Rrrrrrr!*" called Ben, loudly and imperatively. "*Rrrrrrr! Rrrrrrr!*"

This was no sound I had ever heard before. There was fear in it, and urgency, and command, but more than anything else there was warning, warning of great and immediate peril. The great cat stiffened, turned his head slightly, switched his tail once—like a scythe—and leapt away in great bounds. The gun finally roared, but the glistening yard was empty.

Jack rushed in to find me with my arms around both children, the three of us, as he said, "bellowing loud enough to scare all the animals in the canyon." He pooh-phooed the notion that Ben had warned the cougar. "Any noise at all would have driven him off; they're cowards. If you'd barked bow-wow or talked French he would have scampered just the same."

"Oh, Mama," cried Stephanie, still half-hysterical. "He says such *silly* things. Imagine talking French to a mountain lion when we know Ben can speak cat. Oh, Mama!"

I think she was about ten, the last time she called me anything but "Mother." I patted her gently on the back while Jack went on muttering that a man who put a gun in female hands ought to have his head examined. Ben stopped crying and began imitatively patting us both.

"Ma-ma," he said.

I knew he would never talk cat again.

The Jaguar Hunter
by
Lucius Shepard

Lucius Shepard was perhaps the most popular and influential new writer of the '80s, rivaled for that title only by William Gibson, Connie Willis, and Kim Stanley Robinson. Shepard won the John W. Campbell Award in 1985 as the year's Best New Writer, and no year since has gone by without him adorning the final ballot for one major award or another, and often for several. In 1987, he won the Nebula Award for his landmark novella "R & R," and in 1988 he picked up a World Fantasy Award for his monumental short-story collection The Jaguar Hunter. *His first novel was the acclaimed* Green Eyes; *his second the bestselling* Life During Wartime; *he is at work on several more. His latest books are a new collection,* The Ends of the Earth, *and a new novel,* Kalimantan. *Born in Lynchburg, Virginia, he now lives in Nantucket, Massachusetts.*

In the riveting tale that follows, he takes us to the steaming jungles of Central America—a favorite Shepard milieu—for a story about the meaning of the hunt and the nature of the hunter—and the hunted.

* * *

It was his wife's debt to Onofrio Esteves, the appliance dealer, that brought Esteban Caax to town for the first time in almost a year. By nature he was a man who enjoyed the sweetness of the countryside above all else; the placid measures of a farmer's day invigorated him, and he took great pleasure in nights spent joking and telling stories around a fire, or lying beside his wife, Incarnación. Puerto Morada, with its fruit company imperatives and sullen dogs and cantinas that blared American music, was a place he avoided like the plague: indeed, from his home atop the mountain whose slopes formed the northernmost enclosure of Bahía Onda, the rusted tin roofs ringing the bay resembled a dried crust of blood such as might appear upon the lips of a dying man.

On this particular morning, however, he had no choice but to visit the town. Incarnación had—without his knowledge— purchased a battery-operated television set on credit from Onofrio, and he was threatening to seize Esteban's three milk cows in lieu of the eight hundred lempiras that was owed; he refused to accept the return of the television, but had sent word that he was willing to discuss an alternate method of payment. Should Esteban lose the cows, his income would drop below a subsistence level, and he would be forced to take up his old occupation, an occupation far more onerous than farming.

As he walked down the mountain, past huts of thatch and brushwood poles identical to his own, following a trail that wound through sun-browned thickets lorded over by banana trees, he was not thinking of Onofrio but of Incarnación. It was in her nature to be frivolous, and he had known this when he had married her; yet the television was emblematic of the differences that had developed between them since their children had reached maturity. She had begun to put on sophisticated airs, to laugh at Esteban's country ways, and she had become the doyenne of a group of older women, mostly widows, all of whom aspired to sophistication. Each night they would huddle around the television and strive to outdo one another in making sagacious comments about the American detective shows they watched; and each night Esteban would sit outside the hut and gloomily ponder the state of his marriage. He believed Incarnación's association with the widows was her manner of telling him that she looked forward to adopting the black skirt and shawl, that—having served his purpose as a father—he was now an impediment to her. Though she was only forty-one, younger by three years than Esteban, she was withdrawing from the life of the senses; they rarely made love anymore, and he was certain that this partially embodied her resentment of the fact that the years had been kind to him. He had the look of one of the Old Patuca—tall, with chiseled features and wide-set eyes; his coppery skin was relatively unlined and his hair jet black. Incarnación's hair was streaked with gray, and the clean beauty of her limbs had dissolved beneath layers of fat. He had not expected her to remain beautiful, and he had tried to assure her that he loved the woman she was and not merely the girl she had been. But that woman was dying, infected by the same disease that had infected Puerto Morada, and perhaps his love for her was dying, too.

The dusty street on which the appliance store was situated ran in back of the movie theater and the Hotel Circo Del Mar, and from the inland side of the street Esteban could see the bell towers of Santa María del Onda rising above the hotel roof like the horns of a great stone snail. As a young man, obeying his mother's wish that he become a priest, he had spent three years cloistered beneath those towers, preparing for the seminary under the tutelage of old Father Gonsalvo. It was the part of his life he most regretted, because the academic disciplines he had mastered seemed to have stranded him between the world of the Indian and that of contemporary society; in his heart he held to his father's teachings—the principles of magic, the history of the tribe, the lore of nature—and yet he could never escape the feeling that such wisdom was either superstitious or simply unimportant. The shadows of the towers lay upon his soul as surely as they did upon the cobbled square in front of the church, and the sight of them caused him to pick up his pace and lower his eyes.

Farther along the street was the Cantina Atómica, a gathering place for the well-to-do youth of the town, and across from it was the appliance store, a one-story building of yellow stucco with corrugated metal doors that were lowered at night. Its facade was decorated by a mural that supposedly represented the merchandise within: sparkling refrigerators and televisions and washing machines, all given the impression of enormity by the tiny men and woman painted below them, their hands upflung in awe. The actual merchandise was much less imposing, consisting mainly of radios and used kitchen equipment. Few people in Puerto Morada could afford more, and those who could generally bought elsewhere. The majority of Onofrio's clientele were poor, hard-pressed to meet his schedule of payments, and to a large degree his wealth derived from selling repossessed appliances over and over.

Raimundo Esteves, a pale young man with puffy cheeks and heavily lidded eyes and a petulant mouth, was leaning against the counter when Esteban entered; Raimundo smirked and let out a piercing whistle, and a few seconds later his father emerged from the back room: a huge slug of a man, even paler than Raimundo. Filaments of gray hair were slicked down across his mottled scalp, and his belly stretched the front of a starched *guayabera*. He beamed and extended a hand.

"How good to see you," he said. "Raimundo! Bring us coffee and two chairs."

Much as he disliked Onofrio, Esteban was in no position to be uncivil: he accepted the handshake. Raimundo spilled coffee in the saucers and clattered the chairs and glowered, angry at being forced to serve an Indian.

"Why will you not let me return the television?" asked Esteban after taking a seat; and then, unable to bite back the words, he added, "Is it no longer your policy to swindle my people?"

Onofrio sighed, as if it were exhausting to explain things to a fool such as Esteban. "I do not swindle your people. I go beyond the letter of the contracts in allowing them to make returns rather than pursuing matters through the courts. In your case, however, I have devised a way whereby you can keep the television without any further payments and yet settle the account. Is this a swindle?"

It was pointless to argue with a man whose logic was as facile and self-serving as Onofrio's. "Tell me what you want," said Esteban.

Onofrio wetted his lips, which were the color of raw sausage. "I want you to kill the jaguar of Barrio Carolina."

"I no longer hunt," said Esteban.

"The Indian is afraid," said Raimundo, moving up behind Onofrio's shoulder. "I told you."

Onofrio waved him away and said to Esteban, "That is unreasonable. If I take the cows, you will once again be hunting jaguars. But if you do this, you will have to hunt only one jaguar."

"One that has killed eight hunters." Esteban set down his coffee cup and stood. "It is no ordinary jaguar."

Raimundo laughed disparagingly, and Esteban skewered him with a stare.

"Ah!" said Onofrio, smiling a flatterer's smile. "But none of the eight used your method."

"Your pardon, *don* Onofrio," said Esteban with mock formality. "I have other business to attend."

"I will pay you five hundred lempiras in addition to erasing your debt," said Onofrio.

"Why?" asked Esteban. "Forgive me, but I cannot believe it is due to a concern for the public welfare."

Onofrio's fat throat pulsed, his face darkened.

"Never mind," said Esteban. "It is not enough."

"Very well. A thousand." Onofrio's casual manner could not conceal the anxiety in his voice.

Intrigued, curious to learn the extent of Onofrio's anxiety, Esteban plucked a figure from the air. "Ten thousand," he said. "And in advance."

"Ridiculous! I could hire ten hunters for this much! Twenty!"

Esteban shrugged. "But none with my method."

For a moment Onofrio sat with his hands enlaced, twisting them, as if struggling with some pious conception. "All right," he said, the words squeezed out of him. "Ten thousand!"

The reason for Onofrio's interest in Barrio Carolina suddenly dawned on Esteban, and he understood that the profits involved would make his fee seem pitifully small. But he was possessed by the thought of what ten thousand lempiras could mean: a herd of cows, a small truck to haul produce, or—and as he thought it, he realized this was the happiest possibility—the little stucco house in Barrio Clarín that Incarnación had set her heart on. Perhaps owning it would soften her toward him. He noticed Raimundo staring at him, his expression a knowing smirk; and even Onofrio, though still outraged by the fee, was beginning to show signs of satisfaction, adjusting the fit of his *guayabera*, slicking down his already-slicked-down hair. Esteban felt debased by their capacity to buy him, and to preserve a last shred of dignity, he turned and walked to the door.

"I will consider it," he tossed back over his shoulder. "And I will give you my answer in the morning."

* * *

"Murder Squad of New York," starring a bald American actor, was the featured attraction on Incarnación's television that night, and the widows sat cross-legged on the floor, filling the hut so completely that the charcoal stove and the sleeping hammock had been moved outside in order to provide good viewing angles for the latecomers. To Esteban, standing in the doorway, it seemed his home had been invaded by a covey of large black birds with cowled heads, who were receiving evil instruction from the core of a flickering gray jewel. Reluctantly, he pushed between them and made his way to the shelves mounted on the wall behind the set; he reached up to the top shelf and pulled down a long bundle wrapped in oil-stained newspapers. Out of the corner of his eye, he saw Incarnación watching him, her lips thinned, curved in a smile, and that cicatrix of a smile branded its mark on Esteban's heart. She knew what he was about, and she was delighted! Not in the least worried! Perhaps she had known of Onofrio's plan to kill the jaguar, perhaps she had schemed with Onofrio to entrap him. Infuriated, he barged through the widows, setting them to gabbling, and walked out into his banana grove and sat on a stone amidst it. The night was cloudy, and only a handful of stars showed between the tattered dark shapes of the leaves; the wind sent the leaves slithering together, and he heard one of his cows snorting and smelled the ripe odor of the corral. It was as if the solidity of his life had been reduced to this isolated perspective, and he bitterly felt the isolation. Though he would admit to fault in the marriage, he could think of nothing he had done that could have bred Incarnación's hateful smile.

After a while, he unwrapped the bundle of newspapers and drew out a thin-bladed machete of the sort used to chop banana stalks, but which he used to kill jaguars. Just holding it renewed his confidence and gave him a feeling of strength. It had been four years since he had hunted, yet he knew he had not lost the skill. Once he had been proclaimed the greatest hunter in the province of Neuva Esperanza, as had his father before him, and he had not retired from hunting because of age or infirmity, but because the jaguars were beautiful, and their beauty had begun to outweigh the reasons he had for killing them. He had no better reason to kill the jaguar of Barrio Carolina. It menaced no one other than those who hunted it, who sought to invade its territory, and its death would profit only a dishonorable man and a shrewish wife, and would spread the contamination of Puerto Morada. And besides, it was a black jaguar.

"Black jaguars," his father had told him, "are creatures of the moon. They have other forms and magical purposes with which we must not interfere. Never hunt them!"

His father had not said that the black jaguars lived on the moon, simply that they utilized its power; but as a child, Esteban had dreamed about a moon of ivory forests and silver meadows through which the jaguars flowed as swiftly as black water; and when he had told his father of the dreams, his father had said that such dreams were representations of a truth, and that sooner or later he would discover the truth underlying them. Esteban had never stopped believing in the dreams, not even in face of the rocky, airless place depicted by the science programs on Incarnación's television: that moon, its mystery explained, was merely a less enlightening kind of dream, a statement of fact that reduced reality to the knowable.

But as he thought this, Esteban suddenly realized that killing the jaguar might be the solution to his problems, that by going against his father's teaching, that by killing his dreams, his Indian conception of the world, he might be able to find accord with his wife's; he had been standing halfway between the two conceptions for too long, and it was time for him to choose. And there was no real choice. It was this world he inhabited, not that of the jaguars; if it took the death of a magical creature to permit him to embrace as joys the television and trips to the movies and a stucco house in Barrio Clarín, well, he had faith in this method. He swung the machete, slicing the dark air, and laughed. Incarnación's frivolousness, his skill at hunting, Onofrio's greed, the jaguar, the television . . . all these things were neatly woven together like the elements of a spell, one whose products would be a denial of magic and a furthering of the unmagical doctrines that had corrupted Puerto Morada. He laughed again, but a second later he chided himself: it was exactly this sort of thinking he was preparing to root out.

Esteban waked Incarnación early the next morning and forced her to accompany him to the appliance store. His machete swung by his side in a leather sheath, and he carried a burlap sack containing food and the herbs he would need for the hunt. Incarnación trotted along beside him, silent, her face hidden by a shawl. When they reached the ştore, Esteban had Onofrio stamp the bill PAID IN FULL, then he handed the bill and the money to Incarnación.

"If I kill the jaguar or if it kills me," he said harshly, "this will be yours. Should I fail to return within a week, you may assume that I will never return."

She retreated a step, her face registering alarm, as if she had seen him in new light and understood the consequences of her actions; but she made no move to stop him as he walked out the door.

Across the street, Raimundo Esteves was leaning against the wall of the Cantina Atómica, talking to two girls wearing jeans and frilly blouses; the girls were fluttering their hands and dancing to the music that issued from the cantina, and to Esteban they seemed more alien than the creature he was to hunt. Raimundo spotted him and whispered to the girls; they peeked over their shoulders and laughed. Already angry at Incarnación, Esteban was washed over by a cold fury. He crossed the street to them, rested his hand on the hilt of the machete, and stared at Raimundo; he had never before noticed how soft he was, how empty of presence. A crop of pimples straggled along his jaw, the flesh beneath his eyes was pocked by tiny indentations like those made by a silversmith's hammer, and, unequal to the stare, his eyes darted back and forth between the two girls.

Esteban's anger dissolved into revulsion. "I am Esteban Caax," he said. "I have built my own house, tilled my soil, and brought four children into the world. This day I am going to hunt the jaguar of Barrio Carolina in order to make you and your father even fatter than you are." He ran his gaze up and down Raimundo's body and, letting his voice fill with disgust, he asked, "Who are you?"

Raimundo's puffy face cinched in a knot of hatred, but he offered no response. The girls tittered and skipped through the door of the cantina; Esteban could hear them describing the incident, laughter, and he continued to stare at Raimundo. Several other girls poked their heads out the door, giggling and whispering. After a moment, Esteban spun on his heel and walked away. Behind him there was a chorus of unrestrained laughter, and a girl's voice called mockingly, "Raimundo! Who are you?" Other voices joined in, and it soon became a chant.

Barrio Carolina was not truly a barrio of Puerto Morada; it lay beyond Punta Manabique, the southernmost enclosure of the bay, and was fronted by a palm hammock and the loveliest stretch of beach in all the province, a curving slice of white sand giving way to jade-green shallows. Forty years before, it had been the headquarters of the fruit company's experimental farm, a project of such vast scope that a small town had been built on the site: rows of white frame houses with shingle roofs and screen porches, the kind you might see in a magazine illustration of rural America. The company had touted the project as being the keystone of the country's future, and had promised to develop high-yield crops that would banish starvation; but in 1947 a cholera epidemic had ravaged the coast and the town had been abandoned. By the time the cholera scare had died down, the company had become well-entrenched in national politics and no longer needed to maintain a benevolent image; the project had been dropped and the property abandoned until—in the same year that Esteban had retired from hunting—developers had bought it, planning to build a major resort. It was then the jaguar had appeared. Though it had not killed any of the workmen, it had terrorized them to the point that they had refused to begin the job. Hunters had been sent, and these the jaguar *had* killed. The last party of hunters had been equipped with automatic rifles, all manner of technological aids; but the jaguar had picked them off one by one, and this project, too, had been abandoned.

Rumor had it that the land had recently been resold (now Esteban knew to whom), and that the idea of a resort was once more under consideration.

The walk from Puerto Morada was hot and tiring, and upon arrival Esteban sat beneath a palm and ate a lunch of cold banana fritters. Combers as white as toothpaste broke on the shore, and there was no human litter, just dead fronds and driftwood and coconuts. All but four of the houses had been swallowed by the jungle, and only sections of those four remained visible, embedded like moldering gates in a blackish green wall of vegetation. Even under the bright sunlight, they were haunted-looking: their screens ripped, boards weathered gray, vines cascading over their facades. A mango tree had sprouted from one of the porches, and wild parrots were eating its fruit. He had not visited the barrio since childhood: the ruins had frightened him then, but now he found them appealing, testifying to the dominion of natural law. It distressed him that he would help transform it all into a place where the parrots would be chained to perches and the jaguars would be designs on tablecloths, a place of swimming pools and tourists sipping from coconut shells. Nonetheless, after he had finished lunch, he set out to explore the jungle and soon discovered a trail used by the jaguar: a narrow path that wound between the vine-matted shells of the houses for about a half mile and ended at the Rio Dulce. The river was a murkier green than the sea, curving away through the jungle walls; the jaguar's tracks were everywhere along the bank, especially thick upon a tussocky rise some five or six feet above the water. This baffled Esteban. The jaguar could not drink from the rise, and it certainly would not sleep there. He puzzled over it awhile, but eventually shrugged it off, returned to the beach, and, because he planned to keep watch that night, took a nap beneath the palms.

Some hours later, around midafternoon, he was startled from his nap by a voice hailing him. A tall, slim, copper-skinned woman was walking toward him, wearing a dress of dark green—almost the exact color of the jungle walls—that exposed the swell of her breasts. As she drew near, he saw that though her features had a Patucan cast, they were of a lapidary fineness uncommon to the tribe; it was as if they had been refined into a lovely mask: cheeks planed into subtle hollows, lips sculpted full, stylized feathers of ebony inlaid for eyebrows, eyes of jet and white onyx, and all this given a human gloss. A sheen of sweat covered her breasts, and a single curl of black hair lay over her collarbone, so artful-seeming it appeared to have been placed there by design. She knelt beside him, gazing at him impassively, and Esteban was flustered by her heated air of sensuality. The sea breeze bore her scent to him, a sweet musk that reminded him of mangoes left ripening in the sun.

"My name is Esteban Caax," he said, painfully aware of his own sweaty odor.

"I have heard of you," she said. "The jaguar hunter. Have you come to kill the jaguar of the barrio?"

"Yes," he said, and felt shame at admitting it.

She picked up a handful of sand and watched it sift through her fingers.

"What is your name?" he asked.

"If we become friends, I will tell you my name," she said. "Why must you kill the jaguar?"

He told her about the television set, and then, to his surprise, he found himself describing his problems with Incarnación, explaining how he intended to adapt to her ways. These were not proper subjects to discuss with a stranger, yet he was lured to intimacy; he thought he sensed an affinity between them, and that prompted him to portray his marriage as more dismal than it was, for though he had never once been unfaithful to Incarnación, he would have welcomed the chance to do so now.

"This is a black jaguar," she said. "Surely you know they are not ordinary animals, that they have purposes with which we must not interfere?"

Esteban was startled to hear his father's words from her mouth, but he dismissed it as coincidence and replied, "Perhaps. But they are not mine."

"Truly, they are," she said. "You have simply chosen to ignore them." She scooped up another handful of sand. "How will you do it? You have no gun. Only a machete."

"I have this as well," he said, and from his sack he pulled out a small parcel of herbs and handed it to her.

She opened it and sniffed the contents. "Herbs? Ah! You plan to drug the jaguar."

"Not the jaguar. Myself." He took back the parcel. "The herbs slow the heart and give the body a semblance of death. They induce a trance, but one that can be thrown off at a moment's notice. After I chew them, I will lie down in a place that the jaguar must pass on its nightly hunt. It will think I am dead, but it will not feed unless it is sure that the spirit has left the flesh, and to determine this, it will sit on the body so it can feel the spirit rise up. As soon as it starts to settle, I will throw off the trance and stab it between the ribs. If my hand is steady, it will die instantly."

"And if your hand is unsteady?"

"I have killed nearly fifty jaguars," he said. "I no longer fear unsteadiness. The method comes down through my family from the Old Patuca, and it has never failed, to my knowledge."

"But a black jaguar . . ."

"Black or spotted, it makes no difference. Jaguars are creatures of instinct, and one is like another when it comes to feeding."

"Well," she said, "I cannot wish you luck, but neither do I wish you ill." She came to her feet, brushing the sand from her dress.

He wanted to ask her to stay, but pride prevented him, and she laughed as if she knew his mind.

"Perhaps we will talk again, Esteban," she said. "It would be a pity if we did not, for more lies between us than we have spoken of this day."

She walked swiftly down the beach, becoming a diminutive black figure that was rippled away by the heat haze.

That evening, needing a place from which to keep watch, Esteban pried open the screen door of one of the houses facing the beach and went onto the porch. Chameleons skittered into the corners, and an iguana slithered off a rusted lawn chair sheathed in spiderweb and vanished through a gap in the floor.

The interior of the house was dark and forbidding, except for the bathroom, the roof of which was missing, webbed over by vines that admitted a gray-green infusion of twilight. The cracked toilet was full of rainwater and dead insects. Uneasy, Esteban returned to the porch, cleaned the lawn chair, and sat.

Out on the horizon the sea and sky were blending in a haze of silver and gray; the wind had died, and the palms were as still as sculpture; a string of pelicans flying low above the waves seemed to be spelling a sentence of cryptic black syllables. But the eerie beauty of the scene was lost on him. He could not stop thinking of the woman. The memory of her hips rolling beneath the fabric of her dress as she walked away was repeated over and over in his thoughts, and whenever he tried to turn his attention to the matter at hand, the memory became more compelling. He imagined her naked, the play of muscles rippling her haunches, and this so enflamed him that he started to pace, unmindful of the fact that the creaking boards were signaling his presence. He could not understand her effect upon him. Perhaps, he thought, it was her defense of the jaguar, her calling to mind of all he was putting behind him . . . and then a realization settled over him like an icy shroud.

It was commonly held among the Patuca that a man about to suffer a solitary and unexpected death would be visited by an envoy of death, who—standing in for family and friends— would prepare him to face the event; and Esteban was now very sure that the woman had been such an envoy, that her allure had been specifically designed to attract his soul to its imminent fate. He sat back down in the lawn chair, numb with the realization. Her knowledge of his father's words, the odd flavor of her conversation, her intimation that more lay between them: it all accorded perfectly with the traditional wisdom. The moon rose three-quarters full, silvering the sands of the barrio, and still he sat there, rooted to the spot by his fear of death.

He had been watching the jaguar for several seconds before he registered its presence. It seemed at first that a scrap of night sky had fallen onto the sand and was being blown by a fitful breeze; but soon he saw that it was the jaguar, that it was inching along as if stalking some prey. Then it leaped high into the air, twisting and turning, and began to race up and down the beach: a ribbon of black water flowing across the silver sands. He had never before seen a jaguar at play, and this alone was cause for wonder; but most of all, he wondered at the fact that here were his childhood dreams come to life. He might have been peering out onto a silvery meadow of the moon, spying on one of its magical creatures. His fear was eroded by the sight, and like a child he pressed his nose to the screen, trying not to blink, anxious that he might miss a single moment.

At length the jaguar left off its play and came prowling up the beach toward the jungle. By the set of its ears and the purposeful sway of its walk, Esteban recognized that it was hunting. It stopped beneath a palm about twenty feet from the house, lifted its head, and tested the air. Moonlight frayed down through the fronds, applying liquid gleams to its haunches; its eyes, glinting yellow-green, were like peepholes into a lurid dimension of fire. The jaguar's beauty was heart-stopping—the embodiment of a flawless principle—and Esteban, contrasting this beauty with the pallid ugliness of his employer, with the ugly principle that had led to his hiring, doubted that he could ever bring himself to kill it.

All the following day he debated the question. He had hoped the woman would return, because he had rejected the idea that she was death's envoy—that perception, he thought, must have been induced by the mysterious atmosphere of the barrio—and he felt that if she were to argue the jaguar's cause again, he would let himself be persuaded. But she did not put in an appearance, and as he sat upon the beach, watching the evening sun decline through strata of dusky orange and lavender clouds, casting wild glitters over the sea, he understood once more that he had no choice. Whether or not the jaguar was beautiful, whether or not the woman had been on a supernatural errand, he must treat these things as if they had no substance. The point of the hunt had been to deny mysteries of this sort, and he had lost sight of it under the influence of old dreams.

He waited until moonrise to take the herbs, and then lay down beneath the palm tree where the jaguar had paused the previous night. Lizards whispered past in the grasses, sand fleas hopped onto his face: he hardly felt them, sinking deeper into the languor of the herbs. The fronds overhead showed an ashen green in the moonlight, lifting, rustling; and the stars between their feathered edges flickered crazily as if the breeze were fanning their flames. He became immersed in the landscape, savoring the smells of brine and rotting foliage that were blowing across the beach, drifting with them; but when he heard the pad of the jaguar's step, he came alert. Through narrowed eyes he saw it sitting a dozen feet away, a bulky shadow craning its neck toward him, investigating his scent. After a moment it began to circle him, each circle a bit tighter than the one before, and whenever it passed out of view, he had to repress a trickle of fear. Then, as it passed close on the seaward side, he caught a whiff of its odor.

A sweet, musky odor that reminded him of mangoes left ripening in the sun.

Fear welled up in him, and he tried to banish it, to tell himself that the odor could not possibly be what he thought. The jaguar snarled, a razor stroke of sound that slit the peaceful mesh of wind and surf, and realizing it had scented his fear, he sprang to his feet, waving his machete. In a whirl of vision, he saw the jaguar leap back, he shouted at it, waved the machete again, and sprinted for the house where he had kept watch. He slipped through the door and went staggering into the front room. There was a crash behind him, and turning, he had a glimpse of a huge black shape struggling to extricate itself from a moonlit tangle of vines and ripped screen. He darted into the bathroom, sat with his back against the toilet bowl, and braced the door shut with his feet.

The sound of the jaguar's struggles subsided, and for a moment he thought it had given up. Sweat left cold trails down his sides, his heart pounded. He held his breath, listening, and it seemed the whole world was holding its breath as well. The noises of wind and surf and insects were a faint seething; moonlight shed a sickly white radiance through the enlaced vines overhead, and a chameleon was frozen among peels of wallpaper beside the door. He let out a sigh and wiped the sweat from his eyes. He swallowed.

Then the top panel of the door exploded, shattered by a black paw. Splinters of rotten wood flew into his face, and he screamed. The sleek wedge of the jaguar's head thrust through the hole, roaring. A gateway of gleaming fangs guarding a plush red throat. Half-paralyzed, Esteban jabbed weakly with the machete. The jaguar withdrew, reached in with its paw, and clawed at his leg. More by accident than design, he managed to slice the jaguar, and the paw, too, was withdrawn. He heard it rumbling in the front room, and then, seconds later a heavy thump against the wall behind him. The jaguar's head appeared above the edge of the wall; it was hanging by its forepaws, trying to gain a perch from which to leap down into the room. Esteban scrambled to his feet and slashed wildly, severing vines. The jaguar fell back, yowling. For a while it prowled along the wall, fuming to itself. Finally there was silence.

When sunlight began to filter through the vines, Esteban walked out of the house and headed down the beach to Puerto Morada. He went with his head lowered, desolate, thinking of the grim future that awaited him after he returned the money to Onofrio: a life of trying to please an increasingly shrewish Incarnación, of killing lesser jaguars for much less money. He was so mired in depression that he did not notice the woman until she called to him. She was leaning against a palm about thirty feet away, wearing a filmy white dress through which he could see the dark jut of her nipples. He drew his machete and backed off a pace.

"Why do you fear me, Esteban?" she called, walking toward him.

"You tricked me into revealing my method and tried to kill me," he said. "Is that not reason for fear?"

"I did not know you or your method in that form. I knew only that you were hunting me. But now the hunt has ended, and we can be as man and woman."

He kept his machete at point. "What are you?" he asked.

She smiled. "My name is Miranda. I am Patuca."

"Patucas do not have black fur and fangs."

"I am of the Old Patuca," she said. "We have this power."

"Keep away!" He lifted the machete as if to strike, and she stopped just beyond his reach.

"You can kill me if that is your wish, Esteban." She spread

her arms, and her breasts thrust forward against the fabric of her dress. "You are stronger than I, now. But listen to me first."

He did not lower the machete, but his fear and anger were being overridden by a sweeter emotion.

"Long ago," she said, "there was a great healer who foresaw that one day the Patuca would lose their place in the world, and so, with the help of the gods, he opened a door into another world where the tribe could flourish. But many of the tribe were afraid and would not follow him. Since then, the door has been left open for those who would come after." She waved at the ruined houses. "Barrio Carolina is the site of the door, and the jaguar is its guardian. But soon the fevers of this world will sweep over the barrio, and the door will close forever. For though our hunt has ended, there is no end to hunters or to greed." She came a step nearer. "If you listen to the sounding of your heart, you will know this is the truth."

He half-believed her, yet he also believed her words masked a more poignant truth, one that fitted inside the other the way his machete fitted into its sheath.

"What is it?" she asked. "What troubles you?"

"I think you have come to prepare me for death," he said, "and that your door leads only to death."

"Then why do you not run from me?" She pointed toward Puerto Morada. "That is death, Esteban. The cries of the gulls are death, and when the hearts of lovers stop at the moment of greatest pleasure, that, too, is death. This world is no more than a thin covering of life drawn over a foundation of death, like a scum of algae upon a rock. Perhaps you are right, perhaps my world lies beyond death. The two ideas are not opposed. But if I am death to you, Esteban, then it is death you love."

He turned his eyes to the sea, not wanting her to see his face. "I do not love you," he said.

"Love awaits us," she said. "And someday you will join me in my world."

He looked back to her, ready with a denial, but was shocked to silence. Her dress had fallen to the sand, and she was smiling. The litheness and purity of the jaguar were reflected in

every line of her body; her secret hair was so absolute a black
that it seemed an absence in her flesh. She moved close,
pushing aside the machete. The tips of her breasts brushed
against him, warm through the coarse cloth of his shirt; her
hands cupped his face, and he was drowning in her heated
scent, weakened by both fear and desire.

"We are of one soul, you and I," she said. "One blood and
one truth. You cannot reject me."

Days passed, though Esteban was unclear as to how many.
Night and day were unimportant incidences of his relationship
with Miranda, serving only to color their lovemaking with a
spectral or a sunny mood; and each time they made love, it was
as if a thousand new colors were being added to his senses. He
had never been so content. Sometimes, gazing at the haunted
facades of the barrio, he believed that they might well conceal
shadowy avenues leading to another world; however, whenever Miranda tried to convince him to leave with her, he
refused: he could not overcome his fear and would never
admit—even to himself—that he loved her. He attempted to fix
his thoughts on Incarnación, hoping this would undermine his
fixation with Miranda and free him to return to Puerto Morada;
but he found that he could not picture his wife except as a black
bird hunched before a flickering gray jewel. Miranda, however, seemed equally unreal at times. Once as they sat on the
bank of the Rio Dulce, watching the reflection of the moon—
almost full—floating upon the water, she pointed to it and said,
"My world is that near, Esteban. That touchable. You may
think the moon above is real and this is only a reflection, but
the thing most real, that most illustrates the real, is the surface
that permits the illusion of reflection. Passing through this
surface is what you fear, and yet it is so insubstantial, you
would scarcely notice the passage."

"You sound like the old priest who taught me philosophy,"
said Esteban. "His world—his heaven—was also philosophy.
Is that what your world is? The idea of a place? Or are there
birds and jungles and rivers?"

Her expression was in partial eclipse, half-moonlit, half-shadowed, and her voice revealed nothing of her mood. "No more than there are here," she said.

"What does that mean?" he said angrily. "Why will you not give me a clear answer?"

"If I were to describe my world, you would simply think me a clever liar." She rested her head on his shoulder. "Sooner or later you will understand. We did not find each other merely to have the pain of being parted."

In that moment her beauty—like her words—seemed a kind of evasion, obscuring a dark and frightening beauty beneath; and yet he knew that she was right, that no proof of hers could persuade him contrary to his fear.

One afternoon, an afternoon of such brightness that it was impossible to look at the sea without squinting, they swam out to a sandbar that showed as a thin curving island of white against the green water. Esteban floundered and splashed, but Miranda swam as if born to the element; she darted beneath him, tickling him, pulling at his feet, eeling away before he could catch her. They walked along the sand, turning over starfish with their toes, collecting whelks to boil for their dinner, and then Esteban spotted a dark stain hundreds of yards wide that was moving below the water beyond the bar: a great school of king mackerel.

"It is too bad we have no boat," he said. "Mackerel would taste better than whelks."

"We need no boat," she said. "I will show you an old way of catching fish."

She traced a complicated design in the sand, and when she had done, she led him into the shallows and had him stand facing her a few feet away.

"Look down at the water between us," she said. "Do not look up, and keep perfectly still until I tell you."

She began to sing with a faltering rhythm, a rhythm that put him in mind of the ragged breezes of the season. Most of the words were unfamiliar, but others he recognized as Patuca. After a minute he experienced a wave of dizziness, as if his legs had grown long and spindly, and he was now looking down from a great height, breathing rarefied air. Then a tiny dark stain materialized below the expanse of water between him and Miranda. He remembered his grandfather's stories of the Old Patuca, how—with the help of the gods—they had been able to shrink the world, to being enemies close and cross vast distances in a matter of moments. But the gods were dead, their powers gone from the world. He wanted to glance back to shore and see if he and Miranda had become coppery giants taller than the palms.

"Now," she said, breaking off her song, "you must put your hand into the water on the seaward side of the school and gently wiggle your fingers. Very gently! Be sure not to disturb the surface."

But when Esteban made to do as he was told, he slipped and caused a splash. Miranda cried out. Looking up, he saw a wall of jade-green water bearing down on them, its face thickly studded with the fleeting dark shapes of the mackerel. Before he could move, the wave swept over the sandbar and carried him under, dragging him along the bottom and finally casting him onto shore. The beach was littered with flopping mackerel; Miranda lay in the shallows, laughing at him. Esteban laughed, too, but only to cover up his rekindled fear of this woman who drew upon the powers of dead gods. He had no wish to hear her explanation; he was certain she would tell him that the gods lived on in her world, and this would only confuse him further.

Later that day as Esteban was cleaning the fish, while Miranda was off picking bananas to cook with them—the sweet little ones that grew along the riverbank—a Land-Rover came jouncing up the beach from Puerto Morada, an orange fire of the setting sun dancing on its windshield. It pulled up beside him, and Onofrio climbed out the passenger side. A hectic flush dappled his cheeks, and he was dabbing his sweaty brow with a handkerchief. Raimundo climbed out the driver's side and leaned against the door, staring hatefully at Esteban.

"Nine days and not a word," said Onofrio gruffly. "We thought you were dead. How goes the hunt?"

Esteban set down the fish he had been scaling and stood. "I have failed," he said. "I will give you back the money."

Raimundo chuckled—a dull, cluttered sound—and Onofrio grunted with amusement. "Impossible," he said. "Incarnación has spent the money on a house in Barrio Clarín. You must kill the jaguar."

"I cannot," said Esteban. "I will repay you, somehow."

"The Indian has lost his nerve, Father." Raimundo spat in the sand. "Let my friends and I hunt the jaguar."

The idea of Raimundo and his loutish friends thrashing through the jungle was so ludicrous that Esteban could not restrain a laugh.

"Be careful, Indian!" Raimundo banged the flat of his hand on the roof of the car.

"It is you who should be careful," said Esteban. "Most likely the jaguar will be hunting you." Esteban picked up his machete. "And whoever hunts this jaguar will answer to me as well."

Raimundo reached for something in the driver's seat and walked around in front of the hood. In his hand was a silvered automatic. "I await your answer," he said.

"Put that away!" Onofrio's tone was that of a man addressing a child whose menace was inconsequential, but the intent surfacing in Raimundo's face was not childish. A tic marred the plump curve of his cheek, the ligature of his neck was cabled, and his lips were drawn back in a joyless grin. It was, thought Esteban—strangely fascinated by the transformation— like watching a demon dissolve its false shape: the true lean features melting up from the illusion of the soft.

"This son of a whore insulted me in front of Julia!" Raimundo's gun hand was shaking.

"Your personal differences can wait," said Onofrio. "This is a business matter." He held out his hand. "Give me the gun."

"If he is not going to kill the jaguar, what use is he?" said Raimundo.

"Perhaps we can convince him to change his mind." Onofrio beamed at Esteban. "What do you say? Shall I let my son collect his debt of honor, or will you fulfill our contract?"

"Father!" complained Raimundo; his eyes flicked sideways. "He . . ."

Esteban broke for the jungle. The gun roared, a white-hot claw swiped at his side, and he went flying. For an instant he did not know where he was; but then, one by one, his impressions began to sort themselves. He was lying on his injured side, and it was throbbing fiercely. Sand crusted his mouth and eyelids. He was curled up around his machete, which was still clutched in his hand. Voices above him, sand fleas hopping on his face. He resisted the urge to brush them off and lay without moving. The throb of his wound and his hatred had the same red force behind them.

". . . carry him to the river," Raimundo was saying, his voice atremble with excitement. "Everyone will think the jaguar killed him!"

"Fool!" said Onofrio. "He might have killed the jaguar, and you could have had a sweeter revenge. His wife . . ."

"This was sweet enough," said Raimundo.

A shadow fell over Esteban, and he held his breath. He needed no herbs to deceive this pale, flabby jaguar who was bending to him, turning him onto his back.

"Watch out!" cried Onofrio.

Esteban let himself be turned and lashed out with the machete. His contempt for Onofrio and Incarnación, as well as his hatred of Raimundo, was involved in the blow, and the blade lodged deep in Raimundo's side, grating on bone. Raimundo shrieked and would have fallen, but the blade helped to keep him upright; his hands fluttered around the machete as if he wanted to adjust it to a more comfortable position, and his eyes were wide with disbelief. A shudder vibrated the hilt of the machete—it seemed sensual, the spasm of a spent passion—and Raimundo sank to his knees. Blood spilled from his mouth, adding tragic lines to the corners of his lips. He pitched forward, not falling flat but remaining kneeling, his face pressed into the sand: the attitude of an Arab at prayer.

Esteban wrenched the machete free, fearful of an attack by Onofrio, but the appliance dealer was squirming into the Land-Rover. The engine caught, the wheels spun, and the car lurched off, turning through the edge of the surf and heading for Puerto Morada. An orange dazzle flared on the rear window, as if the spirit who had lured it to the barrio was now harrying it away.

Unsteadily, Esteban got to his feet. He peeled his shirt back from the bullet wound. There was a lot of blood, but it was only a crease. He avoided looking at Raimundo and walked down to the water and stood gazing out at the waves; his thoughts rolled in with them, less thoughts than tidal sweeps of emotion.

It was twilight by the time Miranda returned, her arms full of bananas and wild figs. She had not heard the shot. He told her what had happened as she dressed the wounds with a poultice of herbs and banana leaves. "It will mend," she said of the wound. "But this"—she gestured at Raimundo—"this will not. You must come with me, Esteban. The soldiers will kill you."

"No," he said. "They will come, but they are Patuca . . . except for the captain, who is a drunkard, a shell of a man. I doubt he will even be notified. They will listen to my story, and we will reach an accommodation. No matter what lies Onofrio tells, his word will not stand against theirs."

"And then?"

"I may have to go to jail for a while, or I may have to leave the province. But I will not be killed."

She sat for a minute without speaking, the whites of her eyes glowing in the half-light. Finally she stood and walked off along the beach.

"Where are you going?" he called.

She turned back. "You speak so casually of losing me . . ." she began.

"It is not casual!"

"No!" She laughed bitterly. "I suppose not. You are so afraid of life, you call it death and would prefer jail or exile to living it. That is hardly casual." She stared at him, her expression a cypher at that distance. "I will not lose you, Esteban," she said. She walked away again, and this time when he called she did not turn.

Twilight deepened to dusk, a slow fill of shadow graying the world into negative, and Esteban felt himself graying along with it, his thoughts reduced to echoing the dull wash of the receding tide. The dusk lingered, and he had the idea that night would never fall, that the act of violence had driven a nail through the substance of his irresolute life, pinned him forever to this ashen moment and deserted shore. As a child he had been terrified by the possibility of such magical isolations, but now the prospect seemed a consolation for Miranda's absence, a remembrance of her magic. Despite her parting words, he did not think she would be back—there had been sadness and finality in her voice—and this roused in him feelings of both relief and desolation, feelings that set him to pacing up and down the tidal margin of the shore.

The full moon rose, the sands of the barrio burned silver, and shortly thereafter four soldiers came in a jeep from Puerto Morada. They were gnomish, copper-skinned men, and their uniforms were the dark blue of the night sky, bearing no device or decoration. Though they were not close friends, he knew them each by name. Sebastian, Amador, Carlito, and Ramón. In their headlights Raimundo's corpse—startlingly pale, the blood on his face dried into intricate whorls—looked like an exotic creature cast up by the sea, and their inspection of it smacked more of curiosity than of search for evidence. Amador unearthed Raimundo's gun, sighted it along toward the jungle, and asked Ramón how much he thought it was worth.

"Perhaps Onofrio will give you a good price," said Ramón, and the others laughed.

They built a fire of driftwood and coconut shells, and sat around it while Esteban told his story; he did not mention either Miranda or her relationship to the jaguar, because these men—estranged from the tribe by their government service—had grown conservative in their judgments and he did not want them to consider him irrational. They listened without comment; the firelight burnished their skins to reddish gold and glinted on their rifle barrels.

"Onofrio will take his charge to the capital if we do nothing," said Amador after Esteban had finished.

"He may in any case," said Carlito. "And then it will go hard with Esteban."

"And," said Sebastian, "if an agent is sent to Puerto Morada and sees how things are with Captain Portales, they will surely replace him and it will go hard with us."

They stared into the flames, mulling over the problem, and

Esteban chose the moment to ask Amador, who lived near him on the mountain, if he had seen Incarnación.

"She will be amazed to learn you are alive," said Amador. "I saw her yesterday in the dressmaker's shop. She was admiring the fit of a new black skirt in the mirror."

It was as if a black swath of Incarnación's skirt had folded around Esteban's thoughts. He lowered his head and carved lines in the sand with the point of his machete.

"I have it," said Ramón. "A boycott!"

The others expressed confusion.

"If we do not buy from Onofrio, who will?" said Ramón. "He will lose his business. Threatened with this, he will not dare involve the government. He will allow Esteban to plead self-defense."

"But Raimundo was his only son," said Amador. "It may be that grief will count more than greed in this instance."

Again they fell silent. It mattered little to Esteban what was decided. He was coming to understand that without Miranda, his future held nothing but uninteresting choices; he turned his gaze to the sky and noticed that the stars and the fire were flickering with the same rhythm, and he imagined each of them ringed by a group of gnomish, copper-skinned men, debating the question of his fate.

"Aha!" said Carlito. "I know what to do. We will occupy Barrio Carolina—the entire company— and *we* will kill the jaguar. Onofrio's greed cannot withstand this temptation."

"That you must not do," said Esteban.

"But why?" asked Amador. "We may not kill the jaguar, but with so many men we will certainly drive it away."

Before Esteban could answer, the jaguar roared. It was prowling down the beach toward the fire, like a black flame itself shifting over the glowing sand. Its ears were laid back, and silver drops of moonlight gleamed in its eyes. Amador grabbed his rifle, came to one knee, and fired: the bullet sprayed sand a dozen feet to the left of the jaguar.

"Wait!" cried Esteban, pushing him down.

But the rest had begun to fire, and the jaguar was hit. It leaped high as it had that first night while playing, but this time it landed in a heap, snarling, snapping at its shoulder; it regained its feet and limped toward the jungle, favoring its right foreleg. Excited by their success, the soldiers ran a few paces after it and stopped to fire again. Carlito dropped to one knee, taking careful aim.

"No!" shouted Esteban, and as he hurled his machete at Carlito, desperate to prevent further harm to Miranda, he recognized the trap that had been sprung and the consequences he would face.

The blade sliced across Carlito's thigh, knocking him onto his side. He screamed, and Amador, seeing what had happened, fired wildly at Esteban and called to the others. Esteban ran toward the jungle, making for the jaguar's path. A fusillade of shots rang out behind him, bullets whipped past his ears. Each time his feet slipped in the soft sand, the moonstruck facades of the barrio appeared to lurch sideways as if trying to block his way. And then, as he reached the verge of the jungle, he was hit.

The bullet seemed to throw him forward, to increase his speed, but somehow he managed to keep his feet. He careened along the path, arms waving, breath shrieking in his throat. Palmetto fronds swatted his face, vines tangled his legs. He felt no pain, only a peculiar numbness that pulsed low in his back; he pictured the wound opening and closing like the mouth of an anemone. The soldiers were shouting his name. They would follow, but cautiously, afraid of the jaguar, and he thought he might be able to cross the river before they could catch up. But when he came to the river, he found the jaguar waiting.

It was crouched on the tussocky rise, its neck craned over the water, and below, half a dozen feet from the bank, floated the reflection of the full moon, huge and silvery, an unblemished circle of light. Blood glistened scarlet on the jaguar's shoulder, like a fresh rose pinned in place, and this made it look more an embodiment of principle: the shape a god might choose, that some universal constant might assume. It gazed calmly at Esteban, growled low in its throat, and dove into the river, cleaving and shattering the moon's reflection, vanishing beneath the surface. The ripples subsided, the image of the moon reformed. And there, silhouetted against it, Esteban saw the figure of a woman swimming, each stroke causing her to grow smaller and smaller until she seemed no more than a character incised upon a silver plate. It was not only Miranda he saw, but all mystery and beauty receding from him, and he realized how blind he had been not to perceive the truth sheathed inside the truth of death that had been sheathed inside her truth of another world. It was clear to him now. It sang to him from his wound, every syllable a heartbeat. It was written by the dying ripples, it swayed in the banana leaves, it sighed on the wind. It was everywhere, and he had always known it: If you deny mystery—even in the guise of death—then you deny life, and you will walk like a ghost through your days, never knowing the secrets of the extremes. The deep sorrows, the absolute joys.

He drew a breath of the rank jungle air, and with it drew a breath of a world no longer his, of the girl Incarnación, of friends and children and country nights . . . all his lost sweetness. His chest tightened as with the onset of tears, but the sensation quickly abated, and he understood that the sweetness of the past had been subsumed by a scent of mangoes, that nine magical days—a magical number of days, the number it takes to sing the soul to rest—lay between him and tears. Freed of those associations, he felt as if he were undergoing a subtle refinement of form, a winnowing, and he remembered having felt much the same on the day when he had run out the door of Santa María de Onda, putting behind him its dark geometries and cobwebbed catechisms and generations of swallows that had never flown beyond the walls, casting off his acolyte's robe and racing across the square toward the mountain and Incarnación: it had been she who had lured him then, just as his mother had lured him to the church and as Miranda was luring him now, and he laughed at seeing how easily these three women had diverted the flow of his life, how like other men he was in this.

The strange bloom of painlessness in his back was sending out tendrils into his arms and legs, and the cries of the soldiers had grown louder. Miranda was a tiny speck shrinking against a silver immensity. For a moment he hesitated, experiencing a resurgence of fear; then Miranda's face materialized in his mind's eye, and all the emotion he had suppressed for nine days poured through him, washing away the fear. It was a silvery, flawless emotion, and he was giddy with it, light with it; it was like thunder and fire fused into one element and boiling up inside them, and he was overwhelmed by a need to express it, to mold it into a form that would reflect its power and purity. But he was no singer, no poet. There was but a single mode of expression open to him. Hoping he was not too late, that Miranda's door had not shut forever, Esteban dove into the river, cleaving the image of the full moon; and—his eyes still closed from the shock of the splash—with the last of his mortal strength, he swam hard down after her.

The Sin of Madame Phloi
by
Lilian Jackson Braun

Even the common house cat—drowsy, overfed, amiable, trust-
ing, unambitious—may display its own kind of patient intelli-
gence, and, when it must, may devise plans and cunning
strategies of its own; in fact, as the compelling story that
follows slyly demonstrates, it may even be plotting bloody revenge
as it dozes on the rug in a spot of summer sunshine . . . and
plotting it quite well, too.

Lilian Jackson Braun is a prominent mystery novelist.
Among her best-known books are an ingenious series of
mystery novels featuring cats—*including* The Cat Who Went
Underground, The Cat Who Talked to Ghosts, *and* The Cat
Who Knew a Cardinal. *Her short fiction has been collected in*
The Cat Who Had 14 Tales, *a collection of first-rate stories*
about—you guessed it—cats.

* * *

From the very beginning Madame Phloi felt an instinctive
distaste for the man who moved into the apartment next door.
He was fat, and his trouser cuffs had the unsavory odor of fire
hydrant.

They met for the first time in the decrepit elevator as it
lurched up to the tenth floor of the old building, once
fashionable but now coming apart at the seams. Madame Phloi
had been out for a stroll in the city park, chewing city grass and
chasing faded butterflies, and as she and her companion
stepped on the elevator for the slow ride upward, the car was
already half filled with the new neighbor.

The fat man and the Madame presented a contrast that was
not unusual in this apartment house, which had a brilliant past
and no future. He was bulky, uncouth, sloppily attired.
Madame Phloi was a long-legged, blue-eyed aristocrat whose
creamy fawn coat shaded into brown at the extremities.

The Madame deplored fat men. They had no laps, and of what use is a lapless human? Nevertheless, she gave him the common courtesy of a sniff at his trouser cuffs and immediately backed away, twitching her nose and breathing through the mouth.

"*Get* that cat away from me," the fat man roared, stamping his feet thunderously at Madame Phloi. Her companion pulled on the leash, although there was no need—the Madame with one backward leap had retreated to a safe corner of the elevator, which shuddered and continued its groaning ascent.

"Don't you like animals?" asked the gentle voice at the other end of the leash.

"Filthy, sneaky beasts," the fat man said with a snarl. "Last place I lived, some lousy cat got in my room and et my parakeet."

"I'm sorry to hear that. Very sorry. But you don't need to worry about Madame Phloi and Thapthim. They never leave the apartment except on a leash."

"You got *two?* That's just fine, that is! Keep 'em away from me, or I'll break their rotten necks. I ain't wrung a cat's neck since I was fourteen, but I remember how."

And with the long black box he was carrying, the fat man lunged at the impeccable Madame Phloi, who sat in her corner, flat-eared and tense. Her fur bristled, and she tried to dart away. Even when her companion picked her up in protective arms, Madame Phloi's body was taut and trembling.

Not until she was safely home in her modest but well-cushioned apartment did she relax. She walked stiff-legged to the sunny spot on the carpet where Thapthim was sleeping and licked the top of his head. Then she had a complete bath herself—to rid her coat of the fat man's odor. Thapthim did not wake.

This drowsy, unambitious, amiable creature—her son—was a puzzle to Madame Phloi, who was sensitive and spirited herself. She didn't try to understand him; she merely loved him. She spent hours washing his paws and breast and other parts he could easily have reached with his own tongue. At dinnertime she chewed slowly so there would be something left on her plate for his dessert, and he always gobbled the extra portion hungrily. And when he slept, which was most of the time, she kept watch by his side, sitting with a tall, regal posture until she swayed with weariness. Then she made herself into a small bundle and dozed with one eye open.

Thapthim was lovable, to be sure. He appealed to other cats, large and small dogs, people, and even ailurophobes in a limited way. He had a face like a beautiful flower and large blue eyes, tender and trusting. Ever since he was a kitten, he had been willing to purr at the touch of a hand—any hand. Eventually he became so agreeable that he purred if anyone looked at him across the room. What's more, he came when called; he gratefully devoured whatever was served on his dinner plate; and when he was told to get down, he got down.

His wise parent disapproved this uncatly conduct; it indicated a certain lack of character, and no good would come of it. By her own example she tried to guide him. When dinner was served, she gave the plate a haughty sniff and walked away, no matter how tempting the dish. That was the way it was done by any self-respecting feline. In a minute or two she returned and condescended to dine, but never with open enthusiasm.

Furthermore, when human hands reached out, the catly thing was to bound away, lead them a chase, flirt a little before allowing oneself to be caught and cuddled. Thapthim, sorry to say, greeted any friendly overture by rolling over, purring, and looking soulful.

From an early age he had known the rules of the apartment:

No sleeping in a cupboard with the pots and pans.
Sitting on the table with the inkwell is permissible.
Sitting on the table with the coffeepot is never allowed.

The sad truth was that Thapthim obeyed these rules. Madame Phloi, on the other hand, knew that a rule was a challenge, and it was a matter of integrity to violate it. To obey was to sacrifice one's dignity. . . . It seemed that her son would never learn the true values in life.

To be sure, Thapthim was adored for his good nature in the human world of inkwells and coffeepots. But Madame Phloi was equally adored—and for the correct reasons. She was respected for her independence, admired for her clever methods of getting her own way, and loved for the cowlick on her white breast, the kink in her tail, and the squint in her delphinium-blue eyes. She was more truly Siamese than her son. Her face was small and perky. By cocking her head and staring with heart-melting eyes, slightly crossed, she could charm a porterhouse steak out from under a knife and fork.

Until the fat man and his black box moved in next door, Madame Phloi had never known an unfriendly soul. She had two companions in her tenth-floor apartment—genial creatures without names who came and went a good deal. One was an easy mark for between-meal snacks; a tap on his ankle always produced a spoonful of cottage cheese. The other served as a hot-water bottle on cold nights and punctually obliged whenever the Madame wished to have her underside stroked or her cheekbones massaged. This second one also murmured compliments in a gentle voice that made one squeeze one's eyes in pleasure.

Life was not all love and cottage cheese, however. Madame Phloi had her regular work. She was official watcher and listener for the household.

There were six windows that needed watching, for a wide ledge ran around the building flush with the tenth-floor windowsills, and this was a promenade for pigeons. They strutted, searched their feathers, and ignored the Madame, who sat on the sill and watched them dispassionately but thoroughly through the window screen.

While watching was a daytime job, listening was done after dark and required greater concentration. Madame Phloi listened for noises in the walls. She heard termites chewing, pipes sweating, and sometimes the ancient plaster cracking; but mostly she listened to the ghosts of generations of deceased mice.

One evening, shortly after the incident in the elevator, Madame Phloi was listening, Thapthim was asleep, and the other two were quietly turning pages of books, when a strange and horrendous sound came from the wall. The Madame's eyes flicked to attention, then flattened against her head.

An interminable screech was coming out of that wall, like

nothing the Madame had ever heard before. It chilled the blood and tortured the eardrums. So painful was the shrillness that Madame Phloi threw back her head and complained with a piercing howl of her own. The strident din even waked Thapthim. He looked about in alarm, shook his head wildly, and clawed at his ears to get rid of the offending noise.

The others heard it, too.

"Listen to that!" said the one with the gentle voice.

"It must be that new man next door," said the other. "It's incredible."

"I can't imagine anyone so crude producing anything so exquisite. It is Prokofiev he's playing?"

"No, I think it's Bartók."

"He was carrying his violin in the elevator today. He tried to hit Phloi with it."

"He's a nut. . . . Look at the cats—apparently they don't care for violin."

Madame Phloi and Thapthim, bounding from the room, collided with each other as they rushed to hide under the bed.

That was not the only kind of noise which emanated from the adjoining apartment in those upsetting days after the fat man moved in. The following evening, when Madame Phloi walked into the living room to commence her listening, she heard a fluttering sound dimly through the wall, accompanied by highly conversational chirping. This was agreeable music, and she settled down on the sofa to enjoy it, tucking her brown paws neatly under her creamy body.

Her contentment was soon disturbed, however, when the fat man's voice burst through the wall like thunder.

"Look what you done, you dirty skunk!" he bellowed. "Right in my fiddle! Get back in your cage before I brain you."

There was a frantic beating of wings.

"*Get* down off that window, or I'll bash your head in."

This threat brought only a torrent of chirping.

"Shut up, you stupid cluck! Shut up and get back in that cage, or I'll . . ."

There was a splintering crash, and after that all was quiet except for an occasional pitiful "Peep!"

Madame Phloi was fascinated. In fact, when she resumed

her watching the next day, pigeons seemed rather insipid entertainment. She had waked the family that morning in her usual way—by staring intently at their foreheads as they slept. Then she and Thapthim had a game of hockey in the bathtub with a Ping-Pong ball, followed by a dish of mackerel, and after breakfast the Madame took up her post at the living-room window. Everyone had left for the day but not before opening the window and placing a small cushion on the chilly marble sill.

There she sat—Madame Phloi—a small but alert package of fur, sniffing the welcome summer air, seeing all, and knowing all. She knew, for example, that the person who was at that moment walking down the tenth-floor hallway, wearing old tennis shoes and limping slightly, would halt at the door of her apartment, set down his pail, and let himself in with a passkey.

Indeed, she hardly bothered to turn her head when the window washer entered. He was one of her regular court of admirers. His odor was friendly, although it suggested damp basements and floor mops, and he talked sensibly—indulging in none of that falsetto foolishness with which some people insulted the Madame's intelligence.

"Hop down, kitty," he said in a musical voice. "Charlie's gotta take out that screen. See, I brought you some cheese."

He held out a modest offering of rat cheese, and Madame Phloi investigated it. Unfortunately, it was the wrong variety, and she shook one fastidious paw at it.

"Mighty fussy cat," Charlie laughed. "Well, now, you set there and watch Charlie clean this here window. Don't you go jumpin' out on the ledge, because Charlie ain't runnin' after you. No sir! That old ledge, she's startin' to crumble. Some day them pigeons'll stamp their feet hard, and down she goes! . . . Hey, lookit the broken glass out here. Somebody busted a window."

Charlie sat on the marble sill and pulled the upper sash down in his lap, and while Madame Phloi followed his movements carefully, Thapthim sauntered into the room, yawning and stretching, and swallowed the cheese.

"Now Charlie puts the screen back in, and you two guys can watch them crazy pigeons some more. This screen, she's comin' apart, too. Whole buildin' seems to be crackin' up."

Remembering to replace the cushion on the cool, hard sill, he then went on to clean the next window, and the Madame resumed her post, sitting on the very edge of the cushion so that Thapthim could have most of it.

The pigeons were late that morning, probably frightened away by the window washer. It was while Madame Phloi patiently waited for the first visitor to skim in on a blue-gray wing that she noticed the tiny opening in the screen. Every aperture, no matter how small, was a temptation; she had to prove she could wriggle through any tight space, whether there was a good reason or not.

She waited until Charlie had limped out of the apartment before she began pushing at the screen with her nose, first gingerly and then stubbornly. Inch by inch the rusted mesh ripped away from the frame until the whole corner formed a loose flap, and Madame Phloi slithered through—nose and ears, slender shoulders, dainty Queen Anne forefeet, svelte torso, lean flanks, hind legs like steel springs, and finally proud brown tail. For the first time in her life she found herself on the pigeon promenade. She gave a delicious shudder.

Inside the screen the lethargic Thapthim, jolted by this strange turn of affairs, watched his daring parent with a quarter inch of his pink tongue hanging out. They touched noses briefly through the screen, and the Madame proceeded to explore. She advanced cautiously and with mincing step, for the pigeons had not been tidy in their habits.

The ledge was about two feet wide. To its edge Madame Phloi moved warily, nose down and tail high. Ten stories below there were moving objects but nothing of interest, she decided. Walking daintily along the extreme edge to avoid the broken glass, she ventured in the direction of the fat man's apartment, impelled by some half-forgotten curiosity.

His window stood open and unscreened, and Madame Phloi peered in politely. There, sprawled on the floor, lay the fat man himself, snorting and heaving his immense paunch in a kind of rhythm. It always alarmed her to see a human on the floor, which she considered feline domain. She licked her nose apprehensively and stared at him with enormous eyes, one iris hypnotically off-center. In a dark corner of the room something fluttered and squawked, and the fat man waked.

"SHcrrff! *Get* out of here!" he shouted, struggling to his feet.

In three leaps Madame Phloi crossed the ledge back to her own window and pushed through the screen to safety. Looking back to see if the fat man might be chasing her and being reassured that he wasn't, she washed Thapthim's ears and her own paws and sat down to wait for pigeons.

Like any normal cat, Madame Phloi lived by the Rule of Three. She resisted every innovation three times before accepting it, tackled an obstacle three times before giving up, and tried each new activity three times before tiring of it. Consequently she made two more sallies to the pigeon promenade and eventually convinced Thapthim to join her.

Together they peered over the edge at the world below. The sense of freedom was intoxicating. Recklessly Thapthim made a leap at a low-flying pigeon and landed on his mother's back. She cuffed his ear in retaliation. He poked her nose. They grappled and rolled over and over on the ledge, oblivious of the long drop below them, taking playful nips of each other's hide and snarling guttural expressions of glee.

Suddenly and instinctively Madame Phloi scrambled to her feet and crouched in a defensive position. The fat man was leaning from his window.

"Here, kitty, kitty," he was saying in one of those despised falsetto voices, offering some tidbit in a saucer. The Madame froze, but Thapthim turned his beautiful trusting eyes on the stranger and advanced along the ledge. Purring and waving his tail cordially, he walked into the trap. It all happened in a matter of seconds: the saucer with withdrawn, and a long black box was swung at Thapthim like a ball bat, sweeping him off the ledge and into space. He was silent as he fell.

When the family came home, laughing and chattering, with their arms full of packages, they knew at once something was amiss. No one greeted them at the door. Madame Phloi hunched moodily on the windowsill staring at a hole in the screen, and Thapthim was not to be found.

"Look at the screen!" cried the gentle voice.

"I'll bet he got out on the ledge."

"Can you lean out and look? Be careful."

"You hold Phloi."

"Do you see him?"

"Not a sign of him! There's a lot of glass scattered around, and the window's broken next door."

"Do you suppose that man . . . ? I feel sick."

"Don't worry, dear. We'll find him. . . . There's the doorbell! Maybe someone's bringing him home."

It was Charlie standing at the door. He fidgeted uncomfortably. " 'Scuse me, folks," he said. "You missin' one of your kitties?"

"Yes! Have you found him?"

"Poor little guy," said Charlie. "Found him lyin' right under your windows—where the bushes is thick."

"He's dead!" the gentle voice moaned.

"Yes, ma'am. That's a long way down."

"Where is he now?"

"I got him down in the basement, ma'am. I'll take care of him real nice. I don't think you'd want to see the poor guy."

Still Madame Phloi stared at the hole in the screen and waited for Thapthim. From time to time she checked the other windows, just to be sure. As time passed and he did not return, she looked behind the radiators and under the bed. She pried open the cupboard door where the pots and pans were stored. She tried to burrow her way into the closet. She sniffed all around the front door. Finally she stood in the middle of the living room and called loudly in a high-pitched, wailing voice.

Later that evening Charlie paid another visit to the apartment.

"Only wanted to tell you, ma'am, how nice I took care of him," he said. "I got a box that was just the right size. A white box, it was. And I wrapped him up in a piece of old blue curtain. The color looked real pretty with his fur. And I buried the little guy right under your window behind the bushes."

And still the Madame searched, returning again and again to watch the ledge from which Thapthim had disappeared. She scorned food. She rebuffed any attempts at consolation. And all night she sat wide-eyed and waiting in the dark.

The living-room window was now tightly closed, but the following day the Madame—after she was left by herself in the lonely apartment—went to work on the bedroom screens. One was new and hopeless, but the second screen was slightly corroded, and she was soon nosing through a slit that lengthened as she struggled out onto the ledge.

Picking her way through the broken glass, she approached the spot where Thapthim had vanished. And then it all happened again. There he was—the fat man—reaching forth with a saucer.

"Here, kitty, kitty."

Madame Phloi hunched down and backed away.

"Kitty want some milk?" It was that ugly falsetto, but she didn't run home this time. She crouched there on the ledge, a few inches out of reach.

"Nice kitty. Nice kitty."

Madame Phloi crept with caution toward the saucer in the outstretched fist, and stealthily the fat man extended another hand, snapping his fingers as one would call a dog.

The Madame retreated diagonally—half toward home and half toward the dangerous brink.

"Here, kitty. Here, kitty," he cooed, leaning farther out. But muttering, he said, "You dirty sneak! I'll get you if it's the last thing I ever do. Comin' after my bird, weren't you?"

Madame Phloi recognized danger with all her senses. Her ears went back, her whiskers curled, and her white underside hugged the ledge.

A little closer she moved, and the fat man made a grab for her. She jerked back a step, with unblinking eyes fixed on his sweating face. He was furtively laying the saucer aside, she noticed, and edging his fat paunch farther out the window.

Once more she advanced almost into his grasp, and again he lunged at her with both powerful arms.

The Madame leaped lightly aside.

"This time I'll get you, you stinkin' cat," he cried, and raising one knee to the windowsill, he threw himself at Madame Phloi. As she slipped through his fingers, he landed on the ledge with all his weight.

A section of it crumbled beneath him. He bellowed, clutching at the air, and at the same time a streak of creamy brown flashed out of sight. The fat man was not silent as he fell.

As for Madame Phloi, she was found doubled in half in a patch of sunshine on her living-room carpet, innocently washing her fine brown tail.

The Mountain Cage
by
Pamela Sargent

Pamela Sargent has firmly established herself as one of the foremost writer/editors of her generation. Her well-known anthologies include Women of Wonder, More Women of Wonder, The New Women of Wonder, *and, with Ian Watson,* Afterlives. *Her critically acclaimed novels include* Cloned Lives, The Sudden Star, The Golden Space, Watchstar, Earthseed, The Alien Upstairs, Eye of the Comet, Homeminds, The Shore of Women, *and* Venus of Dreams. *Her short fiction has been collected in* Starshadows *and* The Best of Pamela Sargent. *Her most recent book is the novel* Venus of Shadows. *She lives in Binghamton, New York.*

Here she gives us a novel perspective on the human misery of war, and paints a moving portrait of an upheaval so vast and terrible and fundamental that it affects even the birds of the air and the beasts of the earth—among which, of course, we must most definitely number the cats.

* * *

Mewleen had found a broken mirror along the road. The shards glittered as she swiped at one with her paw, gazing intently at the glass. She meowed and hunched forward.

Hrurr licked one pale paw, wondering if Mewleen would manage to shatter the barrier, though he doubted that she could crawl through even if she did; the mirror fragments were too small. He shook himself, then padded over to her side.

Another cat, thick-furred, stared out at him from a jagged piece of glass. Hrurr tilted his head; the other cat did the same. He meowed; the other cat opened his mouth, but the barrier blocked the sound. A second cat, black and white, appeared near the pale stranger as Mewleen moved closer to Hrurr.

"She looks like you," Hrurr said to his companion. "She even has a white patch on her head."

125

"Of course. She is the Mewleen of that world."

Hrurr narrowed his eyes. He had seen such cats before, always behind barriers, always out of reach. They remained in their own world, while he was in this one; he wondered if theirs was better.

Mewleen sat on her haunches. "Do you know what I think, Hrurr? There are moments when we are all between worlds, when the sights before us vanish and we stand in the formless void of possibility. Take one path, and a fat mouse might be yours. Take another, and a two-legs gives you milk and a dark place to sleep. Take a third, and you spend a cold and hungry night. At the moment before choosing, all these possibilities have the same reality, but when you take one path—"

"When you take one path, that's that." Hrurr stepped to one side, then pounced on his piece of glass, thinking that he might catch his other self unaware, but the cat behind the barrier leaped up at him at the same instant. "It means that you weren't going to take the other paths at all, so they weren't really possibilities."

"But they were for that moment." Mewleen's tail curled. "I see a branching. I see other worlds in which all possibilities exist. I'll go back home today, but that cat there may make another choice."

Hrurr put a paw on the shard holding his twin. That cat might still have a home.

"Come with me," Mewleen said as she rolled in the road, showing her white belly. "My two-legged ones will feed you, and when they see that I want you with me, they'll honor you and let you stay. They must serve me, after all."

His tail twitched. He had grown restless even before losing his own two-legged creatures, before that night when others of their kind had come for them, dragging them from his house and throwing them inside the gaping mouth of a large, square metal beast. He had stayed away after that, lingering on the outskirts of town, pondering what might happen in a world where two-legged ones turned on one another and forgot their obligations to cats. He had gone back to his house only once; a banner with a black swastika in its center had been hung from one of the upper windows. He had seen such symbols often, on the upper limbs of people or fluttering over the streets; the wind had twisted the banner on his house, turning the swastika first into a soaring bird, then a malformed claw. A strange two-legs had chased him away.

"I want to roam," he replied as he gazed up the road, wondering if it might lead him to the top of the mountain. "I want to see far places. It's no use fighting it when I'm compelled to wander."

Mewleen bounded toward him. "Don't you know what this means?" She gestured at the broken mirror with her nose. "When a window to the other world is shattered, it's a sign. This place is a nexus of possibilities, a place where you might move from one world to the next and never realize that you are lost to your own world."

"Perhaps I'm meant to perform some task. That might be why I was drawn here."

"Come with me. I offer you a refuge."

"I can't accept, Mewleen." His ears twitched as he heard a distant purr, which rapidly grew into a roar.

Leaping from the road, Hrurr plunged into the grass; Mewleen bounded to the other side as a line of metal beasts passed them, creating a wind as they rolled by. Tiny flags bearing swastikas fluttered over the eyes of a few beasts; pale faces peered out from the shields covering the creatures' entrails.

As the herd moved on up the road, he saw that Mewleen had disappeared among the trees.

Hrurr followed the road, slinking up the slope until he caught sight of the metal beasts again. They had stopped in the middle of the road; a gate blocked their progress.

Several two-legged ones in gray skins stood by the gate; two of them walked over to the first metal beast and peered inside its openings, then stepped back, raising their right arms as others opened the gate and let the first beast pass. The two moved on to the next beast, looking in at the ones inside, then raised their arms again. The flapping arms reminded Hrurr of birds; he imagined the men lifting from the ground, arms flapping as they drifted up in lopsided flight.

He scurried away from the road. The gray pine needles, dappled by light, cushioned his feet; ahead of him, winding among the trees, he saw a barbed-wire fence. His whiskers twitched in amusement; such a barrier could hardly restrain him. He squeezed under the lowest wire, carefully avoiding the barbs.

The light shifted; patches of white appeared among the black and gray shadows. The trees overhead sighed as the wind sang. "Cat! Cat!" The birds above were calling out their warnings as Hrurr sidled along below. "Watch your nests! Guard your young! Cat! Cat!"

"Oh, be quiet," he muttered.

A blackbird alighted on a limb, out of reach. Hrurr clawed at the tree trunk, longing to taste blood. "Foolish cat," the bird cawed, "I've seen your kind in the cities, crawling through rubble, scratching for crumbs and cowering as the storms rage and buildings crumble. The two-legged ones gather, and the world grows darker as the shining eagles shriek and the metal turtles crawl over the land. You think you'll escape, but you won't. The soil is ready to receive the dead."

Hrurr clung to the trunk as the bird fluttered up a higher limb. He had heard such chatter from other birds, but had paid it no mind. "That doesn't concern me," he snarled. "There's nothing like that here." But he was thinking of the shattered mirror, and of what Mewleen had said.

"Foolish cat. Do you know where you are? The two-legged ones have scarred the mountain to build themselves a cage, and you are now inside it."

"No cage can hold me," Hrurr cried as the bird flew away. He jumped to the ground, clawing at the earth. I live, he thought, I live. He took a deep breath, filling his lungs with piney air.

The light was beginning to fade; it would soon be night. He hunkered down in the shadows; he would have to prowl for some food. Below ground, burrowing creatures mumbled sluggishly to one another as they prepared for sleep.

In the morning, a quick, darting movement caught Hrurr's

attention. A small, grayish bird carelessly landed in front of him and began to peck at the ground.

He readied himself, then lunged, trapping the bird under his paws. She stared back at him, eyes wide with terror. He bared his teeth.

"Cruel creature," the bird said.

"Not cruel. I have to eat, you know." He had injured her; she fluttered helplessly. He swatted her gently with a paw.

"At least be quick about it. My poor heart will burst with despair. Why must you toy with me?"

"I'm giving you a chance to prepare yourself for death."

"Alas," the bird sang mournfully. "My mate will see me no more, and the winds will not sing to me again or lift me to the clouds."

"You will dwell in the realm of spirits," Hrurr replied, "where there are no predators or prey. Prepare yourself." He bit down; as the bird died, he thought he heard the flutter of ghostly wings. "I'm sorry," he whispered. "I have no choice in these matters. As I prey upon you, another will prey upon me. The world maintains its balance." He could not hear her soul's reply.

When he had eaten, he continued up the slope until he came to a clearing. Above him, a path wound up the mountainside, leading from a round, stone tower with a pointed roof to a distant chalet. The chalet sprawled; he imagined that the two-legs inside it was either a large creature or one who needed a lot of space. Creeping up to the nearer stone structure, he turned and looked down the slope.

In the valley, the homes of the two-legged ones were now no bigger than his paw; the river running down the mountainside was a ribbon. This, he thought, was how birds saw the world. To them, a two-legs was only a tiny creature rooted to the ground; a town was an anthill, and even the gray, misty mountains before him were only mounds. He suddenly felt as if he were gazing into an abyss, about to be separated from the world that surrounded him.

He crouched, resting his head on his paws. Two-legged ones had built the edifices of this mountain; such creatures were already apart from the world, unable even to hear what animals said to one another, incapable of a last, regretful communion with their prey, eating only what was stone dead. He had always believed that the two-legged ones were simply soulless beings whose instincts drove them into strange, incomprehensible behavior; they built, tore down, and built again, moving through the world as if in a dream. But now, as he gazed at the valley below, he began to wonder if the two-legged ones had deliberately separated themselves from the world by an act of will. Those so apart from others might come to think that they ruled the world, and their constructions, instead of being instinctive, might be a deliberate attempt to mold what was around them. They might view all the world as he viewed the tiny town below.

This thought was so disturbing that he bounded up, racing along the path and glorying in his speed until he drew closer to the chalet. His tail twitched nervously as he stared at the wide, glassy expanse on this side of the house. Above the wide window was a veranda; from there, he would look no bigger than a mouse—if he could be seen at all. Farther up the slope, still other buildings were nestled among the trees.

His fur prickled; he longed for Mewleen. Her sharp hearing often provoked her to fancies, causing her to read omens in the simplest and most commonplace of sounds, but it also made her aware of approaching danger. He wanted her counsel; she might have been able to perceive something here to which he was deaf and blind.

Something moved in the grass. Hrurr stiffened. A small, gray cat was watching him. For an instant, he thought that his musings about Mewleen had caused the creature to appear. In the next instant, he leaped at the cat, snarling as he raised his hair.

"Ha!" the smaller cat cried, nipping his ear. Hrurr swatted him, narrowly missing his eye. They rolled on the ground, claws digging into each other's fur. Hrurr meowed, longing for a fight.

The other cat suddenly released him, rolling out of reach, then hissing as he nursed his scratches. Hrurr licked his paw, hissing back. "You're no match for me, Kitten." He waited for a gesture of submission.

"You think not? I may be smaller, but you're older."

"True enough. You're only a kitten."

"Don't call me a kitten. My name is Ylawl. Kindly address me properly."

"You're a kitten."

The other cat raised his head haughtily. "What are you doing here?"

"I might ask the same question of you."

"I go where I please."

"So do I."

The younger cat sidled toward him, but kept his distance. "Did a two-legs bring you here?" he asked at last.

"No," Hrurr replied. "I came alone."

Ylawl tilted his head; Hrurr thought he saw a gleam of respect in his eyes. "Then you are one like me."

Ylawl was still. Hrurr, eyes unmoving for a moment, was trapped in timelessness; the world became a gray field, as it always did when he did not pay attention to it directly. Mewleen had said such visions came to all cats. He flicked his eyes from side to side, and the world returned.

"There is something of importance here," he said to Ylawl. "A friend of mine has told me that this might be a place where one can cross from one world into another." He was about to tell the other cat of the vision that had come to him while he was gazing at the valley, but checked himself.

"It is a cage," Ylawl responded, glancing up at the chalet. "Every day, the metal beasts crawl up there and disgorge the two-legged ones from their bellies, allowing them to gather around those inside, and then they crawl away, only to return. These two-legged ones are so prized that most of this mountain is their enclosure."

Hrurr stretched. "I would not want to be so prized that I was imprisoned."

"It different for a two-legs. They live as the ants do, or the bees. Only those not prized are free to roam."

Hrurr thought of his two-legged creatures who had been taken from him; they might be roaming even now. He was suddenly irritated with Ylawl, who in spite of his youth was speaking as though he had acquired great wisdom. Hrurr raised his fur, trying to look fierce. "You are a foolish cat," he said, crouching, ready to pounce. Ylawl's tail thrust angrily from side to side.

A short, sharp sound broke the silence. Hrurr flattened his ears; Ylawl's tail curled against his body. The bark rang out once more.

Ylawl scrambled up and darted toward a group of trees, concealing himself in the shadows; Hrurr followed him, crouching low when he reached the other cat's side. "So there are dogs here," he muttered. "And you must hide, along with me."

"These dogs don't scare me," Ylawl said, but his fur was stiff and his ears were flat against his head.

A female two-legs was walking down the path, trailed by two others of her kind. A black terrier was connected to her by a leash; a second terrier was leashed to one of her companions. Hrurr's whiskers twitched with contempt at those badges of slavery.

As the group came nearer, one of the dogs yipped, "I smell a cat, I smell a cat." He tugged at his leash as the female two-legs held on, crooning softly.

"So do I," the second dog said as his female struggled to restrain him.

"Negus!" the two-legs in the lead cried out as she knelt, drawing the dog to her. She began to murmur to him, moving her lips in the manner such creatures used for speaking. "Is that dog loose again?"

"I am sure she isn't," one female replied.

"How she hates my darlings. I wish Bormann had never given her to Adolf." The two-legged one's mouth twisted.

"There's a cat nearby," the dog said. The two-legs, unable to hear his words, stood up again; she was taller than her companions, with fair head fur and a smiling face.

"He must listen to the generals today, Eva," one of the other females said. Hrurr narrowed his eyes. He had never been able to grasp their talk entirely, mastering only the sounds his two-legged ones had used to address him or to call him inside for food.

"Why talk of that here?" the fair-furred one replied. "I have nothing to say about it. I have no influence, as you well know."

Her terrier had wandered to the limit of his leash, farther down the path toward the hidden cats. Lifting a leg, he urinated on one of the wooden fence posts lining the walkway. "I know you're there," the dog said, sniffing.

"Ah, Negus," Ylawl answered. "I see you and Stasi are still imprisoned. Don't you ever want to be free?"

"Free to starve? Free to wander without a master's gentle hand? I think not." He sniffed again. "There is another with you, Ylawl."

"Another free soul."

Negus barked, straining at his leash, but his two-legs was already urging him back toward the chalet. Ylawl stretched out on his side. "Slavish beast." The gray cat closed his eyes. "He has even forgotten his true name, and knows only the one that the two-legs calls him." He yawned. "And the other one is even worse."

"His companion there?"

"No, a much larger dog who also lives in that enclosure." Ylawl rolled onto his stomach, looking up at the chalet. "That one is so besotted by her two-legs that she has begun to lose her ability to hear our speech."

"Is such a thing possible?"

"The two-legged ones have lost it, or never had it to begin with," Ylawl said. "They cannot even hear our true names, much as we shout them, and in their ignorance must call us by other sounds. Those who draw too close to such beings may lose such a skill as well,"

Hrurr dug his claws into the ground. He had never cared for dogs, clumsy creatures who would suffer almost any indignity, but the thought that a dog might lose powers of speech and hearing drew his pity. Mewleen was right, he thought. He had crossed into a world where such evil things could happen. A growl rose in his throat as he curled his tail.

"What's the matter with you?" Ylawl asked.

"I cannot believe it. A dog who cannot speak."

"You can't have seen much of the world, then. You're lucky you didn't run into a guard dog. Try to talk to one of them, and he'll go for your throat without so much as a how-de-do. All you'll hear are barks and grunts."

The worldly young cat was beginning to annoy him. Hrurr swatted him with a paw, Ylawl struck back, and they were soon tussling under the trees, meowing fiercely. He tried to sink his teeth into Ylawl's fur, only to be repulsed by a claw.

Hrurr withdrew. Ylawl glared at him with gleaming eyes. "Now I understand," Hrurr said softly. "I know why I was drawn here."

"And why is that?" the young cat said, flicking his tail.

"I must speak to this dog you mentioned. If she realizes what is happening to her, she'll want to escape. Not that I care for dogs, you understand, but there is more at stake here. The two-legged ones may draw more creatures into their ways, separating us one from another, and then the world will be for us as it is for them. Where there were voices, there will be only silence. The world will end for us."

"It is already ending," Ylawl said pensively. "I have heard the birds speak of burning cities and the broken bodies of two-legged ones amidst the stones. But it is ending for the two-legged ones, not for us. They'll sweep themselves away and the world will be ours again, as it was long ago."

"They will sweep us away with them," Hrurr cried, recalling the blackbird's words.

"Look around. Do you see anything to worry about here? There are the dogs, of course, but one can hardly avoid such animals no matter where one travels. Clearly the creatures who dwell here are valued and carefully caged. If we stay here, we ought to be safe enough."

"I won't live in a cage," Hrurr responded. "Even a dog deserves better. I must speak to her. If she heeds me, she will escape and may be better able to rouse her fellows to freedom than I would be."

Ylawl arched his back. "I see that you must do this thing before you discover how futile it is." He lay down in the shadows again, shielding himself from the bright summer sun.

Hrurr kept his eyes still, and the world vanished once more. Where did it go, he asked himself, and why did it fade away? When he moved his eyes, he found that Ylawl was still with him; the chalet remained on the hill. How many times had he crossed from one world to another without realizing he had done so? Was each world so like every other that no movement could lead him to a truly different place, or was he forever trapped in this one, able only to glimpse the others through windows of shiny glass?

"When will I see this dog?" he asked.

"Soon enough," Ylawl said. "You must wait for her two-legs to lead her outside."

More metal beasts had come to the chalet, leaving their gray-clothed two-legged ones near the door, where the house had swallowed them. The last to arrive had been a man in black; he entered the chalet while two companions, also in black, lingered near his beast, ignoring the group of two-legged ones in gray who were pacing restlessly.

Hrurr, settling on the grass nearby, waited, grooming himself with his tongue while Ylawl scampered about and inspected the beasts. Occasionally, he could discern the shapes of men behind the wide window above.

At last the other two-legged ones came back out of the house, shaking their heads as they walked toward their metal beasts. The waiting men stiffened and flapped their right arms before opening the beasts' bellies. One of the black-clothed creatures stared directly at Hrurr; the man reminded him of something, but the memory was just out of reach. He waited to hear a gentle croon or to receive a pat on the head, but the two-legs turned away, watching as the other beasts roared toward the road.

Someone had appeared on the veranda above the window; Hrurr widened his eyes. Two men were perching on the stone barrier surrounding the balcony; one turned and gazed out over the land. Hrurr continued to stare. Suddenly a head appeared next to the two-legs; it had the long muzzle of a large Alsatian dog.

"There she is," Ylawl said as he strutted over to Hrurr, tail held high. The two-legs had put his hand on the dog's head and was stroking her affectionately; she opened her mouth, showing her tongue.

"I must speak to you," Hrurr called out.

The dog rose, paws on the balustrade, and barked.

"I must speak to you," Hrurr repeated. "Can't you hear me?"

The Alsatian's ears twitched as she barked again. Her two-legs rubbed her back as she gazed at him happily. Hrurr, turning his attention to this creature, saw that his dark head fur hung over part of his forehead; a bit a dark fur over his lip marked his otherwise hairless lower face.

"What is she called?" Hrurr asked Ylawl.

"Blondi," the younger cat answered, tripping a bit over the odd sound. "It is what her two-legs calls her. She, too, has forgotten her name."

"Blondi!" Hrurr cried. The dog barked again. "Are you so lost to others that you can't even hear me?" Instead of replying, Blondi disappeared behind the balustrade. "She doesn't hear."

"I think she did," Ylawl said. "Either she doesn't want to talk to you, or she's afraid to speak in front of her two-legs."

"But he can't hear what she would say." Hrurr, disappointed, trotted down the hill toward the path leading away from the house. When he looked back, the two-legged creatures had vanished.

He groomed himself for a while, wondering what to do next when a band of two-legged ones rounded the corner of the house, marching toward the path. Blondi, unleashed, was among them. She lifted her nose, sniffing.

"Cats!" she cried as she began to bark. Ylawl was already running toward a tree. The dog raced after him, a blur of light and movement, still barking. Hrurr bounded after Ylawl, following him up the tree trunk toward a limb.

The two cats, trapped, hissed as Blondi danced beneath them. She reared up, putting her paws on the trunk. "Go away," she said. "Leave master alone. Nothing here for you."

Her words chilled Hrurr; they were slurred and ill-formed, the sounds of a creature who had hardly learned how to communicate, yet she seemed unaware of that.

"Blondi," Hrurr said, clinging to the limb, "can you understand what I am saying?"

The dog paused; her forelimbs dropped to the ground. "Too fast," she replied. "More slow."

His fur prickled. Ylawl, fur standing on end, showed his teeth, snarling. "You are losing your power of speech," Hrurr said slowly. "Don't you know what that means?"

The dog barked.

"You have lived among the two-legged ones for too long, and have given up part of your soul. You've drawn too close to them. Listen to me! You must save yourself before it's too late."

"I serve master."

"No, he's supposed to serve you. Let him feed you and keep you at his side if he must, but when you lose your power of speech, he asks too much. The world will become as silent for you as it is for him. Don't you understand?"

"Blondi!" The moustached two-legs had stepped away from his group and was calling to her. She hesitated, clearly wanting to harass the cats, then bounded back to him, rolling in the grass as she groveled at his feet. He barked at her and she stood on her hind legs. Picking up a stick, he held it at arm's length and barked again. The dog leaped over it, then sat on her haunches, tongue out as she panted.

Hrurr, sickened by the slavish display, could hardly bear to watch. Hope had risen in him when he saw the dog without a leash; now he knew that she did not need one, that her master enslaved her without it.

Blondi accepted a pat from her two-legs, then bounded ahead of the group as they began to descend the path, walking in two rows. Blondi's two-legs, walking next to the fair-furred female Hrurr had seen earlier, was in the lead. Behind him, the man in black offered his arm to another female; the others trailed behind, reminding the cat of a flock of geese.

"Blondi!" Hrurr called out once more, but the dog kept near her two-legs, leaping up whenever he gestured to her.

Ylawl hunkered down on the tree limb. "You just had to speak to her. You wouldn't listen to me. Now we're trapped. I don't know how we're going to get down."

Hrurr was already backing away toward the trunk. He clung to the bark with his claws, moving backward down the tree.

His paws slipped. He tumbled, arching his body, and managed to land on his feet. "Come on down."

"I can't."

"Don't be such a kitten."

"I can't." The younger cat began to meow piteously as Hrurr fidgeted below.

They had drawn the attention of the two black-clothed creatures near the house, who were now approaching. Hrurr hissed as one of the strangers clucked at him, and retreated a bit, feeling threatened.

One two-legs held out his hands as he boosted his companion, who reached up, grabbed Ylawl by the scruff of the neck, then jumped down. The small cat suddenly dug his claws into his rescuer's arm; the man dropped him, kicking at him with one leather-clad leg. Ylawl dodged him, then ran, disappearing around the side of the house.

One two-legs knelt, holding out a hand to Hrurr as his lips moved. The cat tensed, transfixed by the man's pale eyes and the tiny, gleaming skull on his head covering. His memory stirred. Another man in such a head covering had towered over him as his black-clothed companions had dragged Hrurr's two-legged creatures from their house. He shivered.

"Where are my people?" he asked, forgetting that they could not hear him. The kneeling man bared his teeth; the other began to circle around the cat.

Hrurr leaped up and ran down the hill, the two creatures in pursuit. As he came to a tree, he turned and noticed that the pair had halted. One waved his arms. Giving up the chase, the two climbed back toward the chalet.

Hrurr settled himself under the tree. Had his people been taken to this place? If so, the black-clad men might only have wanted to return him to them. He licked his fur while pondering that possibility. One of his female two-legged ones had screamed, nearly deafening Hrurr as the black-clothed ones dragged her outside; another of his people had been kicked as he lay on the ground. Wherever they were now, he was sure that they would not have wanted him with them; they had not even called out the name they used for him. They must have known that he would be better off on his own.

He should never have come to this place, this cage. He now knew what the broken mirror in the road had meant; his world was shattering, and the black-clad men would rule it along with other creatures who could not hear or speak. He was lost unless he could find his way out of this world.

The two-legged ones were walking up the path, Blondi bounding ahead of them. Hrurr stretched. He had one last chance to speak. Summoning his courage, he sprang out into the dusty light and stood above the approaching people.

Blondi growled, about to leap up the slope toward the cat when her two-legs seized her by the collar, trying to restrain her. Hrurr struggled with himself, wanting to flee.

"Foolish dog," Hrurr said, raising his fur and arching his back. "Strike at me if you can. At least then I'll be free of this world, and become one of the spirits who stalk the night."

The dog hesitated at his words.

"Free yourself," Hrurr went on. "Leave your two-legs before it's too late. Go into the forest and restore yourself before you can no longer hear our words."

"Free?" Blondi replied. "Free now."

"You're a prisoner, like the one who holds you. You are both imprisoned on this mountain."

Blondi bounced on her front paws, then crouched. Her two-legs knelt next to her, still holding her while his companions murmured and gestured at the cat. "Brave, isn't it?" one man said. "What more could you ask of a German cat?"

The two-legs lifted his head, staring at Hrurr with pale eyes. The cat's tail dropped, pressing against his side. He suddenly felt as though the man had heard his words, could indeed see into his soul and rob him of it, as he had robbed Blondi of hers. Hrurr's ears flattened. The man's gaze seemed to turn inward then, almost as if he contained the world inside himself.

"Blondi!" Hrurr's heart thumped against his chest. "I see death. I see death in the pale face of your master. Save yourself. I see wild dreams in his eyes."

"Have food," the dog said. "Have shelter. No prisoner. Go where he goes, not stay here always. Black-clad ones and gray-clad ones serve him, as I do, as all do. I follow him all my life. Free. What is free?"

The two-legs reached inside his jacket, pulled out a leash, and attached it to Blondi's collar. The dog licked his hand.

The procession continued toward the house. Hrurr leaped out of their way, then trailed them at a distance, hearing Blondi's intermittent, senseless barks. Her two-legs turned around to glance down the mountain, waving a hand limply at the vista below.

"There is the mountain where Charlemagne is said to lie," the two-legs said, indicating another peak. "It is said he will rise again when he is needed. It is no accident that I have my residence opposite it."

"What does it mean?" Hrurr cried out, imagining that Blondi might know.

"That he rule everything," Blondi replied, "and that I serve, wherever he goes."

"We shall win this war," the two-legs said. Behind him, two other creatures were shaking their heads. The fair-furred woman touched his arm.

"Let us go inside, my Fuehrer," one man said.

The chalet's picture window was bright with light. Hrurr sat below, watching silhouetted shapes flutter across the panes. Earlier in the night, the fair-furred woman had appeared on the balcony above; she had kindly dropped a few bits of food, glancing around nervously as if afraid someone might see her.

"Well?"

Hrurr turned his head. Ylawl was slinking toward him, eyes gleaming in the dark. "I see that Blondi's still there." The dog, a shadow outlined by the light, was now gazing out the window.

"Her master still holds her," Hrurr said. "I think she would even die for him." He paused. "Come with me, Ylawl."

"Where will you go?"

"Down to the valley, I suppose." He thought of returning to Mewleen, wondering if he would ever find her again.

"It's a long way."

"I wish I could go to a place where there are no two-legged ones."

"They are everywhere. You'll never escape them. They'll swallow the world, at least for a time. Best to take what they offer and ignore them otherwise."

"They serve no one except themselves, Ylawl. They don't even realize how blind and deaf they are." Hrurr stretched. "I must leave."

The smaller cat lingered for moment, then slipped away. "Goodbye, then," Ylawl whispered.

Hrurr made his way down the slope, keeping away from the roads, feeling his way through the night with his whiskers. The mindless bark of a guard dog in the distance occasionally echoed through the wood; the creature did not even bother to sound warnings in the animals' tongue. He thought of Blondi, who seemed to know her two-legs's language better than her own.

By morning, he had come to the barbed-wire fence; slipping under it, he left the enclosure. The birds were singing, gossiping of the sights they had seen and the grubs they had caught and chirping warnings to intruders on their territory.

"Birds!" Hrurr called out. "You've flown far. You must know where I would be safe. Where should I go?"

"Cat! Cat!" the birds replied mockingly. No one answered his question.

He came to the road where he had left Mewleen and paced along it, seeking. At last he understood that the broken mirror was gone; the omen had vanished. He sat down, wondering what it meant.

Something purred in the distance. He started up as the procession of metal beasts passed him, moving in the direction of the distant town. For a moment, he was sure he had seen Blondi inside one beast's belly, her nose pressed against a transparent shield, death in her eyes.

When the herd had rolled past, he saw Mewleen gazing at him from across the road, bright eyes flickering. He ran to her, bounding over the road, legs stretching as he displayed his speed and grace. Rolling onto his back, he nipped at her fur as she held him with her paws; her purring and his became one sound.

"The fragments are gone," he said.

"I know."

"I'm in my own world again, and the dog has been taken from the cage."

"Whatever do you mean?" Mewleen asked.

He rolled away. "It's nothing," he replied, scrambling to his feet. He could not tell Mewleen what he had seen; better not to burden her with his dark vision.

"Look at you," she chided. "So ungroomed—I imagine you're hungry as well." She nuzzled at his fur. "Do you want to come home with me now? They may shoo you away at first, but when they understand that you have no place to go, they'll let you stay."

He thought of food and dark, warm places, of laps and soft voices. Reluctantly, he was beginning to understand how Blondi felt.

"For a while," he said, clinging to his freedom. "Just for a while." As they left the road, several birds flew overhead, screaming of the distant war.

May's Lion
by
Ursula K. Le Guin

Ursula K. Le Guin is probably one of the best known and most universally respected SF writers in the world today. Her famous novel The Left Hand of Darkness *may have been the most influential SF novel of its decade, and shows every sign of becoming one of the enduring classics of the genre; it won both the Hugo and Nebula awards, as did Le Guin's monumental novel* The Dispossessed *a few years later. She has also won three other Hugo Awards and a Nebula Award for her short fiction, and the National Book Award for Children's Literature for her novel* The Farthest Shore, *part of her acclaimed* Earthsea *trilogy. Her other novels include* Planet of Exile, The Lathe of Heaven, City of Illusions, Rocannon's World, The Beginning Place, A Wizard of Earthsea, The Tombs of Atuan, *and the controversial multi-media novel* Always Coming Home. *She has had four collections:* The Wind's Twelve Quarters, Orsinian Tales, The Compass Rose, *and, most recently,* Buffalo Gals and Other Animal Presences. *Her most recent novel is* Tehanu, *a continuation of her* Earthsea *series.*

Here, in a tale that functions as a kind of transitionary prequel to Always Coming Home *and its strangely transfigured California, she gives us a close encounter of a peculiar kind between an old woman and a cat—and in the process spins a moving and bittersweet story with her usual skill . . . which is to say, about as good as it gets.*

* * *

Jim remembers it as a bobcat, and he was May's nephew, and ought to know. It probably was a bobcat. I don't think May would have changed her story, though you can't trust a good story-teller not to make the story suit herself, or get the facts to fit the story better. Anyhow she told it to us more than once,

143

because my mother and I would ask for it; and the way I remember it, it was a mountain lion. And the way I remember May telling it is sitting on the edge of the irrigation tank we used to swim in, cement rough as a lava flow and hot in the sun, the long cracks tarred over. She was an old lady then with a long Irish upper lip, kind and wary and balky. She liked to come sit and talk with my mother while I swam; she didn't have all that many people to talk to. She always had chickens, in the chickenhouse very near the back door of the farmhouse, so the whole place smelled pretty strong of chickens, and as long as she could she kept a cow or two down in the old barn by the creek. The first of May's cows I remember was Pearl, a big, handsome Holstein who gave fourteen or twenty-four or forty gallons or quarts of milk at a milking, whichever is right for a prize milker. Pearl was beautiful in my eyes when I was four or five years old; I loved and admired her. I remember how excited I was, how I reached upward to them, when Pearl or the workhorse Prince, for whom my love amounted to worship, would put an immense and sensitive muzzle through the three-strand fence to whisk a cornhusk from my fearful hand; and then the munching; and the sweet breath and the big nose would be at the barbed wire again: the offering is acceptable. . . . After Pearl there was Rosie, a purebred Jersey. May got her either cheap or free because she was a runt calf, so tiny that May brought her home on her lap in the back of the car, like a fawn. And Rosie always looked like she had some deer in her. She was a lovely, clever little cow and even more willful than old May. She often chose not to come in to be milked. We would hear May calling and then see her trudging across our lower pasture with the bucket, going to find Rosie wherever Rosie had decided to be milked today on the wild hills she had to roam in, a hundred acres of our and Old Jim's land. Then May had a fox terrier named Pinky, who yipped and nipped and turned me against fox terriers for life, but he was long gone when the mountain lion came; and the black cats who lived in the barn kept discreetly out of the story. As a matter of fact now I think of it the chickens weren't in it either. It might have been quite different if they had been. May had quit keeping chickens after old Mrs. Walter died. It was just her all alone there, and Rosie and the cats down in the barn, and nobody else within sight or sound of the old farm. We were in our house up the hill only in the summer, and Jim lived in town, those years. What time of year it was I don't know, but I imagine the grass still green or just turning gold. And May was in the house, in the kitchen, where she lived entirely unless she was asleep or outdoors, when she heard this noise.

Now you need May herself, sitting skinny on the edge of the irrigation tank, seventy or eighty or ninety years old, nobody knew how old May was and she had made sure they couldn't find out, opening her pleated lips and letting out this noise—a huge, awful yowl, starting soft with a nasal hum and rising slowly into a snarling gargle that sank away into a sobbing purr. . . . It got better every time she told the story.

"It was some meow," she said.

So she went to the kitchen door, opened it, and looked out. Then she shut the kitchen door and went to the kitchen window to look out, because there was a mountain lion under the fig tree.

Puma, cougar, catamount, *Felix concolor;* the shy, secret, shadowy lion of the New World, four or five feet long plus a yard of black-tipped tail, weighs about what a woman weighs, lives where the deer live from Canada to Chile, but always shyer, always fewer; the color of dry leaves, dry grass.

There were plenty of deer in the Valley in the forties, but no mountain lion had been seen for decades anywhere near where people lived. Maybe way back up in the canyons; but Jim, who hunted, and knew every deer-trail in the hills, had never seen a lion. Nobody had, except May, now, alone in her kitchen.

"I thought maybe it was sick," she told us. "It wasn't acting right. I don't think a lion would walk right into the yard like that if it was feeling well. If I'd still had the chickens it'd be a different story maybe! But it just walked around some, and then it lay down there," and she points between the fig tree and the decrepit garage. "And then after a while it kind of meowed again, and got up and come into the shade right there." The fig tree, planted when the house was built, about the time May was born, makes a great, green, sweet-smelling shade. "It just laid there looking around. It wasn't well," says May.

She had lived with and looked after animals all her life; she had also earned her living for years as a nurse.

"Well, I didn't know exactly what to do for it. So I put out some water for it. It didn't even get up when I come out the door. I put the water down there, not so close to it that we'd scare each other, see, and it kept watching me, but it didn't move. After I went back in it did get up and tried to drink some water. Then it made that kind of meowowow. I do believe it come here because it was looking for help. Or just for company, maybe."

The afternoon went on, May in the kitchen, the lion under the fig tree.

But down in the barnyard by the creek was Rosie the cow. Fortunately the gate was shut, so she could not come wandering up to the house and meet the lion; but she would be needing to be milked, come six or seven o'clock, and that got to worrying May. She also worried how long a sick mountain lion might hang around, keeping her shut in the house. May didn't like being shut in.

"I went out a time or two, and went shoo!"

Eyes shining amidst fine wrinkles, she flaps her thin arms at the lion. "Shoo! Go on home now!"

But the silent wild creature watches her with yellow eyes and does not stir.

"So when I was talking to Miss Macy on the telephone, she said it might have rabies, and I ought to call the sheriff. I was uneasy then. So finally I did that, and they come out, those county police, you know. Two carloads."

Her voice is dry and quiet.

"I guess there was nothing else they knew how to do. So they shot it."

She looks off across the field Old Jim, her brother, used to plow with Prince the horse and irrigate with the water from this tank. Now wild oats and blackberry grow there. In another thirty years it will be a rich man's vineyard, a tax write-off.

"He was seven feet long, all stretched out, before they took him off. And so thin! They all said, 'Well, Aunt May, I guess you were scared there! I guess you were some scared!' ⟶ I wasn't. I didn't want him shot. But I didn't know what to do for him. And I did need to get to Rosie."

I have told this true story which May gave to us as truly as I could, and now I want to tell it as fiction, yet without taking it from her: rather to give it back to her, if I can do so. It is a tiny part of the history of the Valley, and I want to make it part of the Valley outside history. Now the field that the poor man plowed and the rich man harvested lies on the edge of a little town, houses and workshops of timber and fieldstone standing among almond, oak, and eucalyptus trees; and now May is an old woman with a name that means the month of May: Rains End. An old woman with a long, wrinkled-pleated upper lip, she is living alone for the summer in her summer place, a meadow a mile or so up in the hills above the little town, Sinshan. She took her cow Rose with her, and since Rose tends to wander she keeps her on a long tether down by the tiny creek, and moves her into fresh grass now and then. The summerhouse is what they call a ninepole house, a mere frame of poles stuck in the ground—one of them is a live digger-pine sapling—with stick and matting walls, and mat roof and floors. It doesn't rain in the dry season, and the roof is just for shade. But the house and its little front yard where Rains End has her camp stove and clay oven and matting loom are well shaded by a fig tree that was planted there a hundred years or so ago by her grandmother.

Rains End herself has no grandchildren; she never bore a child, and her one or two marriages were brief and very long ago. She has a nephew and two grandnieces, and feels herself an aunt to all children, even when they are afraid of her and rude to her because she has got so ugly with old age, smelling as musty as a chickenhouse. She considers it natural for children to shrink away from somebody part way dead, and knows that when they're a little older and have got used to her they'll ask her for stories. She was for sixty years a member of the Doctors Lodge, and though she doesn't do curing any more people still ask her to help with nursing sick children, and the children come to long for the kind, authoritative touch of her

hands when she bathes them to bring a fever down, or changes
a dressing, or combs out bed-tangled hair with witch hazel and
great patience.

So Rains End was just waking up from an early afternoon
nap in the heat of the day, under the matting roof, when she
heard a noise, a huge, awful yowl that started soft with a nasal
hum and rose slowly into a snarling gargle that sank away into
a sobbing purr. . . . And she got up and looked out from the
open side of the house of sticks and matting, and saw a
mountain lion under the fig tree. She looked at him from her
house; he looked at her from his.

And this part of the story is much the same: the old woman;
the lion; and, down by the creek, the cow.

It was hot. Crickets sang shrill in the yellow grass on all the
hills and canyons, in all the chaparral. Rains End filled a bowl
with water from an unglazed jug and came slowly out of the
house. Halfway between the house and the lion she set the
bowl down on the dirt. She turned and went back to the house.

The lion got up after a while and came and sniffed at the
water. He lay down again with a soft, querulous groan, almost
like a sick child, and looked at Rains End with the yellow eyes
that saw her in a different way than she had ever been seen
before.

She sat on the matting in the shade of the open part of her
house and did some mending. When she looked up at the lion
she sang under her breath, tunelessly; she wanted to remember
the Puma Dance Song but could only remember bits of it, so
she made a song for the occasion:

> You are there, lion.
> You are there, lion. . . .

As the afternoon wore on she began to worry about going
down to milk Rose. Unmilked, the cow would start tugging at
her tether and making a commotion. That was likely to upset
the lion. He lay so close to the house now that if she came
out that too might upset him, and she did not want to frighten
him or to become frightened of him. He had evidently come for
some reason, and it behoved her to find out what the reason

was. Probably he was sick; his coming so close to a human person was strange, and people who behave strangely are usually sick or in some kind of pain. Sometimes, though, they are spiritually moved to act strangely. The lion might be a messenger, or might have some message of his own for her or her townspeople. She was more used to seeing birds as messengers; the fourfooted people go about their own business. But the lion, dweller in the Seventh House, comes from the place dreams come from. Maybe she did not understand. Maybe someone else would understand. She could go over and tell Valiant and her family, whose summerhouse was in Gahheya meadow, farther up the creek, or she could go over to Buck's, on Baldy Knoll. But there were four or five adolescents there, and one of them might come and shoot the lion, to boast that he'd saved old Rains End from getting clawed to bits and eaten.

Moooooo! said Rose, down by the creek, reproachfully.

The sun was still above the southwest ridge, but the branches of pines were across it and the heavy heat was out of it, and shadows were welling up in the low fields of wild oats and blackberry.

Moooooo! said Rose again, louder.

The lion lifted up his square, heavy head, the color of dry wild oats, and gazed down across the pastures. Rains End knew from that weary movement that he was very ill. He had come for company in dying, that was all.

"I'll come back, lion," Rains End sang tunelessly. "Lie still. Be quiet, I'll come back soon." Moving softly and easily, as she would move in a room with a sick child, she got her milking pail and stool, slung the stool on her back with a woven strap so as to leave a hand free, and came out of the house. The lion watched her at first very tense, the yellow eyes firing up for a moment, but then put his head down again with that little grudging, groaning sound. "I'll come back, lion," Rains End said. She went down to the creekside and milked a nervous and indignant cow. Rose could smell lion, and demanded in several ways, all eloquent, just what Rains End intended to *do?* Rains End ignored her questions and sang milking songs to her: "Su bonny, su bonny, be still my grand cow . . ." Once she had to slap her hard on the hip. "Quit that, you old fool! Get over! I am *not* going to untie you and have you walking into trouble! I won't let him come down this way."

She did not say how she planned to stop him.

She retethered Rose where she could stand down in the creek if she liked. When she came back up the rise with the pail of milk in hand, the lion had not moved. The sun was down, the air above the ridges turning clear gold. The yellow eyes watched her, no light in them. She came to pour milk into the lion's bowl. As she did so, he all at once half rose up. Rains End started, and spilled some of the milk she was pouring. "Shoo! Stop that!" she whispered fiercely, waving her skinny arm at the lion. "Lie down now! I'm afraid of you when you get up, can't you see that, stupid? Lie down now, lion. There you are. Here I am. It's all right. You know what you're doing." Talking softly as she went, she returned to her house of stick and matting. There she sat down as before, in the open porch, on the grass mats.

The mountain lion made the grumbling sound, ending with a long sigh, and let his head sink back down on his paws.

Rains End got some cornbread and a tomato from the pantry box while there was still daylight left to see by, and ate slowly and neatly. She did not offer the lion food. He had not touched the milk, and she thought he would eat no more in the House of Earth.

From time to time as the quiet evening darkened and stars gathered thicker overhead she sang to the lion. She sang the five songs of *Going Westward to the Sunrise,* which are sung to human beings dying. She did not know if it was proper and appropriate to sing these songs to a dying mountain lion, but she did not know his songs.

Twice he also sang: once a quavering moan, like a housecat challenging another tom to battle, and once a long, sighing purr.

Before the Scorpion had swung clear of Sinshan Mountain, Rains End had pulled her heavy shawl around herself in case the fog came in, and had gone sound asleep in the porch of her house.

She woke with the grey light before sunrise. The lion was a motionless shadow, a little farther from the trunk of the fig tree than he had been the night before. As the light grew, she saw that he had stretched himself out full length. She knew he had finished his dying, and sang the fifth song, the last song, in a whisper, for him:

> The doors of the Four Houses
> are open.
> Surely they are open.

Near sunrise she went to milk Rose, and to wash in the creek. When she came back up to the house she went closer to the lion, though not so close as to crowd him, and stood for a long time looking at him stretched out in the long, tawny, delicate light. "As thin as I am!" she said to Valiant, when she went up to Gahheya later in the morning to tell the story and to ask help carrying the body of the lion off where the buzzards and coyotes could clean it.

It's still your story, Aunt May; it was your lion. He came to you. He brought his death to you, a gift; but the men with the guns won't take gifts, they think they own death already. And so they took from you the honor he did you, and you felt that loss. I wanted to restore it. But you don't need it. You followed the lion where he went, years ago now.

The Color of Grass, the Color of Blood
by
R.V. Branham

With only a handful of elegant and intricate stories, like this one, R.V. Branham has established a reputation for himself in the last couple of years as a writer to watch, and as one of the most distinctive and original new voices in SF. Branham's fiction has appeared in Isaac Asimov's Science Fiction Magazine, Midnight Graffiti, Full Spectrum, Writers of the Future, *and elsewhere, and at last report he was at work on a novel. Born in Calexico, California, he put in stints as an assistant X-ray technician, a rape crisis counselor, and an engineering research consultant on his way to becoming a writer, and now lives with his wife in Lawndale, California.*

In the darkly witty story that follows, Branham offers us a sly, cat's-eye view of life with a human family—a view that, as you'll discover, is not exactly a flattering *one. . . .*

* * *

ONE: GOODMORNINGOODMORNIN

It is morning, and it has been a long long time since you lapped up the half and half they left out last night. A long long time.

You push that door farther ajar and step into their room. They're asleep: Your Lady and *That Shit*, a male who always bullies you and feeds you after he's fed *his* Seshat, your Nemesis, a fat brown and beige snotty beast whose eyes are no grey-bluer than yours, but who laid claim to this household years ago, ages ago, nearly decades/millennia/almost eons ago.

It is morning and the sun is up and Your Lady is being a shit (a lowercase shit, but a shit nonetheless), pretending to be asleep. On her side. Now you see the opportunity. She's sleeping on her side. So you leap up and decide to crouch on

153

her ribs. She is a heavy sleeper, but if you knead enough/if you dig your claws into her ribs enough/if you perhaps draw blood the color of grass, then maybe, maybe, you will be fed.

She groans, grunts something, and tosses over, almost crushing little you, sweet little you!

He wakes up, The Shit Turd does! He'll feed you, after he's fed his Seshat. His eyes open for an instant, then shut. There is a noise, an imitation of many bees buzzing buzz. He reaches over, The Shit does, and knocks over the small table, and the buzzing stops.

He gets up and you weave into and out of his steps; he thinks you're so cute, being such a greedy guts for your breakfast . . . the condescending son of a dog. You sometimes fantasize about tripping him . . . he falls against one of the jagged shiny edges in your house. . . . And you drink the blood the color of grass as it pours from his head.

He bends down and strokes you. You purr, involuntarily. And bite him. The bite is voluntary, diabolically so.

He laughs. The Tapered Shit Turd. The Scarab's Delight. The condescending son of a dog-headed demon.

But, wait—? Where's his Seshat—? She looked a bit under last night, wouldn't budge from the sofa, even with all the racing and taunting and teasing you did last night, after Your Lady and That Shit had gone off to snore, loudly.

He leaves the room a moment—you follow . . . he's gone to look after his Seshat, that fat slob with the funny walk and the nice fur who always cleans herself, preening/posing/dozing. Not a fun Seshat at all. Not like you with your Thai-American gramma and Calico mum, your Hokusai bandit's mask and energy and speed and hunger. You're hungry, where's your breakfast?

Goodmorninggoodmornin, you cry out. God, forget about that boring Seshat and feed me! That's what you say, more or less. You also hint about how long you've needed a new collar. One that *kills* fleas, or at least drives them away.

He *finally* comes back, after an eternity, during the which thereof you have watched the layer of tree needles deepen another paw's worth, watched the shadows shift, slightly, but damn if they have not shifted.

He gives you dry food. He always gives his Seshat the wet stuff, the good stuff, with gravy and cereal grain and *real* meat. Not like the dried meat turds. Food pellets. Food shit.

He doesn't give that crap to *his* Seshat!

But you're hungry, so what can you do but dig in? It's a Seshat's life sometimes, sometimes. Like a smug pharaoh he leans to pet your ears, which *sometimes* you *do* enjoy, so you give him your second morning bite.

TWO: THE STRANGE CAGE

He opens a high door and reaches up for something, which he eats. Later, he takes the chair and stands on it. Above the cold food place are two shelves; on the top shelf is a strange cage, which smells:

—faintly of the puddles of oil under chariots, yet the cage is solid instead of liquid,

—of shredded old papers lining the cage's bottom, reminding you of stale dead trees,

—and also of many other Seshats, including your fat Nemesis. You realize it is their *fear* that you smell.

You run to hide.

The last time he took you in that, you had to go in the chariot, with bright lights (and water from sky), and go to a place where they drugged you and cut you open and sewed you back together. All just because you'd wanted to out and see all the males. (Males are not Seshats, who after all are the embodiment of learning and wisdom; nor can they properly be said to be Bast or Sekhet . . . They're just males, seed carriers.)

You've run to hide. But he doesn't go after *you;* he puts *his* Seshat in the strange oblong cage.

You jump on the yellow grey table and look out at the grey blue birds and the trees which someday will bury the world in needles. Needles the color of blood or of grass.

He brings the strange cage into your room, and sets it on the table. You go to see how that fat Seshat is doing. She *must* be sick, she's too tired to file a proper protest. Now, what sort of Nemesis is a very ill and very fat Seshat? You remember another time when *you* were put in that strange oblong cage, taken to *that* place again, where they poked a something that was long up your rectum, *held* it there, and took it out and shook it, and then had the gall to pretend to *examine* it.

You would have gladly feasted on their eyeballs/the balls of their feet/their testes. Anything round enough to play with while eating it. You sometimes wonder if the male seed carriers put Your Lady's male, That Shit, up to it. Is this a male conspiracy against the Seshat?

You decide you have had enough of the strange oblong cage.

THREE: YOUR LADY'S DESK

After The Shit who lives with Your Lady has departed with *his* Seshat, you are *all* alone.

You run gleefully all over the place, finally, in your bedroom (which is only truly your bedroom when That Shit has departed) and find Your Lady still pretending to be asleep on Your Bed. (Your Lady had actually gotten up before That Shit, twice, each time getting the chair That Shit got and standing up on it and reaching for food. And each time Your Lady had ignored your requests for food.) You jump onto the bed, go up to her face, and noticing crumbs of food around her lips, begin to lick. She tosses her hands up, almost hitting you, and turns over. You go over to the other side and begin to clean yourself.

A Seshat's ablutions are a most important daily ritual, almost as important as food and water, clean sand in a clean box, strokes and pats, and the catch of the day.

It is quite tedious, boring, really. Your Lady is sleeping despite your best efforts. Your Nemesis has been taken away by That Shit who never feeds you before *his* Seshat, except when his Seshat's too sick to eat. So you take a nap, dreaming of birds to defeather/to decapitate/of balls with bells in them/of the Great River the color of grass the color of blood and of your friend Pharaoh and his temples you guarded and of granaries you also guarded and of mice/better mousetraps/of dinner.

Wet food.

You wake up, much later in the morning. You can tell it is later by the play of shadow and more shadow on Your Lady.

So you get up. Stretch. Clean yourself again. And go to your favorite space, a work area with two desks. Your Lady's is the best. Stacks of paper to lounge on, drawers to hide in— although Your Lady does not like that. A strange thing happens to you, sometimes, when you are caught in a drawer: a jet of water hits you in the face. It's not *piss*, not from the other Seshat. It is unfathomable, almost preternatural. Where does that water come from?

You find an open drawer, a nice enclosed space like the box your mother kept you in when you were so, so little, so helpless. You climb in and go to sleep.

You hear footsteps, coming nearer. You open your eyes. Your Lady is screaming at you *out Out* OUT! She points something bright, gleaming like the sun, at you, and before you can escape you've been squirted again by that strangely anonymous water *and* been grabbed by the scruff of your neck, mewling and protesting, and taken out the front door.

Then the door slams shut!

You call out for quite a while, to no avail!

Looking up at the damn tree which is deluging the world with needles, day after week after month after season, you remember the nest, the chirrupy cherubs, the tasty baby feathery morsels. *Wet food*.

FOUR: CATCH OF THE DAY

You are halfway up the tree, when who should show up but mama grey blue bird! She is alternately attacking you and going down to the ground to act as a decoy to lead you away from the nest. This is the most frequent tactical error that mama birds make.

You sit there, pretending to clean yourself, as though you'd *already* eaten!

And, slowly, you move a bit further down.

At one point, mama bird makes a fatal error. She is *right* below you, and just as she is about to fly, you pounce onto her, teeth into her back, kicking at her with your hindquarters, trying to disembowel her. You decide to play with her a while, instead, chewing on her wings. The left one and then the right one.

The window to your bedroom opens, as well as the curtains. You see Your Lady, and feel a welling, a surge of pride. Look, Lady, See, Mistress, A Birdie For Our Lunch! She comes out with a mallet, and you run away. That Shit who lives with Your Lady likes to take a mallet and kill your catch before you are even properly through playing with it.

She learned this treachery from him. Your mother told you of male treachery before you'd been weaned. And she was right. Mother Seshats are *always* right.

So, apologizing to Your Lady, you run away with your catch. Your Lady goes muttering mumble muttering back into the house. After an interval you get tired of chewing on the right wing and let go, holding her down with your paws, so you can bite into the left wing again. At that moment, the birdie wriggles out of your killing grasp and hip-hops across the lawn, which, though in need of watering, is the color of blood.

Just then, there is a gleam of silver and a noxious oil smell, also a chariot noise, announcing the arrival of That Shit, probably returning with *his* Seshat.

You run through the piled detritus of tree needles and cones and dog turds, and catch your birdie. You bite into her back and hold her down.

The Shit comes around the corner, holding the oblong strange cage, which is open. How odd, strange. Did your Nemesis die? You'd feel wholly horrible if that were the case.

From your left peripheral vision, you notice a blur, an approaching something. Suddenly your fat Nemesis is before you. Faker, you knew! All along you knew! Faker!

Acting with speed—the sort of speed you had assumed could never be attained with all that fat to act as inertia—she has pounced on your birdie! The malingering faker's taken your bird!

Furthermore, she's stolen the trophy, torn off the head, causing a stream of blood the color of grass to darken the sidewalk.

She runs off, and hides under the house.

The Shit who brought her back from death's door, all he can do is laugh. *Laugh at you.*

What can you do but take your birdie, what's left of it, and finish it in the neighbor's yard?

That afternoon, catching sun and ants and flies, you consider your options:

There's running away.

There's getting even:

—with Your Nemesis,

—with Your Lady, for giving her tacit approval to this wretched status quo. (After all, Pharaoh would have flogged someone for cruelty to Seshats.)

—with That Shit, that Essence of Excrescence who lives with Your Lady, who you might trip as he was about to get into his shiny and gleaming bath, or who you might attack after he started snoring, going for his fluttering testes and hairy eyelids; maybe you could start with small gestures, like pissing on his books or scratching them, or scratching the bookcase, or attacking his favorite wool sweater, and gradually work your way up to a lethal assault,

—Or you could get even with all of them.

You hear a whistle.

To hell with them. For now.

But, wait. That's—

It's Dinner Time!

FOOD!

You run through the historic piles of tree needles, witness to betrayals large and small, from time immemorial, from before you were born even, and run back to have some dinner.

FIVE: GOODMORNINGOODMORNIN

Last night, after your dinner, and after their dinner, Your Lady had left, slamming big and little doors, grumbling mumble. Taken the chariot. Left you alone. All alone, with Your Nemesis, and That Shit.

And a long little time later, there was a noise at the front door and That Scarab's Delight answered—and it was a lady, not *Your Lady,* either, and they hugged each other, then went into the rooms which should be yours, and you tried to follow. But they shut the door in your face, and you heard them laughing. You backed up to a row of books and pissed on them. They still laughed, from behind the door. So you scratched a wall hanging. Chased Your Nemesis everywhere. Knocked down several of That Shit's things—broke a few. And still they laughed, still he laughed. At you. At Your Lady.

It had been a long, long time before the door opened again, and the other lady left—smelling of sweat and of seed. That Shit went with her. And returned a short time later. When he came back alone, he didn't notice you had destroyed many of his things.

It was when he had again shut the door behind him, shut it in your face, it was then you came to a decision.

You pushed that door and pushed that door, and had been about to give up, when Your Nemesis came and reached up and leaned into the door, and opened it. She'd only wanted Your Lady's desk, good.

You'd heard the familiar rhythm, the ebb and flow of That Shit's snoring. Your mother had taught you about veins, especially those around the neck. You leapt onto the bed, and he turned. For the first time in his life, The Shit was co-operating. You stretched, and flexed, drawing claws from paws. And you pounced.

But that was so long ago, a good night ago, and here it is, a goodmorningoodmornin, and no one left anything in the kitchen for you to snack on.

To think he put up less resistance than mama grey blue bird—but he did bleed more. Much more. Still, he was so easy. You must make a note to only pounce on the sleeping. Yet somehow you had expected more excitement—and that much blood is no fun, not fun at all, it makes your fur the color of grass. Still, you're not a kitten anymore; time to put away a kitten's things.

And too bad some of his bits weren't in any shape to stuff back in place. Any Seshat would try, if possible. Pharaoh, after all, usually had a criminal's head sewn back on after its removal. But you are Seshat, not Pharaoh, you want some kitchen food now. Where could Your Lady be?

You hear a chariot approach, and stop. You hear tiny distant jingling become a near jingling, and the door opens. Your Nemesis comes running, demanding food, wet food. Good, it is Your Lady, with another lady, one you vaguely remember. You rush up to her, rub against her, leaving a streak of blood the color of grass. Her friend leans down to stroke your ears, and you playfully bite her. And she laughs.

You hear Your Lady scream and rush back to your room. You are as appalled as she is; you have apparently made some terrible mistake—why else would Your Lady scream like that— isn't it always the Seshat's fault when they scream like that? You rush forward to determine what is wrong, while trying to apologize for whatever rudeness you may have committed. She leaves. Just when you find you've knocked over her plant, she comes back with the mallet. Your Lady has now done something wrong, made the mistake, the silly and stupid grave error. There's no birdie to brain in your room! No birdie at all!

—For Sheila Finch

A Word to the Wise
by
John Collier

The late John Collier was a novelist and poet, but is perhaps best remembered as a writer of short, acerbic, slyly witty stories like "The Touch of Nutmeg Makes It," "Green Thoughts," and "Thus I Refute Beelzy"—stories which brought him international critical acclaim. The bulk of them have been collected in Fancies and Goodnights, *which won the International Fantasy Award, and* The John Collier Reader. *His other books include the novel* His Monkey Wife *and the postholocaust novel* Tom's A-Cold. *Collier died in 1980.*

Here he demonstrates that getting what you want is perhaps not as important as knowing what it's good for. . . .

*　　*　　*

Richard Whitiker drank his milk and carried his serviceable umbrella. When he looked in the glass he saw a face too simple ever to look old, and too worn ever to look young. Clowns have faces of this sort. His hair, well-streaked with grey, looked as if it were a wig, or as if it had been cut at home.

"That," said he, "is the face of someone who has not got very far in life. Damn it, I have hit the nail on the head! I am absolutely right, for nor have I. I have good judgment, you see, yet I have missed the bus on various important occasions."

This bothered him. He consulted the success books, which told him to analyze his past failures, and find out the true reason for them, in order to do better in the future.

This was a tremendous task. He paced up and down the room, he scratched his head; he took his ears in his hands and sat down on the bed to concentrate. At last, as if by a flash of lightning, he saw the very heart of the matter. He sprang up: "There is no doubt about it," he cried, "I should have made none of these silly mistakes. I should have done a thousand

163

times better, I should have been one of the greatest successes
ever known, had I only had a cat that could talk.

"Such an animal would have advised me against that
wretched gold mine.

"It would have told me frankly I could never do well with a
hotel.

"It would have cried 'Look out!' or 'Beware!' or something,
when I brought that Colonel Rankin home and introduced him
to my wife."

He found it a galling thought, to have missed fame and
fortune for lack of a cat and a few words, in a world so
abounding with both. But with the humble persistence of all
wooden-faced men, he resolved to repair the deficiency, and to
make the most of the years that remained to him.

He was not long in supplying himself with a cat, and was
careful to choose one that pursed its lips shrewdly and regarded
the world through a round and owlish eye. "This," said he,
"is the first step, and that is the one that counts. I look forward
to the day when this promising cat shall utter the name of a race
horse or a splendid investment, or tell me how to discover a
delightful young creature who will love a plain middle-aged
fellow like me."

At this thought our friend could hardly contain himself for
joy, which was well salted with impatience. He gave his cat the
best of everything, and talked to it at all hours, taking care to
pronounce his words clearly. He bought a radio for its special
benefit, and turned it on at the time of the stock market reports.
The only trouble was, the cat remained obstinately mute,
which was a source of much mortification to our hero, and of
infinite amusement to his friends.

"I have solved the major problem," he said. "I shall not
allow myself to be defeated by a minor one. Let me see now:
drink makes a man drunk, beef makes a man beefy, milk makes
a man mild. I drink it, and I am mild: I am talking from
experience. Clearly I must feet this cat parrots, and that will
make him talk like an oracle. Besides, the toughness of these
antique birds will strengthen his jaws, and give him more
command of all the muscles of his throat and mouth. One thing

fits in with another: I'll be off to the bird market in the morning."

Next morning he was early at the bird market, and came home with a fine Mexican Yellowhead, whose neck he wrung, and plucked it, and made it into a tasty fricassee which his cat licked up with relish.

Next day he obliged the animal with a well-spoken Amazon Parrot, then with a fluent Panama, then a garrulous Lemon-crested Cockatoo, and on his birthday a magnificent Macaw, and so forth, all talented birds, capable of stopping a horse and van in full career, scaring burglars or embarrassing young men who called with bouquets. But they were done with all that when they fell into the hands of Mr. Whitiker.

The cat opened his mouth fast enough when the birds were set before him, but still kept shut at other times except for an occasional yawn. Meanwhile the cost of this diet was prodigious. Our friend soon felt the strain.

He denied himself everything, he grew very emaciated, his coat wore out at the elbows, his shoes let water at every step, his roof leaked in a dozen places, and everything fell into decay. The little children cried after him in the street as he hurried home from the bird market, fearful lest his cat should be uttering a few crisp words at the moment, and he be missing them.

At last there came a day when he was at the end of all his resources, and could regale the creature with nothing better than a love bird, while he himself dined on despair. On that very day, whether it was astonishment at the scanty portion, or whether his ears deceived him, he could have sworn his cat emitted a low and rather tuneless whistle.

At once his hopes revived, and he saw years of happiness spread shining out before him. "Hurrah!" he cried. "It is beginning to take effect. I shall be rich! I shall be famous! I shall enjoy the embraces of that delicious creature, aged twenty-two or twenty-three, and with a thirty-five inch bust! I wonder if he will give me a tip or two about diet. After all, I have done a lot for him that way."

Nothing like striking while the iron is hot. Next morning our hero went out pawning and borrowing, and scraped together the price of a superb African Grey, the pride of the whole bird market, and, rushing home, he gave it to his cat raw, with the warmth of life still in it. He hoped by this means to insure that none of its virtue should be lost.

The cat swallowed it with avidity, blinked a little, wiped its chops with its paw, and raised its eyes to Heaven, as if in astonishment and gratitude. Then turning them full on Richard Whitiker, it said in a clear and vigorous tone, "Look out!"

The good man clasped his hands in an ecstasy. "He can speak!" he cried. "He can speak! And in what a delightful accent! Soon he will utter the name of a winning horse, or of some stock destined to rise like a rocket. He will tell me to go to such and such a town, to such an hotel, and there I shall meet the ravishing creature, twenty-two years of age, and with a bust measurement of thirty-five. What a moment that will be, when I first . . ."

At this point, however, his neglected ceiling fell with a crash, and our poor friend was stretched lifeless among the debris.

"Now what the hell," said the cat, stepping daintily over his prostrate form. "What the hell is the good of feeding a cat parrots, at such ruinous expense, in order to make it talk, if you take no notice of what it says to you?"

This cat subsequently took up its abode in the home of a Mrs. Straker, where it observed a good deal but thought the less said, the better for all concerned.

Duke Pasquale's Ring
by
Avram Davidson

For many years now Avram Davidson has been one of the most eloquent and individual voices in science fiction and fantasy, and there are few writers in any literary field who can hope to match his wit, his erudition, or the stylish elegance of his prose. His recent series of stories about the bizarre exploits of Doctor Engelbert Eszterhazy (collected in his World Fantasy Award–winning The Enquiries of Doctor Eszterhazy, *and just this year re-released in an expanded and updated hardcover version as* The Adventures of Doctor Ezsterhazy*) and the strange adventures of Jack Limekiller (as yet uncollected, alas), for instance, are Davidson at the very height of his considerable powers. Davidson has won the Hugo, the Edgar, and the World Fantasy Award. His books include the renowned* The Phoenix and the Mirror, Masters of the Maze, Rogue Dragon, Peregrine: Primus, Rork!, Clash of Star Kings, *and the collections* The Best of Avram Davidson, Or All the Seas With Oysters, *and* The Redward Edward Papers. *His most recent books are* Vergil in Averno, *the collection* The Adventures of Doctor Eszterhazy, *and, in collaboration with Grania Davis,* Marco Polo and the Sleeping Beauty.*

In the vivid and evocative story that follows, one of the Doctor Eszterhazy stories, Davidson lovingly crafts a milieu as rich and multi-layered and intricate as the finest mosaic, introducing us to a king without property and to a sinister man who has some sinister ways of getting what he wants . . . and demonstrating in an unsettling fashion the wisdom behind the ancient warning, Touch Not the Cat.

*   *   *

The King of the Single Sicily was eating pasta in a sidewalk restaurant; not in Palermo: in Bella. He had not always been known by that title. In Bella, capital of the Triune Monarchy of

Scythia-Pannonia-Transbalkania, he had for long decades been
known chiefly as an eccentric but quite harmless fellow who
possessed many quarterings of nobility and nothing in the
shape of money at all. But when the Kingdom of the Two
Sicilies (Naples and all of southern Italy being the other one)
was rather suddenly included into the new and united Kingdom
of Italy, ostensibly by plebiscite and certainly by force of
Garibaldean arms, something had happened to the inoffensive
old man.

He now put down his fork and belched politely. The
waiter-cook-proprietor came forward. "Could the King eat
more?" he asked.

"Im[belch]possible. There is no place." He patted the
middle-front of his second-best cloak.

"What damage," said the other. His previous career, prior to
deserting a French man-of-war, had been that of coal-heaver.
But he was a Frenchman born (that is, he was born in Algeria
of Corsican parentage), and this was almost universally held to
endow him with an ability to cook anything anywhere in Infidel
Parts better than the infidel inhabitants could. And certainly he
cooked pasta better and cheaper than it was cooked in any other
cook-shop in Bella's South Ward. "What damage," he repeated. "There is more in the pot." And he raised his brigand
brows.

"Ah well. Put it in my kerchief, and I shall give it to my
cat."

"Would the King also like a small bone for his dog?"

"Voluntarily."

He had no cat; he had no dog; he had at home an old, odd
wife who had never appeared in public since the demise of her
last silk gown. The bone and extra pasta would make a soup,
and she would eat.

With the extinction of the Kingdom of the Two Sicilies
something had gone flash in the old man's brain-pan: surely
Sicily itself now reverted to the status of a kingdom by itself?
Surely he was its rightful king? And to anyone who would
listen and to anyone who would read, he explained the matter,
in full genealogy, with peculiar emphasis on the four marriages
of someone called Pasquale III, from one of which marriages

he himself descended. Some listened. Some read. Some even replied. But, actually, nothing happened. The new King of Italy did not so much as restore a long-forfeited tomato-patch. The ousted King of Naples did not so much as reply. Neither did Don Amadeo, King of Spain (briefly, very briefly, King of Spain). On the other hand, Don Carlos, King of Spain (pretended or claimed), did. Don Carlos was an exile in Bella at the moment. Don Carlos perhaps heard something. Don Carlos perhaps did not know much about Pasquale III, but Don Carlos knew about being a pretender and an exile. He did not precisely send a written reply; he sent some stockings, some shirts, a pair of trousers, and a cloak. All mended. But all clean. And a small hamper of luncheon.

By the time the King of the Single Sicily had dressed in his best and gone to call on Don Carlos, Don Carlos was gone, and—to Bella, as to Spain—Don Carlos never came back.

That was the nearest which Cosimo Damiano (as he chose to style himself) had ever come to Recognition. Stockings, shirts, and trousers had all worn out; the cloak he was wearing even now. And to pay for the daily plate of pasta he was left to his semi-occasional pupil in the study of Italian, calligraphy, and/or advanced geometry.

"To see again," he said, now rising, and setting upon the tiny table a coin of two copperkas.

"To see again," said the cook-shop man, his eyes having ascertained the existence of the coin and its value. He bowed. He would when speaking to Cosimo Damiano refer to him in the third person as the king, he would give him extra pasta past its prime, he would even donate to a pretense-dog a bone which still had some boiling left in it. He might from time to time do more. A half-cup of salad neglected by a previous diner. A recommendation to a possible pupil. Even now and then a glass of thin wine not yet "turned." But for all and for any of this he must have his coin of two copperkas. Otherwise: nothing. So it was.

D. Cosimo D., as sometimes he signed himself, stooped off homeward in his cloak. Today was a rich day: extra pasta, a soup-bone, and he had a half-a-copperka to spare. He might get himself a snuff of inferior tobacco wrapped in a screw of newspaper. But he rather thought he might invest the two farthings in the merchandise of Mother Whiskers, who sold broken nut-meats in the mouth of an alley not far off. His queen was fond of that. The gaunt and scabby walls, street-level walls long since knocked bare of plaster or stucco, narrowed in towards him as he went. The old woman was talking to another customer, not one who wanted a farthingworth of broken nut-meats, by his look. But Mother Whiskers had another profession: she was by way of being a witch, and all sorts of people came to see her, deep in the smelly slums where she had her seat.

She stopped whatever she had been saying, and jerked up her head to D. Cosimo D. "Gitcherself anointed?" was her curious question.

"I fear not. Alas," said D. Cosimo D., with a sigh.

She shook her head so that her whiskers flew about her face, and her earrings, too. "Gitcherself anointed!" she said. "All kinds o' work and jobs I c'n git fer a 'nointed king. Touch fer the king's evil—the scrofuly, that is—everybuddy knows that—and ringworm! Oh my lordy, how much ringworm there be in the South Ward!" Oft-times, when he was not thinking of his own problems alone, Cosimo wondered that there was not much more cholera, pest, and leprosy in the South Ward. "—and the best folks c'n do is git some seventh son of a seventh son; now, not that I mean that ain't *good*. But can't compare to a 'nointed king!"

And the stranger, in a deep, murmurous voice, said No, indeed.

Poor Cosimo! Had he had to choose between Anointing without Crowning, and Crowning without Anointing, he would have chosen the Holy Oil over the Sacred Crown. But he was allowed no choice. Hierarch after hierarch had declined to perform such services, or even service, for him. There was one exception. Someone, himself perhaps a pretender and certainly an exile, someone calling himself perhaps Reverend and Venerable Archimandrite of Petra and Simbirsk had offered to perform . . . but for a price . . . a high one . . . it would demean his sacred office to do it on the cheap, said he. And, placing his forefinger alongside his nose, had winked.

Much that had helped.

"Well, if you won't, you won't," grumbled Old Mother Whiskers. "But I do my best for y', anyway. Gotchyou a stoodent, here. See?"

Taking a rather closer look than he had taken before, Cosimo saw someone rather tall and rather richly dressed . . . not alone for the South Ward, richly . . . for anywhere, richly. There was something in this one's appearance for which the word sleek seemed appropriate, from his hat and his moustache down to his highly-polished shoes; the man murmured the words, "Melanchthon Mudge," and held out his hand. He did not take his glove off (it was a sleek glove), and Cosimo, as he shook hands and murmured his own name, felt several rings . . . and felt that they were rings with rather large stones, and . . .

"Mr. Mudge," said Mother Whiskers; "Mr. Mudge is a real classy gent." And D. Cosimo D. felt, also that—though Mr. Mudge may have been a gent—Mr. Mudge was not really a gentleman. But as to that, in this matter: no matter.

"Does Mr. Mudge desire to be instructed," he asked, "in Italian? In calligraphy? Or in advanced geometry? Or in all three?"

Mr. Mudge touched a glossy-leather-encased-finger to a glossy moustache. Said he thought, "For the present, sir. For the present," that they would skip calligraphy. "Madame here has already told me of your terms, I find them reasonable, and I would only wish to ask if you might care to mention . . . by the way of, as it were, general reference . . . the names of some of your past pupils. If you would not mind."

Mind? The poor old King of the Single Sicily would not have minded standing on his head if it would have helped bring him a pencil. He mentioned the names of a surveyor now middling-high in the Royal and Imperial Highways and to whom he had taught advanced geometry, of several ladies of quality to whom he had taught Italian, and of a private docent whom he had instructed in calligraphy: still Mr. Mudge waited, as one who would hear more; D. Cosimo D. went on to say, "And, of course, that young Eszterhazy, Doctor as he now is—"

"Ah," said Mr. Melanchthon Mudge, stroking his moustache and his side-whiskers; "that young Eszterhazy, Doctor as he now is." His voice seemed to grow very drawn-out and deep.

Plaster and paint, turpentine and linseed oil had all alike long since dried, inside and outside the house at Number 33 Turkling Street, where lived Dr. Engelbert Eszterhazy; though sometimes he had the notion that he could still smell it. At the moment, though, what he chiefly smelled came from his well-fitted chemical laboratory, as well as from the more distant kitchen where—in some matters Eszterhazy was old-fashioned—Mrash, his man-cook, reigned. Old Mrash would probably and eventually be replaced by a woman. In the meanwhile he had his stable repertory of ten or twelve French dishes as passed down through generations of army officers' cooks since the days of (at least) Bonaparte; and when he had run through it and them and before running through them and it again, Mrash usually gave his master a few days of peasant cooking which boxed the culinary compass of the fourth-largest empire in Europe. Ox-cheek and eggs. Beef palate, pigs' ears, and buckwheat. Potatoes boiled yellow in chicken broth with unborn eggs and dill. Cowfoot stew, with mushrooms and mashed turnips. And after that it was back to *boeuf à la mode Bayonne* [sic], and all the rest of it as taught long ago to his captors by some long ago prisoner-of-war.

Today, along with the harmless game of "consulting the menu-book," Mrash had a question, "if it pleased his lordship." Eszterhazy knew that it pleased Mrash to think that he cooked for a lordship, and had ceased trying to convince him of it not really pertaining. So, "Yes, Mrashko, certainly. What is the question?" There might or might not be a direct answer.

"What do they call that there place, my lordship, a boo?"

Philologists have much informed the world that the human mouth is capable of producing only a certain limited number of sounds, therefore it was perhaps no great feat for Eszterhazy at once to counter-ask, "Do you perhaps mean a *zoo?*"

"Ah," said Mrash the man-cook, noncommittally. He might, his tone indicated, though then again he might not.

Eszterhazy pressed on. "That's the short name for the Royal and Imperial Botanical and Zoölogical Gardens and Park, where the plants and creatures mostly from foreign parts are." Mrashko's mouth moved and seemed to relish the longer form of the name. "It's the second turning of the New Stonepaved Road after Big Ludo's Beer Garden," added 'his lordship.'

Mrash nodded. "I expect that's where it come from, then," he said.

" 'Come from'? Where *what* came from, Cooky?"

Cooky said, simply, "The tiger."

Eszterhazy recalled the comment of Old Captain Slotz, someone who had achieved much success in obtaining both civil and military intelligence. Captain Slotz had stated, "I don't ask them did they done it or I don't ask them did they not done it. Just, I look at them, and I say, *Tell me about it*."

"Tell me about it, Mrashko-Cooky."

The man-cook gestured. "See, my lordship, it come up the lane there," gesture indicated the alley. "And it hop onto yon wood-shed, or as it might be, coal-shed. Then it lep up onto the short brick bake-building. Then it gave a big jump and gits onto the roof of what was old Baron Johan's townhouse what his widow live in now all alone saving old Helen, old Hugo, and old Hercules what they call him, who look after her ladyship what she seldom go out at all anymore." Eszterhazy listened with great patience: "and then it climb up the roof and until it reach the roof-peak. It look all around. It put its front-limbs down," Mrash imitated this, "and it sort of just stretch . . . *streeeetch*. . . ."

Silence.

"And then?"

"Then I get back to me work, me lordship."

"Oh."

"Nother thing. I knew that there beast have another name to 't. Leopard. That be its other name. I suppose it come from the book. I suppose it trained to go back. Three nights I've seen it, nor I haven't heard no alarm." He began making the quasi-military movements which indicated he was about to begin the beginning of his leaving.

"Does it have stripes? Or spots?"

Mrash, jerking his arms, moving stiff-legged, murmured something about there being but the one gas-lamp in the whole alley, there having been not much of a bright moon of recent, hoped the creature wouldn't hurt no one nor even skeer the old Baroness nor old Helen; and—finally—"Beg permission to return to duty, your lordship. *Hup!*"

"Granted.—And—Mrash! [Me lord!] The next time you see it, let me know, directly."

The parade-ground manner of the man-cook's departure gave more than a hint that the next meal would consist largely of boiled bully-beef in the mode of the Royal and Imperial Infantry, plus the broth thereof, plus fresh-grated horseradish which would remove the roof of your mouth, plus potatoes prepared purple in a manner known chiefly to army cooks present and past all around the world. Eszterhazy looked out the window and across the alley. At ground level, the stones of the house opposite were immense, seemingly set without mortar. *Cyclopean*, the word came to him. Above these massive courses began others, of smaller pieces of masonry. The last storey and a half were of brick, with here and there a tuft of moss instead of mortar. The steep-pitched roof was of dull grey slate. And though he could see this all quite clearly, he could see no explanation for the story which his old cook, never before given to riotous fancy, had just recounted to him. Long he stared. Long he stared. Long he considered. Then he rang the bell and asked for his horse to be saddled.

The old Chair of Natural Philosophy had finally been subdivided, and the new Chair of Natural History been created. Natural Philosophy included Chemistry, Physics, Meteorology, Astronomy. Natural History included Zoölogy, Ichthyology, Botany, Biology. Dr. Eszterhazy, having bethought him of the knot of loafers always waiting on hand near the Zoo to see whose horse shied at the strange odor when the wind blew so, decided to stop off first at the office of the Royal-Imperial Professor of Natural History, who was *ex cathedra* the Director of the Royal and Imperial Botanical and Zoölogical Gardens and Park. Said, "Your tigers and leopards. Tell me about them."

The Professor—it was Cornelius Crumholtss, with whom

Dr. E.E. had once taken private lessons—said, crisply, "None."
"What's that?"

"The tiger died last year. The Gaekwar of Oont, or is it his
heir, the Oontie Ghook? has agreed to trade us a tiger for three
dancing bears and two gluttons—or wolverines as some call
them—but he's not done it yet. Leopards? We've never had
one. We do have the lion. But he is very old. Shall I have spots
painted on him for you? No? Oh."

Ezterhazy had gone to the Benedictine Library. There were
things there which were nowhere else . . . and, not seldom,
that meant nowhere else . . . once, indeed, he had found the
Papal Legate there, waiting for a chance to see something not
even in the Vatican Library. It was stark and chill in the
whitewashed chamber which served as waiting-room. Who
was waiting for what? Eszterhazy was waiting for Brother
Claudius, for even Eszterhazy might not go up into the vaulted
hall where the oldest books were unless Brother Claudius
showed him up; not even the Papal Legate might do so, and it
was almost certain that not even the King-Emperor
might . . . in the unlikely instance of the King-Emperor's
going to the Benedictine Library to look for a book . . . or
anywhere else, for that matter. E. assumed that the tall, thin
man slumped in the corner was also waiting for Brother
Claudius. By and by, in came the lay-brother who acted as
porter, and wordlessly set down a brazier of glowing coals
before withdrawing.

The man in the corner moved. "Ah, good," he murmured.
"One's hands have grown too cold." He got up, and, moving
to the fire-chauldron, thrust his hands into it and drew them out
filled with hot coals glowing red. His manner seemed abstracted. An odor of singeing hair was very slightly perceptible. Eszterhazy felt his own flesh crawl. Slowly, quite slowly,
the man poured the red hot coals back upon the fire. "You are
Doctor Eszterhazy," next he said.

The statement required no confirmation. "And you, sir?
Who?"

Very slowly the tall body turned. A long finger stroked a

long moustache. "I? Oh. I am the brother of the shadow of the slain. The vanguard of the shadows of the living. I—"

Light. "Ah yes. You are the medium, Mr. Mudge."

"I am the medium. Mr. Mudge. As well. Oh yes.

"I am really very pleased to have this occasion to meet the eminent Dr. Eszterhazy," said Mr. Mudge.

"Indeed," murmured the eminent, very faintly questioning. He himself was certainly very interested at meeting the eminent Mr. Mudge. But, somehow, he rather doubted that he was really very pleased.

"Yes, indeed. Ah. You are not here . . . or perhaps you *are* here . . . to consult the Second Recension of the *Malleus Maleficarum*?"

The doctor said that he was not, not adding that both witchcraft and the fury it had once aroused alike tended to be productive of a definite dull pain between and in back of his eyes. "I am here to consult the Baconian Fragment. If it *is* by Friar Roger. Which is doubtless subject to doubt. If it *is* a fragment; the end of the parchment is rather fragmented, but the text itself seems complete."

Mr. Mudge nodded. He seemed, certainly, to follow the comments. But his manner seemed also to be rather faintly abstracted. "Now, I wish to ask you about your former tutor," he said, and touched his full red tongue to his full red lips, and smiled. In fact the smile was not without a certain appeal, an effect, however, spoiled by . . . by what? . . . by the man's having rather yellow teeth.

"Which former tutor? I have had really a great many, as I began my formal education comparatively late, and was obliged to make up for lost time. So . . ."

"He calls himself sometimes Cosimo Damiano, though I understand that this is not precisely his legal name."

Well. Someone learned enough to read old books in Latin, and he wished to enquire about old—"Yes. And what did you wish to enquire?"

Could Dr. Eszterhazy recommend him? Certainly. The old man's Italian knowledge was encyclopedic, his calligraphy was exquisite, and his knowledge of advanced geometry was . . . well . . . advanced. It was at this point that the door opened and Brother Claudius came in, hands tucked inside the sleeves of his habit. "Come with me," he directed in a hollow voice; and, as he did not say to whom he was saying this, and as he immediately turned and left again, they both followed him. Through many an icy corridor. Up many a worn, yet steep, flight of stairs. Into the vast vaulted hall lined to twice a man's height with books whose ancient odors still had, as far as Eszterhazy was concerned, the power to thrill. The monk gestured him to a table on which a book-box reposed. The monk next gestured Mr. Mudge further on and further on, eventually waving him to another table. On which, or so it seemed at a glance, another book-box reposed. Eszterhazy sat at the bench and opened the box.

Immediately he saw that a mistake had been made, but automatically he turned a few pages. Instead of the rather cramped and fuddled Italian hand which he had expected, massive and heavy 'black letter' met his eye. One line seemed to unfold itself in particular; had it at one time been underlined and the underlining eradicated? For the parchment was scraped under the line. **The mind of a demon is not the same as the mind of a man**. Indeed, no. And the *Malleus Maleficarum* was not the same as the Baconian Fragment.

"Pray excuse me, most reverend Brother," he heard the voice of Mr. Mudge, "but have you perhaps inadvertently given my item of choice to the learned doctor, and his to me?"

The hollow tone of Brother Claudius said, "Each has that which is proper for him now to read." And he removed a small box from his sleeve, and took snuff. The learned doctor, what was it they called Roger Bacon? Ah yes: **Doctor Mirabilis.** Well— Suddenly he looked up; there was Melanchthon Mudge; had he *floated*? Usually the old floor sounded. What? The old floor *always* sounded.

Always but now.

"Brother Claudius has gone now. Shall we change books?"
They changed books.

By and by, he having principally noted what he had come to note, and the day having grown chiller yet, Eszterhazy rose to leave. Without especial thought, he blew upon his hands. With an almost painful suddenness his hand spun round towards the other man; he had not blown upon *his* hands to warm them! But the other man was gone.

It had been intimated to Eszterhazy that his name had been 'temporarily subtracted' from the military Active List for quite some years now, "for the purpose of continuing his education"—that meanwhile he had already obtained the baccalaureate, the licentiate, and two doctorates—and that unless he wished his name moved over to the Inactive List, very well, Engli, better Do Something about this. What he had done was to obtain transfer to the new Militia Reserve (as distinct from the not so new Reserve Militia), and as a result of having done so, found himself the very next weekend serving the twenty-five hours and twenty-five minutes which constituted his monthly service time with the Militia Reserve. (The Reserve Militia, as is well-known, had no monthly service time and instead required an annual service time of three weeks, three days, and three hours.) On reporting to the Armory he learned that although his having obtained a degree in mathematics had automatically shifted him from the Infantry to the Engineers, what was required of him this time had to do with another degree altogether.

"Surgeon-Commander Blauew's got the galloping gout again, Major Eszterhazy, and as you are, it seems, also a Doctor of Medicine, we need you for Medical Officer right now, and you can build us a fortress *next* month; haw haw!" was the adjutant's greeting.

"Very well, Adjutant. Very well. *My* that's a nasty-looking spot on your neck, there, well, well, I'll have a look at it after I've taken care of everything else;" and Temporary-Acting-Medical Officer Eszterhazy, E., moved on away, leaving the adjutant prey to dismal thoughts; and perhaps it would teach him not to play the oaf with his betters. The T.-A.-M.O. examined a number of candidates for the Militia Reserve, passed some, rejected some; made inspections which resulted in the Sanitary Facilities being very hastily and yet very thoroughly doused down with caustic soda and hot water; and delivered a brief and dispassionate lecture on social diseases to officers and men alike: to the great dis-ease of an elderly paymaster who said he doubted it was right to expose the younger men to such scientific language: perhaps not exactly what he meant. Sounds of drill command rang through the large hall with a surprising minimum of echo, in great measure because Eszterhazy (who had not read Vitruvius's *Ten Books* for nothing) was instrumental in obtaining a theater-architect as consultant during the hall's construction.

Eventually it was time for commissioned officers to withdraw for wine and rusks, a snack traditionally taken standing up even where there might be facilities for sitting down. "Seen you in the Bosnian Campaign," someone said; and, the Temporary-Acting-Medical Officer turning his head, recognized a face once more familiar than lately. The face was not only now older, it was much, much redder. "Just dropped in to pay my respects," said the old soldier. "I am just here on my biennial leave. I am just a retired major in my own country, but I am a full colonel in the service of H.H. the Khedive of Egypt. Can I recruit you? Guarantee you higher rank, higher pay, higher respect, *several* servants, and heaps and heaps of fascinating adventure."

The younger man confessed himself already fascinated. He looked the Khedivial colonel in the man's slightly bulging, slightly blood-shot, entirely blue eyes, and said, "Tell me about it."

He listened without a single interruption until Col. Brennshnekkl got onto the subject of hunting in the Southern Provinces of H.H.—the southernmost boundaries of which evidently did not, as yet, exist. "—at least not on any official map; we intend to push 'em as far south as we can push 'em; now where was I? Ah yes! *Hippo!* Ah, you need a champion heavy ball for hippo! Say, a quarter of a pound. Same as elephant. Same as rhino." Perhaps indecisive which of the three to talk about first, Brennshnekkl paused.

Dr. Eszterhazy heard himself asking, "What about tiger?"

"Tiger, eh. Well, you would naturally want a lighter rifle for soft-skinned game. Say, a .500 . . . or better yet a .577 Express—a Lang or a Lancaster or any of the good ones."

Eszterhazy stroked his beard, trimmed closer than in the mode of fashion. "But *are* there tigers in Africa?"

The colonel appeared to be trying to say *Yes* and *No* simultaneously. To aid him he sipped his wine. Then: "Well, strictly to speak, *no*: there are no tigers in Africa. However, lots of chaps call them tigers. Am I making sense? I mean, leopards."

Something somewhere jingled. Or perhaps there was a ringing in the doctor's ears. He repeated, dully, "Leopards?"

Colonel Brennshnekkl explained that in some way leopards were more than tigers. Tigers, like lions, went along the level ground; leopards sometimes hid up trees. And pounced. Carefully setting down his wine, he bared his teeth, turned his hands into paws and his fingers into claws, and gave something in the way of a lunge which was nevertheless certainly intended to imitate a pounce. It seemed to his younger comrade that people for some reason had lately begun to imitate leopards for him. Was it a *trend?*

"What else do they do up trees? Besides prepare to pounce? Do they have their, no, one would not say 'nests,' do they have lairs—?"

No. No, leopards did not have lairs in trees. Well. Not precisely. In the manner of colonels the world over since the beginning of time, this one began to tell a story. "—recollect one day my native gun-bearer, chap named Pumbo—Pumbo? Yes. Pumbo. *Faithful* chap. Pumbo. Came running over to me and handed me my .577 Express. Said, 'Master, tiger,' which is to say, of course, *leopard*, said 'tiger up tree, look-see, shoot-quick!'" He raised an imaginary leopard-gun at an angle. "And as I was sighting, sighting, damn me! what did I see? A bloody young zebra or was it an antelope, bloody leopard had killed it by breaking its neck, as they do, and dragged it up into the upper crutch of the tree where I suppose it could *hang*, you know, all that *gal*loping the wild game there does, making it muscular and tough—'nother thing," temporarily lowering his nonexistent rifle, the colonel got his wine back, looked at Eszterhazy over the rim of the mug; said, " 'nother thing. Hyaenas can't get to it. Once it's up a *tree*. You know. *Well*—"

But that was the last which Eszterhazy was to hear of the matter, for at that moment a whistle sounded to signal a return

to the duties of the twenty-five hours and twenty-five minutes;
a whistle? It was the sort of nautical whistle called a boat-
swain's pipe and it was traditional to sound it at this point. No
one at all knew why. That was what made it traditional.

In what had been the oldest and smallest schloss in Bella, long
since escheated to The Realm, was the chamber of a gentleman
whom rumor connected with the Secret Police. He was called
by a number of names. Eszterhazy called him Max.

"Engelbert Kristoffr."

"Max."

Segars and decanters. "How is the great plan for the
education going?"

"Engelbert Kristoffr" said that it was coming along well
enough. He supposed Max knew that he already had the M.D.
and Phil.D. Yes? And the D.Sc. and D.Mus. were likely next.
Of course degrees were not everything. Right now he was not
taking a schedule of courses for any degree, but he considered
that his education continued daily nonetheless. Max hummed a
bit in this throat. "You shall certainly become the best-
educated man in the Empire. I hope you begin to think of some
great reforms. Everyone thinks that old Professor Doctor
Kugelius is our best-educated man, why? because each year he
gives the same lecture on *The Reconciliation of Aristotle and
Plato* and it is actually fifty lectures and he delivers it in Latin
and what is his conclusion? that, after all, Aristotle and Plato
cannot be reconciled; you did not come to hear me talk about
Aristotle and Plato." Said Max.

The guest shook his head. "I came to hear you talk about
Mr. Melanchthon Mudge," he said.

There was indeed a file on Melanchthon Mudge and Engelbert Kristoffr read it and then they began to talk again. Said
Max: "You well recall a Cabinet decision to hold the laws
against witchcraft in abeyance. It simply would not do, in this
day and age, for our country to start a prosecution for
witchcraft. And as we prefer to believe that the matter is
confined to harmless old women living in remote villages,
there is really no mechanism to handle a latter-day sorcerer."

An ash was flicked off a segar with impatience. "I don't

want the man burned or hanged or shackled, for heaven's sake. We have experts in the sophistry of the law. Can't they simply get an excuse to get the man *out* of our country?"

Max very very slightly poured from the decanter to the mug. "Not so easily. Not when he has a lot of powerful friends. One of whom, are you not aware, is the aunt of your cousin Kristoffr Engelbert, of the Eszterhazy-Eszterhazy line; you are *not* aware? Ah, you were not, but are now. Having read the file." The file reminded him of the Sovereign Princess Olga Helena of Damrosch-Pensk; she was of course not sovereign at all, she was the widow of Lavon Demetrius, whose status as one of the once-sovereign princes of the Hegemony had been mediatized while he himself was yet a minor: the family retained titles, lands, money, and had nothing any longer to do with governation at all; was this a good thing? If they were under the spell of Mr. Mudge, probably.

"Nor is she the only one. Not every name is in the file; listen." Max repeated some of the names not in the file. Engelbert Kristoffr winced. "Is it that they are so immensely impressed because he makes the spirits blow trumpets, move tables, ring bells? In my opinion: *no*. They are so immensely impressed because they are weak in character and he is strong in character and he is very, very *bad* in character and his performances are merely as it were items chosen off a menu. Melanchthon Mudge, as he calls himself, has a very long menu, and if he did not impress the credulous by doing such things, well, he would impress them by doing other things. Was it only because Louis Napoleon and Amadeus of Spain and Alexander of Russia believed the spirits of the dead were at this fellow's command, lifting tables and sounding trumpets and ringing bells, that they gave him jewels? *I* don't think so. And I might ask you to look at what happened afterwards: Louis Napoleon deposed, dying in exile; Amadeus deposed and in exile; Alexander of Russia fatally blown up by political disaffecteds." Max banged his mug sharply on the scarred tabletop. "And another thing. If he *has* such powers, why does he employ them lifting tables and tinkling bells? Why does he content himself with gifts of jewels from kings and emperors?"

Engelbert Kristoffr Eszterhazy thought of another question:

Why is he—via the thought of him?—tormenting me? But he said, suddenly, aloud, "Because the mind of a demon is not the same as the mind of a man."

Said Max, "Well, there you are. There's your answer."

But, wondered Eszterhazy, to which question?

Having left the old, small castle to Max, its present master, Dr. Eszterhazy long wandered and long pondered. Was it indeed his fortune to have become involved with a Count Cagliostro, a century after the original? Was Melanchthon Mudge really "Melanchthon Mudge"? Could anyone be? And if not, who then was he? The learned doctor did not very much amuse himself by conjecturing that perhaps Giuseppe Balsamo had not really died in a Roman dungeon ninety years ago, but—

Of the so-called Pasqualine Dynasty [a learned correspondent wrote Dr. Engelbert] few literary remains exist, and almost without exception they are very dull remains indeed. Only one reference do I find of the least interest, and that is to a so-called Pasqualine Ring. Do your old friends know about it? Legends for a while clustered thick, stories that "it had been worn upon the very thumb of Albertus Magnus," is one of them; I cannot even say if thumb-rings were known in the day of good Bishop and Universal Doctor—you may also have heard it assigned to the thumbs of two anomalous Englishmen named Kelly (or Kelley) and Dee—and one of the innumerable editions of the *Faustusbuch*—but enough! Do think of me when you see your old and noble tutor, and ask him . . . whatever [and here the learned correspondent passed on to another subject entirely].

Why had not Engelbert Eszterhazy, Ph.D., M.D., long since removed his old and (perhaps, who knows) royal tutor and wife to a comfortable chamber in the house at 33 Turkling Street? He had offered, and the offer had with an exquisite politeness been declined. Why had he not bestowed a pension? To this question: the same reply. He had, then, to relieve the burden of want, done nothing? No, not nothing. One day he had encountered the owner of the tottering tenement in which lodged the King and Queen of the Single Sicily in Exile, herself (the owner) a widow incessantly bending beneath the burden of many debts, herself; part in sorrow, part in shame, she said that she would shortly have to double their rent: Dr. Eszterhazy easily persuaded her to mention no such thing to them, but to apply instead to him quarterly for the difference: done. So. There he was one day, visiting, and presently he asked, "And the ring of Duke Pasquale?"

"We have it, we have it," said 'the Queen.' In her haggard, ancient way, she was still beautiful. "We have it. So," she said. "It is all that we have. But we have it. So."

Eszterhazy sat silent. "I will have them bring you a cup of chocolate. Clarinda?" she raised her voice. "Leona? Ofelia?" As, not surprisingly, none of these imaginary attendants answered the summons, the Queen, murmuring an apology, rose to "see what they are all doing," and withdrew into a curtained niche behind which (Eszterhazy well knew) reposed the tiny charcoal brazier and the other scant equipment of their scant kitchen. Politely, he looked instead at the King.

The general outlines of the face and form of him who, with infinite sincerity, called himself 'King of the Single Sicily,' would have been familiar to, at least, readers of the British periodical press; for they were the form and features of Mr. *Punch* (himself originally a native of The Italies, under the name of Signor Punchinello); though the expression of their faces was entirely different. His lady wife did not in any way resemble *Judy*. The King now said, "I shall have the Lord Great Chamberlain bring it." As Cosimo Damiano's former pupil was wondering what piece of gimcrack or brummagem the, alas, cracked imaginations of the pair would work on, the King said, with a gesture, "The view of the hills is remarkably clear today, my son. We are high here. Very high. See for yourself." Eszterhazy politely rose to his feet, went to the window. The window was now graced with a single curtain; there had at one time been two; and some might have seen a resemblance to the other in the garment which the Queen now wore wrapped around her ruined silken dress rather in the manner of a sari.

Clear or not, the view was so restricted by the crumbling walls of the adjacent tenements as to consist of an irregular blur a few feet tall and a few inches wide. Behind him he heard a soft scuffling, shuffling sound. He heard the King say, "Thank you. That is all. You may go." After a moment Eszterhazy felt it safe to say that the view was indeed remarkable. In reply, he was informed that his chocolate was ready. He withdrew slowly from the view, homeopathically of the hills of the Scythian Highlands, and otherwise and very largely of goats, pigs, washing, dogs, children, chickens, rubbishtips, and other features of the always informal great South Ward; and took his seat. And his chocolate.

It was very good chocolate. It should have been. He had given them a canister of it a while ago, and some, with a vanilla-bean in it to keep it fresh. As, each time he visited, there was always a cup given to him, either the canister—like the pitcher of Philemon and Baucis—was inexhaustible, or the royal couple never drank any at all. Well, well. It gave them pleasure to give, and this was in itself a gift.

"And this," said the King, after a moment, "is the ring of Duke Pasquale." And he produced an immensely worn little box not entirely covered anymore with eroding leather and powdering velvet. And, with a dextrous push, sprang up the lid. It made a faint sound.

Eszterhazy with great presence of mind did not spill his hot chocolate into his lap.

Evidently the tarnished band was silver, as—evidently—the untarnished and untarnishable band was gold. They were intertwined and must have been the very devil to keep clean, whenever the task was still being attempted. Though somewhat mis-shapen—perhaps something heavy had rested on it, long ago? while it was being perhaps hidden, long ago?—the width hinted that it might indeed have been a thumb-ring. Long ago. And set into it was a diamond of antique cut, more antique certainly even than the ring-work.

"There were once many," said the old man.

"Oh yes," said the old woman. "The wonder of it, as it must have been. The Pasqualine Diamonds, as they were called. Who knows where the others are. We know where this one is. He besought us to sell. So, so. Conceive of it. Sell? We did not even show."

Eszterhazy brought himself back to his present physical

situation, drank off some of the chocolate. Asked, "And do you wear the ring? Ever? Never? Often?"

The old woman shook her mad old head. "Only on appropriate occasion." She did not say what an appropriate occasion would be; he did not ask. He observed that the ring was on a chain, one of very common metal. His finger touched it. He raised his eyes. "It is the custom to wear it on a chain," she said. "When one wears it, it should be worn on a chain, like a pendant. So, so, so. My late and sainted father-in-law wore it on a silver chain, and his late and sainted father wore it on a golden one. Thus it should be so. Or," the pause could not be called a hesitation, "almost always so. So, so, so. One does not wear it on a finger, not even on the thumb; certainly not on the finger; on the thumb, least of all. It would be a bad thing to do so. So, so, so. Very bad, very bad. It is ours to be keeping and ours to be guarding. As you see. So, so. So, so, so." She coughed.

Her husband the King said, "I shall take it now, my angel." Take it he did; it was done so deftly and swiftly that Eszterhazy was not sure what was done with it. He had some idea. He was not sure.

Need he be?

No.

It was madness to think of these two mad old people living in poverty year after year, decade after decade, when a fortune lay ready to be redeemed. It was made; it was also noble. Turn the ring into money, turn the money into silk dresses, linen shirts, unbroken shoes, proper and properly furnished apartments; turn it into beef and pork and poultry and salad fresh daily, into good wine and wax candles or modern oil-lamps— turn it as one would: how long would the money last? Did the 'King of the Single Sicily' think just then in such terms? Perhaps. He said, as he accompanied his former pupil to the worm-eaten door, this is what he said: "Today's fine food is tomorrow's ordure. And today's fine wine is tomorrow's urine. Today's fine clothes are tomorrow's rags. And today's fine carriages are tomorrow's rubble. And after one has spent one's long and painful years in this world, one wishes to have left behind at least one's honor unstained. Which is something better than ordure, urine, rags, and rubble. Something more than urine, ordure, rubble, and rags. Be such things far from thee, my son. Farewell now. Go with the Good God and Blessed Company of the Saints."

One must hope. Eszterhazy went.

Thus: the Pasqualine Ring.

There had been a meeting of the University's Grand Ancillary Council, to discuss (once again) the private-docent question; and, Eszterhazy being a junior member, he had attended. The conclusion to which the Grand Ancillary Council had come was (once again) that it would at that specific meeting come to no conclusion. And filed out, preceded by dignitaries with muffs and ruffs and chains of office and maces and staves and drummers and trumpeters. About the necessity of all this to the educational process, Dr. Eszterhazy had certainly some certain opinions; and, being still but a junior member, kept them to himself.

The Emperor, who was *ex-officio* Protector, Professor-in-Chief, Grand Warden, and a muckle many other offices, to and of the University, did not attend . . . he never attended . . . but, as always, had sent them a good late luncheon instead of a deputy: this was more appreciated. Eszterhazy found himself in discussion over slices of a prime buttock of beef with a Visiting Professor of one of the newer disciplines, "Ethnology" it was called. Older faculty members regarded an occasional lecture on Ethnology as a permissible amusement; further than that, they would not go. "Where did your last expedition take you?" asked Eszterhazy. Professor De Blazio said, West Africa, and asked Eszterhazy to pass the very good rye bread with caraway seeds. This passed, it occurred to the passer to ask if there were leopards in West Africa. "Although," he added, "that is hardly Ethnology."

De Blazio said something very much like, "Chomp, chomp, gmurgle." Then he swallowed. Then he said, "Ah, but it is, because in West Africa we have what is called the Leopard Society. I believe it to be totemic in origin. *Totem*, do you know the word totem? A North-American Red-Indian word meaning an animal which a family or clan in primitive society

believes to have been its actual ancestor. Some say this
creature changes into human form and back again.—Not bad,
this beef.—Is it Müller who sees in this the source of heraldic
animals? Can one quite imagine the British Queen turning into
a lion at either the full or the dark of the moon? Ho Ho Ho."
Each Ho of Professor De Blazio was delivered in a flat tone.
Perhaps he felt one could not quite imagine it. "Mustard,
please."

Eating the roast beef, for a few moments, speaking English
between mouthfuls, Eszterhazy could think himself in En-
gland. And then the stewards came carrying round the slabs of
black bread and the pots of goose grease. And he knew that
he was exactly where he now thought he was: in Bella, the
sometimes beautiful and sometimes squalid capital of the
Triune Monarchy of Scythia-Pannonia-Transbalkania.

Fourth largest empire in Europe.

The Turks were fifth.

The gas-lights in the great salon in the town-house of old
Colonel Count Cruttz were famous gas-lights. Cast in red
bronze, they were in the form of mermaids, each the length of
a tall man's arm, and each clasping in cupped hands the actual
jets for the gas flames as they, the mermaids, faced each other
in a great circle: with mouths slightly open, they might be
imagined as singing each to each. This was perhaps a high
point of a sort in illumination, here in Bella. Well-dried reeds
were used to soak up mutton-tallow or other kitchen grease,
and these formed the old-fashioned rush-lights which the
old-fashioned (or the poor) still used at night. They smelled
vile. But they were cheap. Their flickering, spurting light was
not good to read by. But they were cheap. They were very,
very cheap. Tallow-candles. Whale-oil. Colza-oil, allegedly
stolen here and there by Tartars to dress their cole-slaw.
Coal-oil, also called paraffin or kerosene. Gas-lamps. From
each pair of red-gold hands the red-gold flames leaped high,
soughing and soaring. Often attempts had been made to
employ the new experimental gas mantles. But Colonel Count
Cruttz always shot them away with his revolver-pistol.

Colonel Count Cruttz looked sober enough tonight; of

course, that was subject to change, although it was customary for nothing but champagne to be served at such soirées, and it was not in accordance with his reputation to become shooting-drunk (even gas-mantle-shooting drunk) on such a ladies' drink as champagne. Still. If a bullet from a revolver-pistol, or two or three, could solve a certain problem of which signs were likely to be shown tonight—if so, gladly would Doctor Eszterhazy ply Colonel Count Cruttz with brandy, vodka, rum, gin, shnapps, and whiskey. Or, for that matter, *alcohol absolutus*. As, however, it was not to be more than thought of, he would have to . . . what would he have to do?

. . . something else.

In one half of the great salon, the soirée looked like any and every other soirée in Bella: that is, an imitation of a soirée in Vienna, which in turn would be an imitation of one in Paris. Few things bored Eszterhazy more than a Bellanese soirée, though they were, barring boredom, harmless. The other half of the great salon, under the soaring gas-lights, was not in the least like every other soirée in Bella, for everyone in that half of the room was gathered around one sole person: a breach of good manners indeed. One might give a 'reception' for a particular person and that person might be lionized, surrounded; this was to be expected. But a soirée was not a reception, at least it was not intended to be, and it was good manners neither in those gathered round one person nor for that one person to allow it. But—*allow it?*

Mr. Mudge reveled in it.

Those in the other half of the room strolled around for the most part by ones and twos, now and then uttering polite words to those they walked with or to those they encountered. What was going to happen? By now Doctor Eszterhazy knew. Someone would give a polite hand-clap. Others would fall silent. Someone would say what good luck they all had. Someone would speak, obliquely, of the Spirits which—or who—had 'crossed over,' and how, for reasons not only not made clear but never mentioned, they sometimes were pleased to make use of the "the justly-famous Mr. Mudge" as the medium of their attempts to contact the living. Eszterhazy had, he hoped, a most open mind: the received opinion of thousands of years to the contrary, the spirits of the dead were *not* where they could neither reach nor be reached? Very well. Let the evidence be presented, and he would form . . . perhaps . . . an opinion. But he knew no evidence that any of the so-called spirits had passed their time, whilst living, in tipping tables or sounding very tatty-looking trumpets or ringing lots of little bells; and so he did not think they would do so, now that they were dead, as a means of proving that they were not really entirely dead after all. Mr. Mudge did it (assuming it to be Mr. Mudge who did it); Mr. Mudge did it all very well.

But did any of it need to be done at all?

Eszterhazy could not think so.

He was not altogether alone.

"Engli, need we got to have all this?" asked a man, no longer at all young, with a weather-beaten and worn . . . worn? eroded! . . . face, stopping as he strolled.

"Not if you do not wish it had, Count."

The Count almost doubled over in an agony of conviction. "I *don't!* I *don't!* Oh, I thought nothing when Olga Pensk asked it of me, that was a month ago, always have had a soft spot in me heart for her, *lovely* young girl her daughter is—But oh I've heard such a lot in that month. And I can't get back to talk to Olga about it. She won't see me. She's become that creature's creature. Look at her, doesn't take her eyes off him, let me tell you what I have heard."

But Eszterhazy, saying that perhaps he had heard it, too, urged that this be put off to another time.

"Do something, do something, do something," begged the Count and Colonel. "I know what I'd love to do, and would *do*, hadn't all of us in the Corps of Officers given our solemn vow and oath to his Royal and Imperial Majesty neither to fight duels nor commit homicides; wish I *hadn't*. Engli. Engli. You're a learned chap. You lived how many a month was it with the Old Men of the Mountains, didn't you learn—"

But Eszterhazy was lightly clapping his hands.

Afterwards, he had brief misgivings. *Had* he been right to have done it at all? To have done it the way he had done? That Melanchthon Mudge thought this-or-that about it: on this he

did not need to waste thought. The Sovereign Princess of
Damrosch-Pensk, would she *ever* forgive him? Too bad, if she
would not. But suppose that collegium of white wizards, the
Old Men of the Mountains, to hear of it; what would *they*
think? Well, well, he had not depended on what they had
taught him for everything he'd done in the great salon of
Colonel Count Cruttz's townhouse. Even the common sorcer-
ers of the Hyperborean High Lands dearly loved the rude, the
bawdy, the buffoon; they did not rank with the Old Men, but he
had taken some pains to learn from them, too.

And though he told himself that he did not need think about
Mr. Mudge, think about Mr. Mudge he did. If he had
denounced Mr. Mudge as a heretic; a heresiarch, satanist, and
diabolist; if he had made him seem black and scarlet with
infamously classical sins? Why, certainly the man would have
loved it. Swelled with pride. Naturally. But he, Eszterhazy,
had not done it. Nothing of the sort. He had parodied the usual
ritual of the séance. He had reduced the introductory words to
gibberish and, worse by far than merely that, to *funny*
gibberish. He had made the table tip, totter, fall back, to the
audible imitation of an off-color street-song, as though accompanied on, not one trumpet, but a chorus of trumpets, as played
by a chorus of flatulent demons. He had done something
similar with his summoning-up, in mockery, of the spirit bells.
Was it not enough to show how others could do it? Did he *have*
to have them ring in accompaniment to the naughty
(recognizable—but who would admit it?) song on the 'trumpet'?

Well, 'need.' *Need makes the old dame trot*, went the
proverb.

He had *done* it.

The whole doing was a mere five minutes long; but it had,
of course, made it utterly impossible for Mudge, with or
without others, to give his own performance. Absolutely
impossible, right afterwards. And who knows for how long
impossible, subsequently? He had lost the best part of his
audience, for certainly the effect was ruined. If he would
indeed try a repetition, elsewhere, a week, a fortnight, even a
month, months later, he would hardly dare do so in the

presence of any who had been there then. A single guffaw would have meant death.

And eloquent of death was the man's face as his eyes met Eszterhazy's. It was but for a moment; then the face changed. No hot emotion showed as he came up to Eszterhazy, the Colonel Count rather hastily stepping up to be ready, in case of need, to step between them. But no. "Very amusing, Doctor," said Mr. Mudge. He bowed and said a few courteous words to the host. Then he left. Leaving with him, her own face as though carved in ice, was the Sovereign Princess Olga Helena. Not icy, but perhaps rather confused, was the face of her daughter, the Highlady Charlotte, own cousin to Eszterhazy's own cousin. Had she, too, believed? Well, it were better she should now doubt. That there were sincere people in the ranks of the spiritualists, the doctor did not doubt. That some were not alone sincere, but, also, even, *good*, he was prepared to admit. But Mr. Mudge was something else, and if indeed he were sincere, it was in the sincerity of evil.

It made of course no difference to the chemistry of Glauber's Salts what name was given them or who had first discovered them. But it was a hobby-horse of Eszterhazy's, one which he so far trusted himself never to ride along the nearer paths which lead to lunacy, that the pursuit of inorganic cathartics marked the real watershed between alchemy and chemistry. The 'philosopher' who, turning away from the glorious dreams of transmuting dross to gold, sought instead a means of moving the sluggish bowels of the mass of mankind and womankind, had taken his head out of the clouds and brought it very close to the earth indeed. **Quaere:** How did the dates of Ezekkiel Yahnosh compare with those of Johann Glauber? **Responsum:** Go and look them up. That the figures in the common books were unreliable, E.E. knew very well. He had also known (he now recalled) that there was a memorial to the great seventeenth-century Scythian savant somewhere in the back of the Great Central Reformed Tabernacle, commonly called the Calvinchurch, from the days when it—or its predecessor—was the only one of that faith in Bella.

Q.: Why might he not go right now and copy it? **R.:** Why not?—unless it were closed this hour on Sunday night. But this caveat little recked with the zeal of Predicant Prush, even now ascending into the pulpit, as Eszterhazy tried to collect his information as unobtrusively as possible from the marble plaque set in the wall. "My text, dear and beloved trustworthy brothers and sisters," boomed the Preacher from beneath the sounding-board, "is Jeremiah, V, 6. *Wherefore a lion out of the forest shall slay them, and a wolf of the evening shall spoil them,* **a leopard shall watch over their cities:** *everyone that goeth out shall be torn to pieces: because their transgressions are many, and their backslidings are increased.* **Miserable sinners, there is nevertheless hope in repentance!**" cried out the Predicant in a plenitude of Christian comfort. And went on to demonstrate that the animals mentioned in the text were *types*, which is to say, *foreshadowings*, with the lion signifying the Church of Rome, the wolf implying Luther; and the leopard, recalcitrant paganism. As for transgressions and backsliding, Dr. Prush gave them quite a number for exempla, ranging from Immodest Attire to Neglect Of Paying Tithes. "Woe! Woe!" he cried, smiting the lectern.

But Eszterhazy was not concentrating on the sermon. There rang incessantly in his ear, as though being chanted into it by something sitting upon his shoulder, only the words **a leopard shall watch over their cities** . . .

And, when back at home, he examined his scant notes for the dates of Ezekkiel Yahnosh, he found that, really, all that he had written in their place was *Jeremiah*, V, 6.

Many a set of hoopshirts worn in Bella in their time, many a crinoline worn in Bella in its time, many a bustle worn in Bella (around about then or not a long span later being their time) had been fashioned in the ever-fashionable stablishment of Mademoiselle Sophie, Couturière Parisienne. Mlle. Sophie was a native of a canton perhaps better known for its cuckoo-clocks than its *haute couture*, but she had nevertheless plied a needle and thread in Paris. She had plied it chiefly in replacing buttons in a basement tailor-shop until her vast commonsense told her to get up and go out of the basement into the light and air. She hadn't stopped going until she reached Bella, and if her trip and

her beginnings in business had indeed been 'under the protec-
tion' of a local textile merchant who sometimes visited Paris on
business, why, whose affair was that? That is, who else's
affair? Nevertheless, most of the women's garments in Bella
owed nothing to the fact that Mlle. Sophie gained her bread by
the pricks of her needle; and perhaps a slight majority of the
women's garments in Bella owed nothing at all to what was
worn in Paris. Even as Eszterhazy paused to throw down and
step upon a segar, several woman—evidently sisters—passed
by dressed in the eminently respectable old high burger style:
costly cloth stiff with many a winter day's embroidery, the
bodices laced with gold-tipped laces, each stiff petticoat of
bright color slightly shorter than the one underneath. No one
else even much noticed.

Still, someone laughed, and it was not a nice laugh.
Eszterhazy did not move his head, but his eyes slightly moved.
Just across the narrow street was Melanchthon Mudge, clad in
fur-coat and fur-hat whose gloss must have represented a
fortune in sable and other prime pelts: what was he laughing at?
Slowly approaching was a woman by herself. She moved with
difficulty. She had been limping with a side-to-side motion
which caused her short and heavy body to rock in a manner that
allowed little dignity. Nothing about her was rich, and certainly
not the rusty black cloth coat which covered the upper part of
her dingy black dress: truth to tell it was not even over-clean.
Her face was not young and it was not comely and it seemed
fuddled with effort. Such things as gallantry and pity aside, if
one thought the grotesque laughable, then one would under-
standably laugh at the sight of her. But such laughter, merely
the comcomitant of a country culture which laughed at cripples
and stammerers, was more puzzling when it came from
Mudge. The woman clearly heard the laugh, was clearly not
indifferent to it. She tried to walk on more swiftly, rocked and
swayed more heavily; there was another laugh; abruptly Mudge
walked off.

On the poor woman's head was a bonnet of the sort which
had been favored, perhaps a generation ago, by fashion in the
North-American provinces. So, on the spur of the moment,
Eszterhazy, lifting his own hat, addressed her in English.

"You don't have such picturesque native costume," the slightest inclination of his head towards the wearers of the local picturesque costume, "in your own country, I believe, ma'am."

She slowly rocked to a stop and looked at him with, at first, some doubt. "No, sir," she said, "we don't, and that's a fact. We haven't had the time to develop it. Utility has been our motto. Maybe too much so. You don't know who I am, do you? No. But I know you, Mr. Esthermazy, if only by sight, for you've been pointed out to me. Reverend Ella May Butcher, European Mission, First Spiritualist Church, Buffalo, N.Y." She extended her hand, he—automatically—had begun to stoop to kiss it—she gave a firm shake—he did not stoop. "My late husband was very well acquainted with President Fillmore. But you don't know President Fillmore here." She was in this correct. Neither Eszterhazy personally nor the entire Triune Monarchy had known President Fillmore: there . . . or anywhere.

"I've come to show those deep in sorrow that their beloved ones have been saved from the power of the shadow of death. It ain't for me to say why the spirits of those who've passed over are sometimes pleased to use me as my medium, Mr. Esthermazy. We have settings on Mondays, Wednesdays, Fridays, and Sundays, the Good Lord willing, at eight o'clock P.M. in the room at the head of the stairs in the old Scottish Rite hall. No admission charge is ever made; love offering only." If Reverend Ella May Butcher was offered much such love, there was nothing to show it. The flat level of her voice did not vary as she asked, "Do you know that man who laughed at me just now?"

The shouting of the teamsters and the clash of hooves on the stone blocks obliged him to raise his voice. "We have met," he said.

Widow Butcher looked at him with her muddy eyes. "There are spirits of light, sir; and there are spirits of darkness. That one's gifts never came from the light. I have to go on now. I hope to see you at one of our settings. Thank you for your kindness." He bowed slightly, lifted his hat, she lifted her skirts as high as was proper for a lady to lift them (a bit higher than would have been proper perhaps in London, but surely not too high for Bella and doubtless not too high for Buffalo, New York, where her late husband had been very well acquainted with President Fillmore), and prepared to cross the broader street. At this signal the filthy scarecrow which was the crossing-sweeper leaned both hands on the stick of his horrid broom and plowed her a way through the horse-dung. Eszterhazy watched as she poked in her purse for a coin; then a knot of vans and wagons went toiling by, laden high with barrels of goose-fat and rye meal and white lard and yellow lard. And when they had gone, so had she.

He had not expected to meet Mr. Mudge within the week, but he had not expected to be in the South Ward within the week, either. Someone had reported to him that a certain item of horse-furniture was in a certain popular pawnshop there, and someone had said that—not having been redeemed when the loan expired—the item (it was a mere ornament, but then, too, perhaps the horse which first had borne it had also borne the last Byzantine Emperor) was now for sale.

"Impossible," said a familiar voice. Outside the pawnship.

And another voice, less familiar, but . . . familiar . . . said . . . asked, " 'Impossible'? Impossible for you to do it when two Emperors and one King have already done it?"

There was D. Cosimo D., looking as though he would be away, and there was Mr. Mudge, looking as though he would not let him go. "I do not know other than nothing of it," said Cosimo.

Mudge said he would 'explain the matter yet again.' The briefly reigning King Amadeus of Spain had been pleased to give Mr. Mudge a gift of jewels. Louis Napoleon, Emperor of the French, had given him some other jewels. And a third such royal gift had come from Alexander, late Czar of all the Russians. "By the merest coincidence," said Mudge, "they contained elements of the so-called Pasqualine Diamonds. That is to say, I now have them all. I can show you the Deeds of Gifts."

"I wish not to see them. *Gifts!*"

"That is to say, all but the thumb-ring of Duke Pasquale.

Without it, the set is incomplete. You may name a price. Money, lands; lands and money—whatever. I shall execute a will demising the jewels all to your noble house. I—"

"*I*, sir. Know nothing. Have nothing to sell. Desire nothing to obtain. Ah, my son"—to Eszterhazy—"You have heard? Am I not right?"

And Eszterhazy said, "The King of the Single Sicily is right."

A week later, as Eszterhazy emerged from his club in Upper Hunyadi Street, a tall man seemed to uncoil from a bench, and, in an instant, stood before him. It was Melanchthon Mudge. Melanchthon Mudge was before him, the bench was alongside of him, a stone pillar of the colonnade was behind him. Only one way of passage remained, but he did not seek to take it. The man wished to do it so? well, let him do it so, then.

"Be quick," he said.

"Dr. Eszterhazy," said the tall, thin man, earnestly; "you have twice affronted me." Eszterhazy looked at him with a face which was absolutely expressionless, and said absolutely nothing. Mudge seemed rather disconcerted at this; and, a moment having passed, he compressed his lips, something like a frown beginning to appear: this vanished almost at once. A smile replaced it; one might easily see how very many had regarded it as a charming smile. Very often. "You have, Doctor, twice affronted me, I say. But I cannot believe that you ever meant to do so. This being the case, you will take no affront when I explain to you what the affronts were"—and still, Eszterhazy did not move. He continued to gaze with motionless eyes.

Mudge cleared his throat. Then he held up one finger of his left hand and he pressed upon it with one finger of his right. "To begin with, although perfectly aware of my perfect reasons for wishing to purchase the Pasqualine Ring, you urged its present owner not to part with it." He paused. No reaction. No reply. A second finger came forward on the extended left hand, was pressed upon with the forefinger of the right. "You also, doubtless purely as a jape, counterfeited—by some species of parlor trick which in another and lesser man I should term 'charlatanry'—counterfeited those great gifts which are mine as donatives of the Spirits. Now, sir, I do urge you, Dr. Eszterhazy, not to presume to affront me a third time. I am in process of taking a most important step in my personal life. It would mean that we would meet so very often that I should desire to be upon no terms with you save the very friendliest. But if you—"

Eszterhazy's eyes shifted suddenly, transfixed the other man with such a sort of look that the man winced. A brief cry, as of pain, was torn from his throat. "Wretch, rogue, and scoundrel," Eszterhazy said; "I well know that you have it in your black mind to propose marriage to my cousin's cousin, the Highlady Charlotte of Damrosch-Pensk. This, it does not lie within my power to prevent; that is, her mother being in something close to vassalage to you, we both know why, you may propose. I shall tell you what does lie within my power. By the terms of her late father's will, the Highlady Charlotte is in effect a ward of the Emperor until her thirtieth year—unless she is lawfully married before that day. I have already seen to it that a full statement of your depraved behavior in other countries, your disgusting statements set by your own hand in writing in regard to another lady, and the abhorrent circumstances under which you became, first famous, and then rich—I have with a great and grim pleasure seen to it that the Lord President of the Privy Council now knows it all. The present Emperor will never give his assent without consulting the Lord President. And—"

But this next sentence was scarcely begun when something unseen stuck Eszterhazy a blow and sent him with great force reeling against the pillar from where he had been standing several feet away. It was of course painful, it left him breathless and without power of speech: all his effort went into remaining upright; he clutched the pillar, backwards, with both his hands.

Even as he felt himself stagger, he saw the medium, face set for one fearful second into a rictus of rage, go striding away and down the steps. His cloak flew almost level with the ground. There was another voice echoing in Eszterhazy's ears, very faint it was, very faintly echoing. *There are spirits of*

*light, sir; and there are spirits of darkness. That one's gifts
never came from the light. . . .*

Eszterhazy, coming up the slum stairs to where the old couple
lived, was not at first surprised to hear the sounds of alterca-
tion. The place was, after all, a *slum*, and slum-dwellers tend
when angered not merely to speak out but to shout. What
surprised him was to hear the old noblewoman's voice raised,
even briefly. What could—Ah. Ahah. The local muckman was
trying to collect garbage-fees. So. True, that the work was
damnably hard. True that in the South Ward the fees were often
damnably hard to collect. True, that it was hard to imagine the
old couple's scanty diet producing enough garbage to be worth
feeing. And, true, bullying was a time-established way of
collecting the fees. Or trying to.

A fat, foul smell, filthy and greasy, announced its owner
even before the sight of the fat, foul body on the landing by the
door—fat, foul, smelly, greasy—voice coarse, loud, hector-
ing. "—wants me entitles!" the voice shouted. "Wants me ten
copperkas!" Fat, smeary shoulders thrusting at partially-closed
door. " 'r I takes the tea-pot off the cloth and the cloth off the
table and—" The third take was never mentioned, the door
flew open wider, there stood the dauntless little 'Queen,'
something glinted, something flashed. The muckman gave a
hoarse howl and fell back, struggling for balance. The door
closed. The muckman whirled around, flesh quivering; flesh,
where a hand fell for a moment away, flesh bleeding. Scratches
on the rank, besmeared arm. Made by—made by what? "That
she-cat," grumbled the man, fear giving way to mere astonishment and dull defeated rage—made by small embroidery
shears? or—

"That she-cat has claws," said the muckman, and stumped
away down. The rank smell of him alone remained.

Inside, a moment later, there was of course no mention of it
all. They seemed a bit more haggard, a bit more harried than
usual. He asked if there were not, was there not? something
wrong. They looked at him with wasted eyes. "The ring. Duke
Pasquale's ring. The ring. He shall never have it. Never."

* * *

"Cosimo, I saw a very curious thing."

"And what was that, my dear one?"

"I saw a leopard, Cosimo, leaping from roof to roof, till it was out of sight. Was that not curious?"

"Indeed, my dear one, that was curious indeed. Not many people are vouchsafed to see visions. By and by, perhaps, we will understand. The soup is now very warm. Let me feed you, as I already have our spoon."

If this were a nightmare, thought Eszterhazy, then he would presently shout himself awake, and . . . "*If* this were a nightmare"! And suppose this were *not?* But these thoughts were all peripheral. He felt things he had never felt before, sensed that for which he knew no terms of sensation. Impressions immensely deep, and immensely unfamiliar. And then some sort of barrier was broken, and he felt it break, and things ceased to be immeasurably alien; but he was not comforted by this, not at all, for everything which was now at all familiar was very horribly so: he heard very ugly sounds made by things he could not see and he saw (if only fleetingly or on the periphery of vision) very ugly things doing things he could not hear. In so far as it resembled anything it resembled the grotesque paintings of the Lowlander Jan Bos: but mostly it resembled nothing. Fire bubbled in his brain like lava. To breathe was to be tortured by his own body. Terror was a solid thing sucking marrow from his bones. He caught sight of a certain known face and on the face, its mouth slightly parted and wet yellow teeth exposed, was an expression of lust and glee.

Who was this, suddenly seizing his arm, face now a chalky mask with charcoal smudges under the eyes? "My son, he will not grant it, he will not grant it! I said to his secretary, 'Father, forget that I am the rightful King of the Single Sicily and consider only that I am a child faithful to Mother Church and with a wife who is sick, Father, sick!' But he will not grant it! *Marón!*"

What Cosimo Damiano was doing in the Mutton Market of the Tartar Section, Eszterhazy did not know; but then he did not know at all what he himself was doing there. And if he himself had, in a state of confusion of mind, wandered far—why then, why not his old tutor? "Sir. Who will not grant what?"—though, already, he had begun to guess.

"Why, license for an exorcism! Our parish priest reminds me that he himself, though willing, cannot do so without a faculty from the bishop . . . in this case the archbishop . . . that is, the Prince-Patriarch of Bella. I begged the secretary, 'Father,' I said—But it doesn't matter what I said. Away he went with his head to one side and back he came with his head to the other side, and he shook his head. His Eminence will not grant it. . . ."

Ancient custom, having the force of canon law, decreed that the Archbishop and Prince-Patriarch of Bella be called "His Eminence" just as though he were a cardinal; and His Eminence's secretary was Monsignor (not merely "Father") Macgillicuddy. Msgr. Macgillicuddy was descended from those Erse warlords whose departure from their afflicted Island has been compared to the flight of the wild geese: unlike the nonmetaphorical ones, those wild geese never flew back, but drifted slowly from one Catholic kingdom to another. Msgr. Macgillicuddy had been 200 years out of Ireland and no one still in Ireland looked as exquisitely Irish as did Msgr. Macgillicuddy. Perhaps it was a shame that there was no Gaelic monarch at whose court he might be serving instead, and perhaps he did not think so. He belonged to no order, he was attached to no ethnic faction of the Empire or the Church, and if he said that the Prince-Patriarch-Archbishop would allow no exorcism, then that—absolutely—as Eszterhazy well knew— was that.

To one side a bow-legged Tartar made a sudden dive at a scaping ram, bucked it shoulder to shoulder, slipped arm and hand between the beast's forelegs, seized a hind leg and pulled forward; the ram went backward, the Tartar swiveled around and, having dropped the leg, from behind seized the animal's shoulders. The ram sat upright, and could not move. Along came the butcher's men with their ropes. Escape had been short-lived. A covey of quaint figures, the old Tartar women of the Section, huddled into shawls and veils and skirts and pantaloons, began to gather, each intent on the fresh mutton for the evening's shashliks. Escape had been very short-lived. For a while the ram had been king of the mountains, defending his meadow of grass and wild thyme and his harem of ewes. But that was over now.

As to *why* Cosimo Damiano wanted a faculty for his parish priest to perform an exorcism, the old man would be anything but specific. His cracked old brain was cracking wider now under the strain of—of what? Of something bad, of bad things, things which were very, very bad: and happening to *him*. And to his sick old wife. Charms were not enough, amulets and talismans not enough, holy water and prayers and Latin Psalms: not enough. Any more. *Cornuto*, usually efficacious against the *strega?* Not enough.

"But . . . Sir . . . do give me an example?—a single sample?"

Almost as though not so much obeying or answering his former pupil as being made a thrall by something else, in a second the body of the old man twisted and the face of the old man twisted and the voice of the old man changed . . . swift, sudden: movement, sound: frightful . . . Eszterhazy tottered back. Another second and the old man was as before, and trembling with terror. With a stifled croaking wail he scuttled off.

The aged females of the Tartar Section were wending their ways to their homes, each with a portion of mutton-meat wrapped in a huge cabbage-leaf. Eszterhazy paid no attention. In the face of the old man a moment ago, in the body of the old man then, in the grum, grim voice, he had for one second, but for a significant one, recognized and been horribly reminded of the same frightful features of his own recent nightmare . . . if such they were . . . the phrase *psychic assault* came to his mind. What was there in his clean, well-furnished laboratory to help them all against this? Eszterhazy muttered, "*Aroint thee, Satan.*" And he spat three times.

And all these . . . these assaults . . . against himself, against the old man and the old wife . . . why? Merely affront and pride? Because, come down to common denominators, what were *they*? What was *it*? It was the ring of Duke Pasquale, that antique family heirloom with which the aged couple would not part. Was it indeed because he coveted the jewel as part of a set otherwise incomplete, that the current enemy was setting these waves of almost more than merely metaphysical assault? Could he not obtain, with his own wealth, a replica of real silver, real gold, real diamond? And . . . yet . . . if that was not why he wanted the Pasqualine Ring . . . then why did he want the Pasqualine Ring?

As long as he lived, Eszterhazy was never to be entirely sure. But he was to become sure enough.

And still the assaults continued.

About ten A.M. and there was Colonel Count Cruttz. Unusual. For one thing; for another, what was it the older man was muttering to himself? It sounded like *Saint Vitus*. An invocation? Perhaps. Perhaps not. In Bella—

The Hospice of Saint Vitus in Bella at the time of its founding had been just that—a hospice for pilgrims seeking cure for what might have been (in modern terms) chorea, cerebral palsy, ergot poisoning, certain sorts of lunacy, or . . . many things indeed. By and by most people had learned not to bake bread from mouldy rye, and the rushing torrents of the pilgrimages had slowed to trickles; still, the prolongedly lunatic had to be lodged somewhere, it being no longer fashionable to lose them in the forest or lock them in a closet: and so, by the time of King Ignats Salvador (the Empire did not yet exist), the Hospice had become the Madhouse and St. Vitus's Shrine its chapel. It *was* quite true that besides the common enclosures there was a secluded cloister for insane nuns and, far on the other side, one for mad monks and priests; it was *not* true, common reports not withstanding, that there was also one for barmy bishops.

"Good mid-morning to you, Colonel Count Cruttz; very well, then: *Fritsli*."

"Mi' morning, Engli. Say, you are a gaffer at St. Vitus, ain't you?"

"I am one of the Board of Governors, yes."

"Well, I want a ticket. Morits. One of my footmen." The colonel-count looked haggard.

Dr. Eszterhazy reached out from a pigeon-hold a dreaded

"yellow ticket," a **Form For Examination Prior to Commit-ment:** sighed. "Poor Morits. Well, this should get him seen to, promptly;" he signed it large. And, did he not, "poor Morits" indeed might gibber and howl for hours in the public corridors, waiting his turn on standby. "What has happened to him? Morits, mmm. *Pale* chap, isn't he?"

Master confirmed that man was indeed a pale chap. That was him. What had *happened*? Man had gone mad, was what happened. In the night, not long before dawn. Screams had rocked the house—and it was an old house with thick walls, too. Insane with terror, Morits. "Mostly he just screamed and tried to hide himself in his own armpits, but when you could make out what he was saying while screaming, why, it was always the same thing. Always the same thing. Always." Cruttz turned his haggard gaze on Eszterhazy.

Who asked, "And what was that? This . . . 'the same thing' . . . ?"

Cruttz wet his lips. Repeated, " 'On the ceiling! On the ceiling! The witch-man! On the ceiling!' "

"The . . . 'witch-man'? Who and what was that?"

Heavily: "That is who and what and which the people call this Hell-hound, Melanchthon Mudge."

Silence. Then, "Very well, then. One understands 'the witch-man.' But. What and what does he mean by 'on the ceiling'?"

A shrug. "I am damned if I know. And I feel that just by knowing the fiend I might be damned. And so poor Morits has been screaming, struggling, be-pissing himself for hours now, and brandy hasn't helped and neither has holy water nor holy oil and so I've come for the yellow ticket. See?"

Eszterhazy saw only scantly. "Had the man . . . Morits . . . ever before showed signs of—?"

Reluctantly: "Well . . . yes . . . sort of. *Nervous* type of chap, always was. Which is all that keeps me from shooting down that swine like a mad dog with my revolver-pistol." That, and—the Emperor having indicated a keen dislike for having people shot down like mad dogs with revolver-pistols— that and the likelihood of such an action's being surely followed by a ten-year exile to the remote wilderness of Little

Byzantia, where the company of the lynx, the bear, and the wild boar might not suffice for the loss of more cosmopolitan company.

Colonel Count Cruttz took up the "yellow ticket" and as he was doing so and murmuring some words of thanks and farewell, his eyes met Eszterhazy's. The latter felt certain that the same thought was in both their minds: was Mudge punishing the house in which he had been humiliated? Was Mudge doing this? Was Mudge not doing this?

And, if so, what might Mudge not do next?

One was soon enough to learn.

Quite late that morning as he was being examined in St. Vitus by the Admitting Physician, pale Morits not only ceased struggling, but—upon being instructed to do so—had stood up. Quietly. Dr. Smitts applied the stethoscope. And Morits, pale Morits, gave a great scream, blood gushed from his nose and mouth, and—"I caught him in my arms. The stethoscope was pulled from my ears as he fell, but I had heard enough," said Dr. Smitts.

"What did you hear?"

"I heard his heart leap. And then I heard it stop. Oh, of course, I did what I could do for him. But it never started again. No. Never."

"Never. . . ."

Was this what Mudge had done next?

Eszterhazy thought it was.

Later, some years later, Eszterhazy was to acquire as his personal body-servant the famous Herrekk, a Mountain Tsigane, who stayed on with him . . . and on and on. . . . But that was later. This year the office was being filled (if *filled* was not too strong a verb) by one Turt, who had qualified by some years as a barber; and if experience folding towels well enough had not made Turt exquisite in the folding and unfolding of and other cares pertaining to Eszterhazy's clothes . . . well . . . one could not have everything. Could one? Turt awoke him; Turt brought, first, the hot coffee, and next the hot water and the scented shaving-soap. Next Turt would bring the loose-

fitting breakfast-gown and on a tray the breakfast, which—
perhaps fortunately—Turt did not himself cook. Turt meant to
do well, Turt clearly meant to do better than he did, and it was
not Turt's fault that he breathed so very heavily. Turt (short for
Turtuscou) was a Romanou, and it was a fact of social life in
the Triune Monarchy that sooner or later one's Romanou
employee would vanish away on what the English called
"French leave": and return . . . by and by . . . with some
fearsome story of dreadful death and incapacitating illness
amongst far-away family; if/when this ever happened, Eszterhazy had determined to terminate Turt's service. But Turt,
though not bothersomely bright, was bright enough, and either
saw to it that all his near of kin stayed in good health or else he
simply allowed them to die without benefit of his attendance in
whatever East Latin squalor pertained to them around the
mouth of the Ister.

On this morning Eszterhazy, dimly aware of great pain, was
more acutely aware of Turt's breathing more heavily than
usual. Had Turt gasped? Had Turt cried out? If so, *why*?
Eszterhazy sat bolt up in bed. *"Dominû, Dominû!"* exclaimed
Turt.

"What? What?"—heavily, anguished.

For reply Turt pointed to the floor. What was on the floor?
Turt's *Lord* looked.

Blood on the floor.

Instantly the pain flared up. Instantly, Eszterhazy remembered. He had been sleeping soundly and calmly enough when
something obliged him to wake up. Some dim light suffused
the room. Some ungainly shape was present, visible, in the
room. Something long, attenuated, overhead. Something overhead. Something barely below the ceiling. Something which
turned over as a swimmer turns over in water. Something with
a human face. The face of Mr. Mudge, the medium. How it
glared at him, with what hate it glared down at him. Its lips
writhed up, and, *The ring!* it said. ***The ring, the ring! I must
have the ring!*** It made a swooping, scooping gesture with one
long, long incredibly long lengthened arm. That was the first
pain. What was it which the hand now held and showed to
him? It was a heart which it held and showed to him; a human

heart. And, whilst the words echoed, echoed, **Ring! Ring!** the fingers tightened and the fingers squeezed and that was the second pain. The third. The—

It had been a dream, a bad, bad, dream; a nightmare dream. Only that, and nothing more. In that case, why this dreadful pain upon his heart? And why the blood upon the—

"A nosebleed," he heard himself say. And heard Turt say, "No, sir. No. Not."

"Why not?"

Turt began making many gestures, the burden of them being that, for one thing, there was no blood upon his master's nose and none upon his master's sheets. That, furthermore, blood dropping from the side of the bed to the floor would have left a stain of a certain size, only. And that this stain was of a larger and a wider size. Which meant that it had fallen from a greater height. And as Turt's hand went up and pointed to the ceiling, the hand and all the rest of Turt's body trembled; the Romanou are of all the races of the Empire of Scythia-Pannonia-Transbalkania the most superstitious by far, and their legends teem and pullulate with accounts of *uampyri* and werewolves and werebears and werebats and werecats; and of ghoulies and ghosties and things which do far worse in the night than merely go *boomp*.

—then why this fearsome pain? Eszterhazy started to sit up, cried out, gestured towards the cabinet, gasped, "The small blue bottle—" The elixir of foxglove made him feel better, then (Turt supplying this next bottle unbid) the spirits of wine made him feel better yet. Then he gestured to the still red stain, directed, "Clean it up."

Turt, so often metaphorical and metaphysical, chose now to be literal. And simply sopped a corner of the napkin in the still-steaming coffee, stooped, wipe, wipe: 'twas done. He made the dirtied cloth vanish. Straightened up. Smoothed his sallow face. "My *Dominǔ's* coffee," he said. Soon afterward he brought the shaving-water and the scented soap. Eszterhazy had for a while little to do and much to think about (there was not, considering his beard, much to shave, either: the neck and the cheekbones; but Turt trimmed also).

Eszterhazy, while his servant scraped and clipped, consid-

ered his own peril. Presumably, Mudge was anyway somewhat
in fear of him, whereas he had been in no way afraid of poor
Morits. Presumably, he himself was therefore . . . safe?
Well . . . safer. . . .

But for how long?

He recalled that face, high up, hateful. To prove the cheat of
the servers of the Idol of Bel at Babylon, Daniel had scattered
ashes on the floor; would it now be necessary to scatter them
on the ceiling?

Eszterhazy was in bed. Bed. Boat. Boat. As he drifted by in the
darkness he heard the sound of the district watchman rapping
the butt of his staff on the flagstone pave at the corner.
Presently he would hear it rapping on the other corner. He did
not. He was not there. He was somewhere else. He knew and
did not know where. It was in a great yard somewhere, an open
waste of rubble and huts. The South Ward, somewhere. Behind
a mouldering tenement. Between it and a riven old wall. Up
there in that room, that room *there*, with the broken shutter
banging aslant, lived an old man and an old woman, there,
there in the night. Here, down *here*, concealed in a half-sunken
pit, someone was hiding and biding time. Someone tall and
sleek and grim. Someone muffled in a cloak. Was waiting. The
cracked old bell began to toll in the tower of the Madhouse of
Saint Vitus. Someone chuckled. It was not a nice sound. At
once Eszterhazy knew who it was. *I am the brother of the
shadow of the slain, the vanguard of the shadow of the living.
I am the medium, Mr. Mudge. As well.*

Mr. Mudge moved up out of the half-dug pit, and who knew
for what gross usage the pit was to have been digged; moved
forward, ahead, face intent. Nearer to the tottery old tenement,
nearer to the window behind the broken slant shutter, Eszterhazy desperate to stop him, but paralyzed, unable to call out, to
move. To *breathe*. Shutter suddenly springing open. Clap.
Bang. Cough. Someone springing out and down. Some*one*?
Some*thing*? Dark, dark, very dark. Fluid movement, there in
the dark. Warn Mr. Mudge? *Why?* No. Mr. Mudge not there.
Where? His cloak flying, floating, in the blackness night; Mr.
Mudge fleeing before it as though, paws on its shoulders, it

coursed him through the night. *No*: Something else coursed him through the blackness night. Scorn and contempt on his face giving way to concentration, concentration to effort, effort to—*Run, Mudge, run!*—to concern, to care, to alarm, faster, *faster, faster*, leap and run and climb and clamber and jump and clamber and climb and run and leap; close behind him something followed faster yet and something else for a second flashed and glinted, something else gleamed at or about the neck of . . . something . . . as sometimes one sees a glint or gleam where the fond master of an animal has fastened a metal sigil advising of its name and owner; or like some ring on a hand moving suddenly in the dim and flaring lamps—

—screamed, Mr. Mudge; **Quaere:** What did Mr. Mudge scream? **Responsum:** Mr. Mudge screamed for help. **Q.:** How did Mr. Mudge scream for help and to what or whom? **R.:** To *"Belphegor, Belzebub, Baphomet, Sathanas, à mon aide O mes princes, aidez-moi, à moi, à moi, à—"* The prayer, if prayer it was, decayed into a continuous repetition of the broad **a**-sound as Mr. Mudge fled, leaping; as . . . something . . . leaping, coughing, followed after him; a great, sudden, abrupt coughing sound, a great forelimb chopping down Mr. Mudge: and all his imprecations sank powerlessly beneath even the level of derision. . . .

Eszterhazy, body spent with having followed the hazards of the chase, awoke bathed in sweat and in bed.

One thing alone remained still quick within his ears, and though it seemed not to be for this night before, yet perhaps it somehow was. *That she-cat has claws*, an odd voice said.

That she-cat has claws.

Dawn.

Mrash.

"Your Lordship, that tiger come a-wandering again-time!"

Eszterhazy lifted dulled, fatigued eyes. "The—? Ah . . . the leopard? You saw it running along and up the roofs?" What was it he felt, now? It was unbalanced that he felt now. He had with infinite difficulties maintained a stance against attack, assault, terror, pain, and worse. He felt this was gone now. But he was infinitely tired now. *Infinitely* tired. He dared be infinitely careful, lest he fall, now. What had and what was happening?

Mrash said, "No, lordship. I seen it running *down* the roofs. And as I looked, so I seen. 'Seen what'? Why, seen summat as was not the tiger nor the leopard. Look out the window there, me lordship. Look out, look up. Look up."

Where was bluff old Colonel Brennshnekkl, who had hunted leopard in Africa, thinking them more dangerous than lion or tiger which course the level ground along? Back in Africa, out of which, always something new. So Plautus says. Pliny?

Mrash again gestured to the window. "My lordship, look," he said. Added, "There cross the alley, on the roof of old Baron Johan house. On the ridge o' the roof, by the chimbley; look, sir."

Eszterhazy looked; shielding with his hand against the obscuring reflection of the gaslight on the window glass, straining his eyes, wishing—not for the first time—that someone would invent a *light*, a quite bright light, which could (unlike the theatrical limelight) be cast *up* or *across*, across a distance. Well. Meanwhile. Meanwhile, something flapped in the wind, there on the rooftop, on the ridge by the chimney. "What, Mrashko? Some old clothes? Carried by wind—eh?"

"Nay, my lordship," Mrash said. "Clothes, yes. Old or new. But I doubt the wind be that strong tonight to—No matter. That be a cloak and a full suit of clothes, sir, and I be a veteran of more nor one war and I'll tell thee what, Master: inside the suit of clothes does a dead man lie."

Mrash was hired to perform only the duties of a man-cook, but Mrash was no fool, he had indeed been in more than one war, nor had he spent all that time cloistered in the cook-tent; nor had his eyes been worn by much reading. His master said, "Sound the alarm." In a moment the great iron ring rang out its clamor of **ngoyng ngoyng mramha mram, ngoyng ngoyng mramha mram**. In the very faint glim of the single small gaslamp at the alley's far end men could be seen running, casting odd and oddly-moving shadows. But what was on the rooftop cast no shadow. And it never moved at all.

By and by they came with the hooks and the ladders and the bull's-eye lanterns and the grapples and the torches. They climbed up from inside the great old house across the alley and then they climbed up the steep-pitched roof. And Eszterhazy climbed with them. (Had he made this climb before? He *had . . . had*n't he?)

"Aye, he be dead. And have *been*. He'm *stiff*." This from a volunteer fireman, a coal-porter by his sooty look. "See how wry his neck? He did fell and bruck it." And:

"Am these *claw*-marks?" asked another. Answering himself, "Nay, not here in The Town," meaning Bella. "I expects he somehow tore himself when he fall . . . for fall to his dread death 'tis clear he did, may the Resurrected Jesus Christ and all the Saints have mercy on him and us. Aye. Man did fell. . . ."

Dread death. . . . Mercy. . . .

The very-slightly-odd lordship who lived in the smaller and lower house which faced Turkling Street the other side of the alley, he shook his head. "If so, how came he here?" was his question, almost as though asking of himself. "Here—high above the street on the peak of a house with no higher one to fall from? Dead men fall *down*. They don't fall *up*."

It was so. There being no more to say to that, they brought the dead man down.

Old Helen, Baroness Johan's old housekeeper-cook, served them the traditional hot rum-and-water. While they were sipping it: "Sir Doctor. Pardon, sir. The police want to know who 'tis. The late deceased. Can Sir Doctor—living 'cross the lane—tell them who 'twas and what was doing there?"

Sir Doctor started to nod. What indeed? Had it all been a dream which he had earlier seen as he lay upon his bed? Or "a vision of the night"? Or—His mouth moved silently; then, "The deceased called himself 'Melanchthon Mudge,'" he said. He took another swallow of the grog. It was very strong.

Just as well.

Just as well? Aye, well, add it up. That there were rings which were rings of power was a mere commonplace in the lore of legend. And what Dr. Eszterhazy knew about the lore of legend was more, even, than he knew about anything in which he had ever been granted a degree—though who would grant him a degree in it? The thumb-ring of Duke Pasquale (*which*

Duke Pasquale? did it even matter?) was a very late entry into
the lore of legend, and had come to Eszterhazy's attention only
yesterday, as it were. How had Melanchthon Mudge learned of
it?—whoever "Melanchthon Mudge" really was? hunted down
as though by a leopard and killed as though by a leopard and
left high up aloft as though by a leopard. *What* had he done for
the third Napoleon of France and the second Alexander of
Russia and the first and last Amadeus of Spain, all men of
subsequent ill-fate, that they should have given him (doubtless
at his request) portions of the time-scattered Pasqualine jewels?
Nothing *very* good, one might be sure. (Was it all adding up?
Well, one would see. Get on with it. Go on. Go on.)

Was the power of Duke Pasquale's ring that it gave one a
capacity to turn for a while into an animal, a beast, a wild
beast? Well could one imagine the glee of roaming wild and
free of human form—Well. And once again he marvelled at
what must have been the long, *long* restraint (if this were all
true) of the self-imagined Royal couple in never having made
use of the Pasqualine ring. Never? "Never" was a longer word
than its own two syllables; *never*? Surely neither of them, old
King, old Queen, would ever (never) have used it for mere glee
or mere power. Only an inescapable need for defense, for
self-defense, the defense of Eszterhazy and the house of Count
Cruttz and perhaps of that whole great city of Bella (. . . *a
leopard shall watch over thy cities* . . .) against the great evil
thing, the vengeful and killing thing which called itself
Melanchthon Mudge, could have impelled them to make use of
it. *If* this were all true: *could* this all be true? all of it? any of
it?—for, if it was not, what was the other explanation? If there
was another explanation.

Try as he might, as he added all this up, Eszterhazy could
think of no other explanation.

A dozen frontiers were being "rectified." A dozen boundaries
were changing shape, none of them large enough to show upon
a single map in an atlas; but, as to matters of straightening here
and bending there, here a square mile and there some several
kilometres: a dozen frontiers and boundaries were changing
shape. And for every *quid* a *quo*, with dust being blown off a

thousand parchment charters. In order to assure that a certain area in the Niçois Savoy be restored to its natural outlines, it was necessary to compensate . . . to, well, compensate two municipalities, one diocese, and . . . and what was *this*? to compensate *the heirs of the fourth marriage-bed of the august Duke Pasquale III*, in lieu of dower-rights, rights of conquest, rights of man, rights of women . . . *rights*.

What cared the historians and the cartographers? and for that matter, what cared the minor statesmen around this particular "green table," for the right or plight of *the heirs of the fourth marriage-bed* etc? nothing. Save that if it were not taken care of, then neither could other boundaries and rights be taken care of, and a certain sand-bar in the Gambia would remain out of bounds and no-man's-land, to vex the palm-oil and peanut-oil trade of certain citizens of certain Powers.

"So, you see, Doctor," said Stowtfuss of the Foreign Office of the Triune Monarchy, "you were quite right in your suggestion and *we* passed it on and *they* passed it on; and, now, well, the King of the Single Sicily is still not really King of the Single Sicily and never will be . . . a good thing for Sicily, and a better thing for him. But now at least he can pretend his pretensions at a healthily higher standard of living. A tidy little income, that, from the old estate in the Nice-Savoy."

Eszterhazy nodded. "And his wife needn't scrub the floor on her aged knees," he said. Old woman, old wife, old she-cat with claws. And with that one ring of power which wanton Mr. Mudge had so terribly wanted. That he, too, might have claws? And, turning, changing his spots—and more than alone his spots—use such claws in the night?

"Yes, yes," said Stowtfuss, pityingly. "Yes, poor chaps, the poor old things. He and his old wife are cousins, you know. They are also related to . . . what's the name? her maiden name? . . . a relation to the poet, same as the old man's mother's maiden name, to the poet Count Giacomo—ah yes! Leopardi! Leopardi! Count Giacomo Leopardi was their cousin. I suppose you may guess the animal in that coat of arms."